EMPIRE OF JEGGA

By
DAVID V. REED

I0541405

ARMCHAIR FICTION
PO Box 4369, Medford, Oregon   97501-0168

For more information about Armchair Books and products, visit our website at…

www.armchairfiction.com

Or email us at…

armchairfiction@yahoo.com

THE POWER OF THE EMPIRE...

Nick Brewster and the crew of the rocket ship "Trailblazer II" didn't know what to think when they arrived drunk, injured, and confused on the surface of the moon. They had expected to die, but they instead landed in a scene of utter chaos. Brewster and his crew soon found themselves in the middle of an interplanetary conflict, filled with what seemed like daily assassinations and political machinations. But Nick, who possessed scientific knowledge that was coveted by all sides in the conflict, found himself in the company of beautiful women, posing for the fawning military personel, and generally having what appeared to be a grand 'ol time. Nick's crew, however, had other plans. They were going to be part of a cosmic revolution...with or without him.

Packed to the brim with action and intrigue, and featuring an unforgettable climax, David V. Reed spins an epic tale in the Burroughs tradition. "Empire of Jegga" is a true science fiction classic.

CAST OF CHARACTERS

NICK BREWSTER
Arrogant, self-righteous and…rich. This man was loved by women and loathed by men—which didn't bother him at all.

JOE ABBOTT
He was Brewster's Chief Engineer, but being paid to like a guy and actually liking him are two different things…

DR. JOHN STEVENS
Inventor of the first ever moon rocket he and his thirteen-member crew left Earth—never to be heard from again.

CAPTAIN AKAR
An ambitious Warlord, he made quite an impression as Mar's Ambassador. Would he be able gain the Earthmen's favor?

SUBA MARANNES
She was a golden-haired Venusian with an agenda all her own. Was she to be a friend or foe? Only time would tell.

VRITA
This Martian beauty was mysterious and her amorous attentions highly desirable—but her passion burned in unexpected ways…

PORO
A big, loutish, green-skinned brute of Jupiter, who was either very dim…or very bright.

FOREWORD

Empire of Jegga is a fine science fiction novel. Some people, after reading it, might be inclined to call it a lost classic. It's got one thing going against it, though. It was published in *Amazing Stories* during Raymond A. Palmer's tenure as editor. That—in and of itself—is often enough to make many science fiction critics turn their noses up. When some sci-fi historians hear Palmer's name, they automatically think of the wild Richard S. Shaver tales and all the pop-gun sci-fi that he crammed into both *Amazing Stories* and *Fantastic Adventures* during the 1940s. And it's true, a lot of the tales in both these magazines during that time period were far from stellar. However, in spite of what seemed like Palmer's best efforts to destroy both publications, there were still many fine tales published in them during that era. Unfortunately, a lot of them get lost in all the criticism and gobbledygoop that surrounded the Palmer merry-go-round. When one compares the lineup of writers in *Astounding Science Fiction, Startling Stories,* and *Thrilling Wonder Stories* (Asimov, Heinlein, Simak, etc.) to some of those in Palmer's stable (Wilcox, Shaver, Yerxa, etc,) it's really a pretty laughable comparison. But one mustn't forget that other Palmer regulars like Robert Bloch, Edgar Rice Burroughs, Rog Phillips, and Edmond Hamilton were certainly no slouches when it came to writing good science fiction.

One writer from the Palmer era who is often over-looked is David V. Reed (born David Levine). Reed gets thrown in with Wilcox and others (though we admittedly have a weakness for some of Wilcox's over-the-top tales) and this, in our humble estimation, is most unfair. The first Reed work we published was a terric novel, *Murder in Space*, written around the same time as *Empire of Jegga*. Reed also wrote a lot of crime and mystery tales for Palmer's *Mammoth Detective*, and his expertise in that genre is most evident in *Murder in Space*.

For *Empire of Jegga*, though, Reed undertook to create an epic tale of space opera, complete with an evil empire, an underground revolutionary movement, spaceships, ray guns, beautiful women, Martian scoundrels, political intrigue, etc.—all the kinds of things we came to worship decades later in movies like *Star Wars*. And it works. Reed's development of the Nick Brewster hero/anti-hero character is very engaging. The story doesn't ever really let up, and the climax puts you right on the edge of your seat.

You will have to put up with some of Ray Palmer's footnotes, though. For some who have waded through Palmer's footnotes in the Richard

Shaver tales, this might be enough to send you running for the hills, but in all fairness, Palmer's footnotes in *Empire of Jegga* are nowhere as intrusive and they do actually help one understand some of the complexities of Reed's Jeggan Empire. One footnote in particular, *Notes on the Introduction to the Civilization of the Empire of Jegga,* is several pages long. We have therefore placed this at the end of the volume. It is, however, required reading before continuing on with the rest of the novel.

So sit back in your favorite armchair and enjoy what is probably David V. Reed's best work, *Empire of Jegga.* Admittedly, it may not be quite on the same level as Asimov's *Foundation* series or Heinlein's *Double Star,* but we suspect many in the sci-fi field might be pleasantly surprised.

—Greg Luce
Editor-in-chief,
Armchair Fiction

CHAPTER ONE

FIFTEEN minutes before midnight the batteries of searchlights were turned on, and huge white fingers began to play in the dark skies over Long Island. Columns of light flashed down to earth, sweeping briefly over countless thousands of people as if in an attempt to discover where the massed throngs ended. Deafening cheers roared over the countryside, tons of confetti swirled aloft to be caught for an instant in the lights and transformed into myriad gems. Once a shaft of light stabbed into the center of the crowds and gleamed on silver. There, resting on the ground at an angle, was a long, cylindrical vessel, slender as a bullet. The mob surged forward against the cordon of police that isolated the ship. Excitement burned in the night air like a wearying fever.

"And here come another party, escorted by a squad of state troopers. Listen to those sirens!"

The sirens were echoing by radio in a score of countries; half the civilized world was listening. The radio and television men filled the great colonial veranda of the Brewster mansion, and dozens of voices hummed together, describing the scene, interpreting, elaborating.

"That's Governor Horton of Texas down there, folks. He's the short man trying to duck the photographers. You may remember Governor Horton was here once before to bid Nick Brewster goodbye—last year when the *Trailblazer I* made the first attempt to reach the Moon by rocket ship. I don't have to remind you that Brewster stayed up in the Canadian woods *that* night. Look at them milling down there..."

A COPY boy came running through the city room of the *New York Post*, two large sheets of paper flying before him, work stopping in his wake. He skidded to a stop before the managing editor's desk and faced the assembled brains of the newspaper.

"Hold up the first front page," said the editor. The copy boy raised one of the sheets in trembling hands.

TRAILBLAZER II OFF ON PERILOUS JOURNEY TO MOON!

"Okay. Let's see the alternate."

BREWSTER QUITS AGAIN

"Fine," said the editor. "Only one change. I want a—"

"Excuse me, chief, but don't you think we're going a little too far with that alternate headline? I mean, saying that Brewster quits again. He didn't really quit last year and I don't think—"

"Whadd'ya mean he didn't quit? He damn well did quit. That first ship of his took off without him on it, didn't it? He was supposed to be there, wasn't he? And where was he? Up in that expensive Canadian hunting lodge of his, dead drunk after a five day celebration and orgy, and up to his ears in dames!"

"But he didn't tell the ship to leave without him. If he'd had a chance to sober up, and the ship had waited, he'd have gone with it."

"If? *If!* We don't deal with *Ifs* on the *Post!* Maybe he'd have gone and maybe he wouldn't. The fact is that the ship left and never was heard from again. Fourteen men gambled with death on that experiment of his, and the chief experimenter wasn't there when they lost, and in my book and the public's book, that means quitting. If he goes off tonight, we run the first head. If he doesn't, we call him a two-time quitter and everybody agrees with us. Now here's the change I want. Break out that lousy story on the Treasury Department and give me a three-column cut of Brewster. Here's the picture I want you to use."

The editor held up a glossy print, a picture of a young man with deep-set eyes that looked out at the world half in contempt, half in amusement, with a strong jaw that was relaxed in a lazy smile.

"Handsome rat, isn't he?" said the editor. "Run this caption under it:

Nick (Sure Thing) Brewster, Millionaire Adventurer Who Reached For the Moon. Got that? Okay, where's rewrite? You got that story on the life of Brewster ready?"

"Not so it's readable."

"Read me what you have. Just the highlights."

Nick Brewster, famous, foolhardy adventurer, went the limit tonight when he took off for the Moon in the second of his two million-dollar experimental rocket ships. Born with a silver spoon in a mouth usually given to sneering, young Brewster inherited five million dollars at his father's death in 1951. Six years later, according to FORTUNE'S estimate of last year, he had run the figure well up past forty million, earning the nickname of Sure Thing Brewster, leaving behind him a history of escapade and scandal, danger and enterprise.

Today, aged twenty-seven, he could call few men his friends, his unpopularity ascribed to many reasons. Chief among these were the facts of his continual absence from the United States within the past two years, his arrogance, and his often-mentioned record with ladies, the last named supposedly having chased him before he was old enough to vote. Those who knew him considered him extremely intelligent, hard as granite.

Last year, June 12, 1958, Brewster alienated more people with a single blow than ever before. Backing the invention of Dr. John Stevens for a rocket ship capable of reaching the Moon, he sank two million dollars into it. Leading scientists who examined the vessel agreed that it had every chance of success. The night the ship left, carrying Dr. Stevens and thirteen men of the crew, Nick Brewster, who had announced that he would be aboard for the dangerous experiment, was left behind.

Various stories filled the press, explaining Brewster's defection, but chiefly credited was Dr. Stevens' statement that he had received word that Brewster was in Canada, attending a farewell party so enthusiastically that he was unable to leave at the appointed time. Dr. Stevens left without him.

The ship was never heard from again. When the telescopes lost it, the "Trailblazer I" ceased to exist. Its signals died away and the great magnesium flares it was supposed to light up on the Moon were never seen...

"THAT'S enough," said the editor. "Great stuff. Go on from there and work on Brewster. The inside story of the wild party in that hunting lodge, but keep it clean; this is a family newspaper. Soft-pedal the woman angle and play up the rumors. You know—Brewster never intended to go on that trip. Cold feet or something. Sure Thing Brewster never took a really long chance—"

"What about his being a hunter and explorer?"

"Hunter my foot! Say he shot tigers from behind expensive guns, explored the Arctic in ermine sleeping bags. Lives mean nothing to him. Play up the way he was booed and hissed in public. Get out the pictures of him being rescued from that angry mob at that ball game in Chicago. Dig up the dirt biographies. Run that story of that girl who took a shot at him in Maine, that girl whose brother was one of the crew in the first ship."

"But he never pressed charges against her."

"Because he was afraid to show his face in a courtroom. Find me a juicy financial scandal of his. Do two or three paragraphs on his chief engineer—what's his name—Joe Abbott? Abbott's been out of a job for two years. Talented engineer, down on his luck, old classmate of Nick Brewster's, bought with gold—that kind of stuff. We got half an hour to hit the streets, so hop to it. I got a date with the television cast of the big event, *if* it comes off."

The editor switched on the screen behind his desk and fiddled the dials. The dark screen began to glow and the outlines of a panorama shot grew clearer. An enormous, well-kept estate, its shrubbery trampled, its gates broken, people everywhere, lights in the sky...

"...and still they come, folks. The roads to the Brewster estate have been closed for a week, ever since the news got out that Brewster had built a duplicate of the first *Trailblazer* for a new try, but right now an army couldn't keep order here! Not much time left now, if it's really going to happen. Hold on, folks, here come more sirens! It looks like...just a moment, please—yes, it's..."

"I DON'T give a damn who it is," said Nick Brewster, evenly. "I don't want to see anybody."

"He doesn't want to see anybody," Joe Abbott said to the police captain at the door. The captain went out quickly, but for a moment the confusion and noise from the rest of the packed house sifted through and marred the silence that lay in the library.

"They're all here," said Abbott, quietly. "The Hollywood contingent, and Wall Street and Washington, and a couple of ambassadors and senators and governors. But Governor Horton was your father's best friend. Maybe you could see him without offending the others. He came all the way from Texas."

"To hell with Horton and the rest of them," said Brewster.

"Nick," said Abbott, "you can't just—"

Brewster interrupted him with a wave of his hand. "Not now, Joe. There isn't time. We're different people, you and I, and you won't get any satisfaction talking to me. Call it anything you like; that's the way I am, that's Nick Brewster." He lit a fresh cigarette from a butt, and his gray eyes traveled over his cupped hands to Abbott. "All the same," he added, "I want you to know that I'm grateful for the way you stuck by me."

"You paid me for it, didn't you?" said Abbott.

"Yes," said Brewster, slowly, "I paid you, but I don't think I could have bought your friendship. I've had that all along. We'll be following the *Trailblazer I* in a little while, and none of us knows what's in store for us. That's why I'm telling you thanks, now."

Abbott got up and walked to one of the great windows that formed a bay in the library. He parted the closed curtains with a hand and looked out. Presently, he said, "I think it's almost time. They've got the searchlights on the ship."

As he spoke, the windows shivered from the cheering outside. A door opened, and the police captain was in the library. "Mr. Whiteside says the ship is ready, Mr. Brewster. I've got an escort of fifty men waiting just outside. We've cleared the hall."

"Thank you," said Brewster. He threw his leather coat over his shoulders, and as Abbott reached him, he punched Abbott lightly on the shoulder. "Let 'er go, Joe," he smiled, and followed the captain out.

The police had pushed the visitors, distinguished and otherwise, against the walls. As Brewster and Abbott emerged from the library, a few people called to them. Brewster waved a hand perfunctorily and walked swiftly through the policed lane to the veranda. There he stopped for a moment, blinded by the series of flash-bulb explosions as the photographers shot their pictures.

"How about a smile, Mr. Brewster? Waving goodbye?"

"Mr. Brewster! Mr. Brewster! One with you and Governor Horton shaking hands? Just a quick shot, please!"

Before Brewster could say anything, Governor Horton had pushed through the crowd and had taken Brewster's hand. As the lights exploded all around them, Horton said, "I've been trying to see you all day."

"I know," said Brewster. "Were you going to tell me what you told the *Life* reporters in that picture series they ran on me? That my father should have left his money to a home for mongrels?"

HE SHOOK his hand free, and nodding to the captain, started down the stairs on the two hundred yard walk to the ship, Abbott following. Pandemonium broke loose. Furious waves of people surged against the protective dikes of police, screaming, yelling, trying to get closer to Brewster. One of the searchlights knifed down and provided a brilliant white lane to the ship. Fantastic showers of confetti filled the air, and the hoarse voices of tens of thousands hammered like a gigantic drum. Brewster walked on, head down, looking neither to right nor left, as if there was no one there. When he reached the glistening ship, Abbott caught his hand and held him at the massive lock long enough for the photographers to shoot a few pictures, then both men went in.

Inside, Harry Whiteside, who was Abbott's assistant, gravely shook hands with both men, then turned the power screws that sealed the lock. The rest of the crew was ready, most of them already strapped in their heavy belts.

"Fire the port tubes," said Abbott to Whiteside. "That crowd out there is too close." He led Brewster forward to control room, and as they got there, a muffled series of blasts went off. Looking through one of a row of circular portholes in the outer bulkheads, they saw the crimson flash of the rockets light up the countless faces outside, and the crowds melting away, as if from the heat of the tubes.

Abbott adjusted mouthpiece and earphones. "Set?" he spoke into the phone at his lips. "Fire in order, one to six." The blasting grew louder, and the people had disappeared from view. "Fire in series, one to twenty."

Instantly, the blasting increased until it was a steady, splitting thunder. The crimson became tinged with yellow, then faint bits of blue edged into the flames that ringed the ship. One by one, the searchlights faced the slender hundred-foot length of the ship, but they scarcely paled the fire.

"Cease fire and stand by," said Abbott.

The silence seemed overpowering. Nothing existed now except the metal bulkheads of the ship's bowels, gleaming in dull convolutions of coils and instruments and meters and dials, and outside there was darkness pierced by a circle of cold white eyes. Abbott pressed a finger down on a switch, and they could hear the quiet mesh of gears as the prow of the vessel began to tilt heavenward. Brewster fastened his belt and stared out of a porthole. The ship stopped moving at a sixty-degree angle.

Over the flat horizon, a fat rust-colored autumn moon waited serenely. A thin layer of clouds lay high in the sky, tinted underneath with soft orange.

"Aft tubes only, one to seventy. Fire together."

IT WAS over a moment after it had begun, but the moment was an eternity of pain. There was a single, all encompassing sound, and something tore at their hearts and throats. There were endless seconds in which there was no sight, and a mist through which glittering objects began to take form, a copper wire, a red-gleaming light. There was a moment when being ceased, and ever so slowly, thought became possible, and sluggishly, memory returned, and Brewster remembered the distant moment after Abbott had last spoken, and then he had turned in his belt and grinned somberly and tried to shake hands. And Brewster remembered how he had thought—how calm Joe's voice is. Then agony, dull and insistent and gnawing, and the strain against the glassite belts was beginning to ease and they could hear it creaking softly.

In the vast stillness that followed, Brewster wiped away the tears that had streamed down his face. His vision sharpened, and he saw Abbott before him. Abbott's face had frozen in a mask of astonishment, and the first tiny cracks of fear were appearing in it.

"*Look...*" Abbott whispered.

But Brewster had already seen it. It was no trick of his eyes, no after-image. The moon, white as plaster, was an enormous ball, a sphere so great that it completely filled the sky. There was nothing but its unbelievable immensity ahead.

"What's happened?" said Brewster.

Abbott turned to him slowly and shook his head. "I don't know," he said. "Something's gone wrong. We're much too close..."

He turned to a screen that projected the rear view from the ship and switched it on. The screen flashed on an image of a city. They saw a river separating the city, and they could make out bridges, the faint phosphorescence of a ferry's wake in the water, houses, lights.

It was impossible. They couldn't be so close to Earth. Their initial velocity should have taken them far beyond such a view or the ship would have dropped back to Earth before it had cleared the atmosphere. And yet the moon was so enormous before them that they must have been very close to it.

"Is there a telescopic lens in the projector?" asked Brewster.

"No," said Abbott, trying to shake off his daze. "We've got to go aft and see what's happened."

He unhitched his belt and started to take a step, then suddenly he grabbed at the belt and held on. His feet had left the deck completely, and he was floating in mid-air. He pulled himself down, and all at once Brewster was laughing. Abbott looked at him in wonder, and the laughter had done the trick.

"Forgot," he mumbled, half grinning at Brewster. "We're in free space. You'd better put those magnetized shoes on too." Hurrying now, he unfastened two pairs of metal-shod shoes from a tier on the bulkhead and threw a pair to Brewster. A moment later, both were clambering down the companionway.

"Joe! Mr. Brewster! Follow me, quick!" Whiteside had come running from the stern and met them halfway. They followed him back to the aft observation room. Half the crew was there, staring out of the large portholes.

THERE, as it appeared, directly behind them, was the Earth, a dark, blue-green ball. Its proportions, when they could maneuver themselves into such postures as to see all of it at once, were unbelievable. Sometimes they could see all of it, then, by moving their heads an inch or so, they lost the mass and saw only a segment, but with such clarity and in such detail that it could have been possible only from an airplane hovering a few miles above Earth. It was utterly impossible to see both the entire diameter of Earth and yet be able to see segments of it in such powerful magnification. But they were seeing it.

"That city we saw before," said Peters, "the one with the river running through it—that was two cities, St. Paul and Minneapolis. I know them inside out. It was like looking through a magnifying glass."

"Like...looking through a...magnifying glass," Brewster murmured. He shifted his head a bit. "It keeps happening. Suddenly you get a new angle and everything grows sharp…they way I thought I saw the Andes Mountains in South America, as if it was a relief map, close to us…"

"Stand over here," said Steinberg, "just where I am. See it? *That's* Manhattan. There's the Washington Bridge, and the Hudson, and there's Newark Bay. And if you move just a bit to the right, you can see Long Island—and those searchlights from where we took off…"

Abbott brushed a hand across his face. "It just isn't possible," he repeated. "Maybe the instruments have a clue to this." He turned to the crew, whose faces revealed the same bewilderment that lay on his. "Everybody back on duty," he said. "You can tell your alternates what's happening, but keep your heads. We'll work it out and let you know."

He started after Brewster back to the control room.

Abbott's practiced eyes swept over the banked array of instruments. Slowly he sank down to his chair and spoke into his phone, his hands trembling as they held the mouthpiece.

"Harry? Fire all bow tubes. Immediately."

Whiteside's puzzled voice rang from the earphones from where they lay on the control board. "Did you say bow tubes?"

"Yes. Quickly."

"But we've got all the stern tubes firing in series and they've been set for the next six hours. You may interfere with the acceleration and—"

"Those are orders."

"Aye, aye, sir."

"Acceleration…" Abbott breathed heavily, staring at the control board. "We've got to stop it somehow…"

Nick Brewster crossed over to him, and seizing him by the arms, he shook Abbott. His voice was cold and decisive when he spoke. "Snap out of it! What's wrong?"

"Wrong?" said Abbott, slowly. "Everything's wrong. Everything but these instruments, and they check each other. And if they're right, I think I know what happened to the *Trailblazer I.*"

"What happened?"

"Look at the planometers. The one that measures our distance from the moon. Now look at the timer. We've been up eighteen minutes. Our initial velocity was 7 miles a second. Allowing a gradual deduction we're traveling at approximately 25,000 miles an hour."

"What are you getting at?"

"Look at the planometers!" cried Abbott. "Eighteen and a half minutes now—and we've covered 7770 miles. But look at our distance from the moon—50,230 miles. Don't you see what that means?" The veins in his throat were like iron bands. "The moon isn't 240,000 miles from Earth. It's less than 60,000. If our instruments are right, and everything points to it—then in a little more than two hours we'll crash into the moon while we're *still* accelerating."

CHAPTER TWO

NICK BREWSTER gripped the steel arms of his chair. "What are you talking about?" he demanded.

"It's all there in the instruments," said Abbott, hoarsely. "They all check. The distance from the sun to Mars isn't registering as 141,000,000 miles. It says 33,000,000. The distance from the sun to Mercury isn't 36,000,000 but less than a fifth of that. And the vast distance from the sun to Neptune—almost three billion miles—registers here as less than a thirteenth of that distance…"

"The instruments have all gone haywire," said Brewster. "Even the ratios are wrong…"

Abbott kept staring at the control board. "Are the instruments wrong?" he repeated. "We have evidence here to show that they're right. We know the moon is in reality very close to us now. We have only to look out there to see that the meter reading 49,310 miles must be correct. Its size alone tells us that.

"And now, look through this observation porthole—there—to that green star, that enormous ball of cold fire. It could only be Neptune, and according to our charts, it *is* Neptune. But Neptune should be invisible to the naked eye… Why do we see it so clearly? Why is the moon so close? Both the instruments and our eyes tell us the same story. Only the measurements that we always accepted seem wrong. *The measurements must be wrong!*"

"But what about the way we see Earth?" asked Brewster.

"The same thing," Abbott nodded. "When we see all of the Earth, we see it as it should be seen from 8,000 miles away, where we now are. The flaw here is the way we suddenly see parts of it so closely. We know, however, that we can't be as close as we seem to be at those times because our initial velocity, without which we could never have left Earth, must have taken us far beyond the detailed view we get. Our first two seconds of flight carried us beyond such close views.

"So something, some agent we don't know about, makes it *appear* that we are much closer to Earth than we know we are. That same thing has always made everything else appear much farther away than we now know they were. Something warps our point of view…and there's only one answer to that that I can see."

Brewster waited for him to continue.

"It can only be that the dense atmosphere of the Earth acts as a lens," said Abbott. "Looking out into space from Earth is like looking through the wrong end of a telescope. Can anything be measured accurately when it's seen through a magnifying lens—a lens that's been turned the wrong way?"

Abbott switched on the rear view mirror again and both men looked into it.

"Now," Abbott continued, "we see that the converse is true. The reason we suddenly see large segments of Earth so clearly is because we catch the lens right. When we do, we see details that only a tremendous magnification could show. It adds up…"

Brewster said, "Then we're going to crash?"

Joe Abbott nodded. "We allowed six hours for acceleration and four to ease off in. We set the tubes that way and there's nothing we can do about it. We're less than two hours from the moon."

"And that," said Brewster, quietly, "is what happened to the *Trailblazer I*. Without any means of communicating with Earth while she was in space, she went to her doom." He pronounced the last word hollowly, as if he were mocking it. When Abbott looked at him, because of the way he had said it, Nick Brewster had a faint, bitter grin on his face.

HALF an hour later the moon had grown so large they couldn't see all of it at once. It looked like a great ball loosely wrapped in shriveled, pockmarked skin, and given a slight rosy color by the jets of flame from the fore rockets.

"Is there a chance?" said Brewster.

"Very slim. We have more power in our fore rockets than the first *Trailblazer*, because we thought maybe that was one of the reasons she didn't land safely and we—"

"You're repeating yourself," said Brewster. "Don't give me that engineering crap again. Just answer the question: is there a chance?"

"I won't know for another half hour."

Without a word, Brewster got up, lit a cigarette, and walked out of the control room. Presently he came back, lugging a heavy wooden case, which he had evidently taken from the supply hold. Then he sat in his wicker chair across the long, narrow room from Joe Abbott, looking out at the moon and occasionally glancing at the timer as the slow minute hand turned on its axis.

When the planometer passed 16,000 Brewster said, "Well, Joe?"

Abbott shook his head grimly. "If we had another hour and a half, maybe some of us could live through the crash. We've decelerated 6800 miles per hour, and at that rate—"

"Save it," said Brewster. "At that rate only posterity will be interested in the figures, and none of us are going to be part of posterity. Call the crew together here. All of them."

He took a wrench from the tool rack and smashed open the case, pausing long enough to allow Abbott to pipe the crew. Then, strewing fistfuls of straw over the metal deck, he started to take out a bottle when he saw the straw rising weightlessly from the deck and moving slowly up to the overhead, where, for some reason, it clung. When the first of the crew came into the control room, Brewster was laughing.

"Look at that," he pointed. "I wondered where my cigarette butts disappeared to. Thought someone was cleaning up after me."

One by one the crew came into the room, until all twelve were there, standing quietly in the narrow confines along the panels of dials.

"I'll make it short and sweet, men," said Brewster. "We're going to crash on the moon in about an hour. If you're interested in finding out why, Joe Abbott can tell you. It'll give you something to do. If you're not interested, maybe you'll take my suggestion and one of these bottles, and to hell with it. Some of you have been with me before, some of you haven't, but I know, having chosen you carefully, that none of you is afraid to die. If you want it, here it is: the best Scotch on the market, twenty-year-old stuff. Only hold on tight to it, or you'll have to go after it with a ladder."

Holding the case between his legs, Brewster passed the first bottle to Drake. "Thank you, sir," said Drake, tersely. They followed him in line, Morrow, Oberman, Rogofsky, Peters, Callahan, Lindstrom, Steinberg, Fredericks, Stewart, Purdom. Harry Whiteside was last and he smacked his lips appreciatively. Some of them spoke, most of them were silent. They sat down on the deck, against the bulkheads, keeping their metal-shod shoes as flat as they could.

"Have one?" asked Brewster.

"Don't mind if I do," said Abbott.

"Keep the cork in between drinks," said Brewster. "Here's how."

A few minutes later, Brewster went out, returning soon afterward with a portable phonograph and a batch of records. "Had it specially built for this trip," said Brewster. "It has springs to keep the pickup in position."

HE STOOD over the men, looking down at them, watching the way their eyes kept turning to the planometer. Brewster was an uncommonly tall man, a little over six foot three, and standing there now he looked taller than ever, and with the little, bitter ironic smile on him and his cold eyes, he looked almost satanic.

"Joe," said Brewster. "Switch the planometers off. Nobody's really interested in them anymore."

Abbott threw in several switches, and the moon planometer froze at 13,441. Then he got up and pulled steel shutters down over the face of the observation ports. The brilliant whiteness that had been pouring into the room gave way to the blue-white of artificial light. The phonograph whirred quietly, and a dance band played one of the current hit tunes. Brewster turned it up louder and began to whistle along, pausing now and then to uncork his bottle.

He was putting on the third record when Stewart suddenly got to his feet and hurled his bottle at the moon planometer. "Why doesn't it move?" he shouted. "I'm not afraid! Let it move!" The bottle had smashed into bits, the fragments of broken glass and the liquor hung in odd shapes near the planometer. "Damn it!" Stewart raved. "Damn—"

Nick Brewster took two quick steps to Stewart, spun him around by his arm and smashed a fist into his face. The impact of the savage blow was enough to knock the man off his feet, and as he fell unconscious to the deck, Callahan tied him down with a glassite belt. The third record began to play, and Rogofsky and Oberman sang the words thickly.

Minutes passed, and the odor of Scotch whiskey grew heavier. Several others had joined in the singing. Morrow kept time by beating his bottle gently on the deck. Rogofsky's eyes were closed. It was very noisy now with the singing and the music, and Abbott leaned far over in his fixed chair and tapped Brewster.

"Drunk?" he asked.

"Only my first bottle," Brewster grinned, mirthlessly. "I wish I were. My doctor used to tell me that someday I'd be sorry if I kept drinking. Well, I'm sorry now, because now it's going to take too long to get drunk."

"Zat all you're sorry for?" asked Abbott, swaying the least bit.

"That's all."

"You're a hard guy, Nick, a really—"

"Cut it," said Brewster, sharply. He smiled again. "I'm afraid I have to give you the same answer as always…there isn't time now. We pioneers don't philosophize, do we, Joe?" His lips curled sarcastically.

"Tell me one thing," Abbott persisted. "You went on this ex— exped—ishun just to show them up, didn't you? Just to ssshhow 'em up."

"No," said Brewster. "I went because I wanted to go. It was as simple as that. I know you don't understand it."

Abbott's head rolled loosely. He took his thumb off the neck of his bottle and took a long drink. Then he sat there, staring at nothing.

THE *Trailblazer II* went plummeting down. Little by little, the singing died away. Fredericks lurched out of the room, and they could hear him retching in the companionway. The lights twinkled and dimmed and never recovered their full power. In the silence a steady hum had become audible, as if it were the momentum of the ship itself making itself heard, crying a song of death as it hurled its long, sleek length down toward the lifeless world below. The phonograph played on.

Brewster had lost all sense of time when he got out of his chair. The end was moments distant, he knew vaguely. His mind was clear and awake, and a thousand swift thoughts raced torturously through the various levels of his consciousness. Even now, he knew, he was unable to accept the inevitable blindly, and though part of him recoiled at the notion that had seized him, his desire to know what was happening was stronger—to be there, a final witness to catastrophe, though the evidence would be buried with him.

His mouth was a thin, set line as he raised an edge of the steel shutters and looked through. For a moment he was blinded by the impact of whiteness on his eyes. He saw only an illimitable expanse of chalky land, the outlines blurred with the colors of the spectrum, and colored concentric rings swimming up toward him. Then he saw the surface of the moon, its placid sweep of empty valleys, its dry ravines, its mountains like ivory sculpture...

It was during these fleeting instants of sight that Brewster realized that the ship had stopped falling...that she hovered perhaps a hundred feet over the surface of the moon.

Dazed momentarily, Brewster let the shutters fall, and whirling around, he climbed through the squatting men and raced down the companionway to the stern of the ship. There he saw that the aft rockets were still spitting their powerful fire. There was power enough in them to have buried the ship in the crash...but they hadn't crashed. What had stopped them?

The ship was leveling off. Slowly, the stern came down until the vessel was hovering parallel to the surface. It continued to drop foot by foot, as imperceptibly as an elevator, until it was no more than fifty feet in the air. The force of the rockets was being uselessly spent in the atmosphere—they had ceased to affect the ship at all.

And something, some prodigious might not resident in the ship had cushioned and eased and stopped its momentum, and was now holding it in its grasp...

Staring down, Brewster knew that his eyes were playing tricks on him. It had seemed to him that there had been movement below, that the soil had shifted and that the white rocks were moving—then the shattering realization was on him—because the rocks had moved. Only they weren't rocks. They were beings of some sort, life—

Suddenly two thin bars of white substance reared up from the ground, higher and higher, until the topmost ends leaned against the sides of the ship. There were crossbars all the way up—it was a ladder... And now, separating itself from the ground, something white was climbing up that ladder to the ship.

SPELLBOUND, Brewster watched the being come up. It was only when the thing was a few feet below that he saw it was human—or as near human as any living creature could be without actually being human. It was a man, no more than five feet tall, with a pale skin and deep, luminous, black-red eyes, and hair the color of platinum. He was swathed in a voluminous white cloak that blended perfectly with the landscape, and it was only when his head appeared from under the cloak that Brewster understood why he had thought at first that the rocks were moving.

When the *man* had climbed to the level of the ship, he clenched his hands and began beating against the sides. Brewster heard the faint boom of his hammering and did nothing. The man reached inside his cloak and held a cone-shaped rod in his hand, and from the apex of the cone a thin, green stream like liquid fire played on the metal sides. It had no effect on the ship.

Then, quite by accident, though the man seemed alarmed and was looking about, the man's eyes lifted until he looked through the stern port where Brewster was standing, and his eyes met Brewster's.

What was he saying? Brewster gazed into the ruby eyes and watched the little man gesticulate and mouth phrases. He was trying to tell Brewster something. He was indicating that Brewster come down, that he leave the ship. Was this, thought Brewster, one of the beings responsible for the mighty force that had inexplicably saved the vessel? Why was he so perturbed? What made him assume that Brewster, or the men in the ship, were friendly beings? Why did he seem to think that they could leave the ship at all?

His mind working slowly, still unable to comprehend fully what had happened, Brewster gazed at the man and saw his chest moving, saw his nostrils dilate. He was…but of course he was breathing. Why shouldn't… Brewster shook his head violently. He had to be able to think clearly. The man was trying to tell him something, something that was evidently of great importance.

Suddenly Brewster had made his decision. Back he ran, down the ship, to the vaulted doors of the air lock, paused a moment, then went into the control room. The men looked up at him in a stupor. It would be impossible to rouse them. He opened a stowage chamber and began piling out oxygen helmets and tanks. Laboriously, he fixed a helmet on each of the men, and took one himself.

Joe Abbott stirred and looked through his helmet at Brewster. His eyes unconsciously darted down to the wristwatch he had hidden under a sleeve of his leather coat, and suddenly he was roused. He got up unsteadily and took Brewster's arm.

"What happened?" His voice echoed through the helmet speaker with metallic resonance.

"See that the men are all right," Brewster snapped, "then come to air lock." Something was telling him to hurry.

WHEN he got back to the lock there was no hesitation. He threw in its power switch and stood back. Slowly, the massive door began to swing open. Brewster had fastened a glassite belt around his middle, expecting a tremendous rush of air from the ship to the outside, but when it came its mildness amazed him.

With the door opened, he gripped the edge and peered out over the side. There was no movement down below, but the man on the ladder at the stern was still there, still hammering. As Brewster's helmeted head stuck out of the ship, the man saw him.

All at once, another ladder seemed to raise itself from the ground, reaching up to the lock. As the first man swiftly slid down his ladder, a second appeared, climbing up the new ladder. Up he came, several rungs at a time, until his head was level with Brewster's feet. He looked up at Brewster, and Brewster's hand tightened on the automatic pistol he held.

"Quick," said the man. "How many of you are there?"

He had spoken in English…in slightly accented, yet unmistakably accurate English…

"Answer at once!" the man cried. "How many?"

"Fourteen," Brewster choked.

"Take them out at once!" the man cried. "Come down below to us as quickly as you can! Your lives depend on it!"

Brewster turned back toward the control room, and in turning he bumped into Joe Abbott. Abbott was standing there as if paralyzed.

"Come on!" Brewster shouted.

CHAPTER THREE

BY THE time Brewster had half carried the first of the crew to the lock, the man had disappeared from the ladder. When he looked down there was no one in sight.

Brewster regarded Abbott and said, tersely, "You're too unsteady. Get the men in here. I'll carry them down." He lifted Stewart's inert form over his strong shoulders and lowered himself to the ladder. The ladder was as smooth as glass to his touch. It was a long way down.

Reaching bottom, he stepped carefully on the crusty soil and deposited Stewart, then quickly went up again. Almost at the top, he glanced down. Stewart had disappeared, and on the spot where Brewster had left him, only his helmet remained.

Suddenly the soil moved, and Brewster saw what had happened. There were many men down below, all of them carefully camouflaged with white cloaks. When they lay quietly on the ground, and the stiff cloaks formed haphazard folds, they were indistinguishable from the terrain. One of these men had hidden Stewart with a cloak. Now he reached for the helmet he had taken off Stewart and covered that.

Startled, Brewster climbed into the ship and took off his own helmet. The first experimental breath reassured him. The air was cold and dry, but sufficiently dense to breathe. He found nothing strange in this; matters had long since passed the stage of normal reaction.

Several men had already assembled at the lock, and Abbott came in, dragging Tom Drake. "You think you can go down yourself, Peters?" said Brewster. "And you, Callahan?" Both men nodded, though they seemed to be having trouble standing erect. "Go ahead," Brewster said. He lifted Drake like a sack and slowly edged back on the ladder. By the time he had reached bottom, Peters and Callahan were gone. He put Drake down, and a cloak swirled up and hands pulled Drake away, under it.

He started the long, perilous climb up again, fatigue pulsing through him, numbing his body. Abbott had taken the helmets off the others and had doused them with water, but only Purdom seemed to be aware of his surroundings. Lindstrom had struggled to his feet, and Rogofsky was blinking his eyes and groaning weakly. The others were too drunk to move or do more than look around, stupefied.

At a word from Brewster, Purdom started down, and Lindstrom, staggering, went after him. Doggedly, Brewster lifted Rogofsky up and went back to the ladder. He saw only Purdom climbing down, halfway from the ground. A few feet from the bottom of the ladder he saw Lindstrom. He had fallen and hit the ground in a grotesque posture. A cloak moved to him and covered him up, and the man who had been under the cloak began to climb swiftly up the ladder.

The little man reached the ship. "Leave the others," he said. "The Jeggites are coming. To be caught by them is death!" He pointed toward the horizon. A clustering group of dark stains were advancing.

"But we can't leave these men here!" cried Abbott.

"Help Rogofsky down, Joe," said Brewster, quickly. "I'll take Morrow instead."

"But what about—"

"We'll come back for them."

He eased Rogofsky down after Abbott. The moment they were clear he ran down the companionway to the stowage hold. A moment later, carrying an enormous carton, he returned and stooped down under Morrow, adjusting both burdens. Powerful as he was, his face tightened in pain as he reached the ladder, and oddly enough, a single thought went through his mind. With the lesser gravity of the moon he should have felt much more weightless, much stronger. But he felt only weariness, and the ground below seemed to waver as he gripped the ladder with one hand.

THE little man remained in the ship until Brewster was halfway down, then followed. He jumped down the last rungs and began tipping the ladder over. Abbott cried out and clutched the ladder, starting to say something, when Nick Brewster gripped his arms. Abbott wrenched free and Brewster pursued, winding his arms around Abbott's throat, pulling him down.

From somewhere a huge cloak was thrown over the struggling men, and hands pulled at them until they both fell over, lost in the folds and choking in the swirling particles of dust. Relentlessly, Brewster tightened his murderous embrace.

"You must be quiet," a voice close to them whispered. "Our one chance against the Jeggites is surprise." A body moved cautiously, close to them, parting the folds until a transparent portion of the concealing cloak was disclosed...and suddenly, Abbott stopped fighting.

There, on the brow of a hill, thirty yards away, stood three strange vehicles. They looked like deep bowls balanced on a tripod of three wheels. They were colored a dead, dusty white that might have remained invisible even though they had stopped on the crest of the hill and higher hills behind them had to supply protective blending. But men came out of the vehicles, four men out of each of them, looking up at the *Trailblazer II*.

They looked like men, though they were utterly unlike the little white men who had concealed Brewster and the others. They were tall, at least six feet in height, dark-visaged, and dressed in tight-fitting uniforms of black, shining cloth, with peaked caps on their heads.

Brewster felt the anticipatory chill of danger as he regarded them. These were undoubtedly advance guards of the larger group that he had seen from the ship. They seemed uneasy as their eyes swept the valley below the vessel. They waited for minutes, without speaking to each other, until the larger party reached them.

There were perhaps fifty men all told, standing abreast in a long, precise column that extended over the hill. As they started down into the valley, behind them an enormous vehicle rolled up to the crest. It was made of a dull, reddish, substance, mounted on numerous wheels, its sides covered with gleaming instruments beside which black-clad attendants walked, keeping pace with the machine. From the top of the machine protruded a squat, hollow tube like a cannon, revolving with the ease of a weathervane as the vehicle moved, so that the tube remained always pointed at the *Trailblazer II*, high above them.

BURNING with curiosity, Brewster watched the long column march into the valley. He felt an intense admiration for their precision, for their silent thoroughness. They were military men, he knew, and...

At that moment, without an instant's warning, dozens of fiery green streaks of light blazed into being. There was a scarcely audible hissing sound, and more than half of the advancing column tumbled over and rolled down the rest of the hill. Half the remaining men fell flat on the ground, taking whatever cover was afforded by the lined, pitted valley, and from their hands, holding small cones, came an answering fire, not a haphazard, wild spray, but a series of patient thrusts, each to one of the spots where green light had issued.

The other half of the platoon raced back to the bowls, but before they had reached them the peaks that surrounded the valley, which towered over the low hill, were filled with more of the green, thin flames. Man after man slumped over as the concealed fire kept blazing. There was no knowing which arid spot of land would suddenly become a deadly stream of fire. But the men in black never wavered, never broke.

Somehow they contrived to give each other a secret signal, and all together they began backing to the vehicles, firing steadily as they retreated. Of the more than fifty who had been there a moment before, three lived long enough to gain their vehicles. Of these, one toppled over at the door. The second vehicle remained where it stood. The third whirred and slowly moved away.

Immediately there was action in the valley. Scores of cloaks were swept aside and gathered up. The man in Brewster's cloak scrambled to his feet; he was holding a cone he hadn't had occasion to use. There were hundreds of the little men in the valley. A large number of them, more than twice the number of the dead tall men, had been killed, but the outcome of the battle had never been in doubt. The tall men had been outnumbered at least six to one.

Already many of the little men were running out of the valley. Numerous voices called out in English for the men from the *Trailblazer* to follow. The men hesitated in confusion, for though the monstrous battle they had witnessed had swiftly restored their minds, they heard Abbott shouting for them to wait—and they saw that somehow the *Trailblazer* had settled down until it now hovered no more than ten feet from the ground.

Abbott was running back toward the ship.

"Go back!" a dozen voices screamed in alarm. "There is no—" Several of the little men were running after him when Brewster knifed through their ranks, hurled his body forward and brought Abbott down.

At that moment the *Trailblazer's* bow kicked into the air. A muffled explosion roared out and a jagged hole appeared just short of the prow. A second, than a third blast rocked the ground together, and the thunder of the explosions, freed by the gaping wounds in the ship, rolled out from the stricken vessel with such force that the rush of air alone knocked scores off their feet. Again and again some mighty agent within the ship roared, blowing away huge sections of metal, strewing the valley with debris and dust. Finally the midship smashed apart, flying in every direction, and seeming to do it so slowly that it looked like a terrible flower blossoming...

WHEN it was over, and Brewster and Abbott arose, they saw, without fully understanding, that many of the little men had been killed by the convulsive explosion of the ship. And of their own, Morrow's face had been splattered away by a chunk of metal. He lay dead, a few feet from the remains of Lindstrom.

Four men had been left in the ship.

There was nothing there now but sections of molten carcass. A fire licked yellowly in the white sand.

His head still reeling from the impact of the sound, Brewster heard faintly the cries of the little men. They were pointing to the direction from which the Jeggites had come. Far off, a new black wave was speedily advancing toward them.

Brewster remembered little after that. He and the others fled, following the little men. Misty impressions remained in his mind; the sight of many little men who stopped running and lay down again under their white cloaks, waiting to ambush the new pursuers. The pools of drying blood...the sudden surge of bitterness as he remembered leaving the carton behind...the tremendous exhilaration he felt when he finally climbed out of the valley, as if he were flying, for every step sent him bounding into the air, covering twenty feet at a leap...

It was the same for the others from the ship—as if invisible shackles had been broken. They leaped high above their guides, frequently outdistancing them and forced to wait. Once, when Brewster looked behind, he saw green flame again in the valley, and dark bodies falling. And then, running into a tortuous zigzag of peaks, a small cavernous opening gave from a mountainside, and they were following the little men into the shelter of darkness...

"YES," said Brewster, slowly, staring down at the two mutilated bodies. "Their names were Hoake and Worth. They were combustion engineers on the first *Trailblazer* with Dr. John Stevens..." The corpses were mummified and shriveled, the features scarred and broken.

"You see," said the little man, earnestly. "Only six survived out of the entire crew. Though the Jeggites had been waiting for a ship to leave your world for centuries, they were unprepared when it came, and it crashed. Of the six survivors, we know that Dr. Stevens is still a prisoner of the Jeggites, and perhaps three others are still alive." The little man's eyes glinted as he looked at the bodies. "But these two men were tortured to death. We stole their bodies from a ship that intended to carry them away—"

"But we don't understand," said Abbott. Wearily, he brushed a hand across his face. "We don't know what you're trying to tell us. All this about the Jeggites and... We don't even know how you speak our language..."

Abbott turned to Brewster, as if to speak to him, but changed his mind when he looked at Brewster's curious expression. Brewster shrugged as if to say that it was useless. They had been talking to one, then another of the little men, and the hurried conversations had all been the same—nervous, repetitious explanations that got nowhere, that explained nothing ultimately, though they seemed overburdened with fact.

All that time there had been feverish, though it seemed aimless, activity around them. They were standing in one corner of an enormous-domed cavern, and there were scores of the little men about. They had been leaving and arriving in steady streams through the winding catacombs buried in the bowels of the mountain. Many of them sat along the tiers that formed an amphitheater of the cavern, little beings wrapped in their white shrouds, looking pale and ill in the light that flared from numerous torches.

"But you see we do speak your language," said the little man, as if he were helpless in the face of the fact. "Our spies among the Jeggite servants learned it from the men of your first expedition, and the Estannar teachers taught it to all. People of all the races can speak it. We learn it as the language of freedom."

"What kind of freedom?" said Brewster.

The little man frowned and looked more helpless than ever. He answered in a tone that implied that his answer was very obvious. "We want only one freedom—freedom from the Jeggites." His anxious eyes looked from Brewster to Abbott and traveled along the faces of the other men. "You do not believe me," he said, "but soon one of the Estannar will be here. He will tell you the same things, and then you will know they are true."

He gestured toward the mummified bodies. "That is why we kept these bodies—to show you that we spoke the truth, and that you must go with the Estannar when he comes to take you away."

"Take us away?" said Abbott, perplexed. "Where?"

"To safety, where you can help in the plan of the Estannars."

"Who are the Estannars?"

"They are our teachers. Some of them were sent here to live with us and direct our tasks. Everyone knew that once a ship had come from your world of Kren, others would follow. The Estannars worked out the plan to steal you from the Jeggites."

ABBOTT groaned in despair. He said to Brewster, "What do you make of this mess?"

"Save your breath," said Brewster. "Can't you see they're all idiots? He's told us a dozen times that these Estannars rule them, and one of them seems to be expected, so let's wait for that."

"You do no understand," said the little man. "The Estannars do not rule us. Only the Jeggites rule." Hatred blazed in his voice so fiercely that it gave a new dimension to this vapid, muddled being. "The Jeggites rule the Borons, Estannars, Ermos, Phylades, Hruthes…" He broke off, as if unable to continue a list so terrible to him.

Sudden, keen interest flickered on Brewster's expressionless face. "You mean these Jeggites rule the moon, and all the races of the moon are rebelling against them?" The little man nodded and would have spoken if Brewster had let him. "Think of it," said Brewster, softly, with an ironic twist on his lips. "The *barren* moon. Hundreds of thousands of people of different races, locked in a terrific fight against one of them…"

There was a fresh burst of activity at the far end of the cavern and a string of torches emerged from one of the tunnels that gave into it. As if it were a long awaited signal, the men seated in tiers rose and a subdued murmur swept up into the half-darkness.

The torchlight revealed a man walking quickly toward the group of humans. His rapid stride parted the white cloak, which, like his torch bearers and escort, he wore, and revealed an undergarment that looked like a suit of mesh armor, composed of hammered, beaten rings, gleaming as bright, fiery gold. He was scarcely taller than the men around him, but he appeared to tower over them. It might have been his erect carriage, or the way he held his head—he had a high, imposing forehead and wore his blond hair short—but whatever it was, there was something purposeful and strong about him.

When he stopped before the Earthmen, standing on the other side of the dead, leathery-hued corpses, and looked at each man individually, they met the frankness of his steady, blue eyes. He was a very handsome man by an Earthly standard, which was the only standard one could have applied to him, for there was no difference at all between him and an Earthman.

He said, "Do you have a spokesman?"

"I'm the spokesman," said Brewster.

"I am Dramon, an Estannar. Tell me your names."

THE Estannar stepped around the corpses and shook hands, like an Earthman, first with Brewster, then with each of the men as Brewster gave their names: Abbott, Stewart, Peters, Callahan, Drake, Purdom and Rogofsky. "There were six more of us," said Brewster, "who were—"

"I know," said Dramon. "They were lost in your escape from—"

"Four of them were blown up!" Abbott interrupted suddenly. The anger and baffled helplessness that had churned in him overflowed, as if here, finally, was someone who could be held accountable. "We don't know where we are," he said, "or what we've gotten into, but—"

"Suppose you let me tell you," said Dramon, quietly. A brief smile lit his face up. "We seem to be interrupting each other. Since we have little time now, and I have the answer to the countless questions I know must be in your minds, let me tell you what I think you have to know immediately."

He made a little gesture with his hands and he said, "You have been plunged into a situation of enormous complexity. At this moment the most important element of that situation is its danger. Though you have had no part in its creation, that danger threatens you more immediately than any of us. I speak not only of the danger to your lives. It is much more than that. But since I cannot undertake speaking to you now, I can only ask for your trust and your willingness to follow me."

"Where?" asked Brewster.

"I want to avoid the questions that must follow that answer."

Brewster said, "I'm afraid you can't avoid them."

"Very well," said Dramon. "Our plans are almost completed. We are taking you to Estannar."

"I thought Estannar was the name of a race."

Dramon breathed in audibly. "It is also the name of the place where that race lives. You know Estannar as the planet Venus."

In the stunned silence, the Estannar's intelligent eyes traveled over the semi-circle of men before him. "Yes," he nodded, slowly, "it is an overwhelming conception for you. I understand…

"The universe is filled with life, life that will appear familiar to you, and life so strange that its existence will be utterly incomprehensible. There are different races on each of the planets, and there are many breeds among these races. All the life of the universe, save yours, is the domain of the Jeggites—the inhabitants of the planet you call Mars. The Jeggites…the Martians…are the lords and conquerors of the universe.

"The Martians have waited centuries for mankind to come, for only you can help them complete their conquest. Only through you can they hope to conquer the planet we call Kren, and which you call Earth."

NICK BREWSTER tried to find coherence in the chaos of his mind. He looked away from the blond man before him, then he looked back again. His lips moved uncertainly, and finally he laughed. It was a troubled laugh. He didn't know where to begin.

He said, "You're saying that you—I mean all of you, these different races you speak of—can space-travel?"

"Interplanetary commerce existed a thousand years ago. Our sciences developed differently, more quickly on some planets than others but in many ways interplanetary science far outstrips your own. The destructive power alone of the Martians is prodigious, though—"

"If the...the Martians," said Brewster, pronouncing the word hesitantly, "wanted to conquer Earth, why didn't they try?"

"They've never stopped trying. The atmosphere that surrounds the Earth, hardly paralleled in density anywhere in the solar system, created such friction that the Martian vessels were burned. Martian vessels have reached the Earth, but only as cinders."

Brewster said, "It didn't burn our ship."

The Estannar made his gesture again, turning his palms outward and closing his fists. "I must ask you again to trust me. I can tell you everything, but not now. There is no time, believe me."

Brewster's eyes were clouded as he stared at the Estannar. "We don't know anything," he said. "We don't begin to understand you, let alone trust you. All we know is we're in the middle of something that's so big it...it..." Brewster said, "We've no reason to trust you."

Dramon held his fists closed so tightly that white spots appeared over his knuckles. "The Martians were waiting for a ship like yours," he said. "Our sciences never mastered metals. We created what your Dr. Stevens called a plastic civilization. Our plastics burned where your metals didn't. That is why we destroyed your ship—to make certain that it did not fall into the hands of the Martians."

The Estannar held up a restraining hand as Brewster said something about Stevens. Brewster flushed and went on speaking, but Dramon turned from him to the others, and instead of raising his voice as Brewster had done, he spoke more quietly.

"I cannot hope for your understanding," he said. "The Martians are beyond your understanding. The universe they rule is an empire built on hatred and violence. Its teeming billions of people are the slaves of Mars in one form or another, and all, to varying degrees, pay it tribute. Mars is a world of unreason, with a morality of its own, a morality so repugnant to the rest of the universe that it has fought the Martians for centuries.

"You are now part of that fight. You belong among us. But whether or not you want to help us—for potentially you are the greatest of our allies—returning to your own world is now impossible. Therefore, I must again ask you, will you come with me?"

The Estannar stepped back and regarded the men, and then, as he saw their eyes turn to Nick Brewster, he waited for Brewster to speak.

A CHANGE had come over Brewster. Listening to the Estannar, a host of conflicting thoughts and emotions had raced through him. His deep-set eyes glinted grayishly as he asked, "Would you say that the things you've told us are facts—or opinions?"

"Facts."

"No one would disagree with you?" Brewster persisted, quietly. "There aren't races...individuals, people, say, who see these things a little differently?"

"What are you trying to say?"

Brewster stroked his chin reflectively. "I'm saying it," he said. "I don't see why we must assume you're telling the truth."

Somberly, Dramon said, "It is a tragic fact that since I am of Estannar, I always speak the truth. I cannot lie."

Nick Brewster smiled. "I won't pretend to understand that. I do know, however, that every fight has two sides. At least two. It might just happen that we had fallen on one side, when we might have chosen the other, given our choice."

The little white men who were standing behind Dramon came in closer. Softly, the Estannar said, "You might choose... conquest...murder...slavery...injustice?"

"It depends," said Brewster. "It depends on your point of view." He faced his companions as he went on. "Not that we approve of murder, but murder, violence, injustice—even if they exist—are just words, opinions. The Indians of our west burned people alive, and from their point of view they were right because they were defending themselves. The pioneers conquered them, and from their point of view they were right because they needed land where they could live. If you, as an Estannar, landed in the Indian country a hundred years ago, the Indians would have told you that the pioneers were conquerors and murderers, but it would be only a partial truth. Maybe, if you'd had a choice, you'd have chosen the pioneers. Maybe they'd turn out to be more our kind."

The Estannar said, "You speak more to your friends than to me, but I do not see how you can think the Martians might be more your—"

Brewster interrupted. "Do we have a choice?"

"Earthmen," said Dramon, "speak for yourselves. Brewster will not believe me, but what do you say, Drake? And you, Purdom?" He had remembered the names perfectly. "What have you to say, Abbott?"

Joe Abbott said, "I believe you, if only because you saved our lives."

"Did he?" Brewster snapped. "We were stopped from crashing by a machine, but the *Martians* had that machine."

"What you say is true," the Estannar admitted, as the men waited. "The Martians had the machine, but it was stolen from us. We Estannars, Venusians, invented the machine long ago, anticipating—"

"Not interested!" said Brewster. "We don't know whose the machine was. We know the Martians used it. If we're to be thankful for being alive, we'll thank them!"

"It seems to me, Mr. Brewster—" Glenn Purdom began.

"Shut up!" said Brewster.

Dramon said, "But their purpose in saving you was only to—"

Brewster demanded, *"Do we have a choice?"*

THE Venusian let his hands fall limply to his sides. "No," he said, very quietly. "There never has been any question of a choice. You forget that more than your desires are involved." He flung his cloak over his shoulders and spoke a few words in a strange tongue to the little men around him. They cried out his orders, and the cavern echoed with their voices. "You will do as I say," said the Venusian to the Earthmen. "If you disobey, we will be forced to kill you."

"That," Brewster sneered, "is tyranny enforced by murder."

Dramon nodded. "If you prefer."

The little men had come pouring down from the overhanging tiers. They formed triple lines along the cavern floor, each of them holding a cone in his hands. At a signal, they started walking quickly into one of the tunnels from which many of them had come. Torchbearers went in with them at regular intervals, as the immense cavern emptied its lights into the tunnel, it grew more shadowy and dimensionless.

When half the little men had gone in, Dramon told the Earthmen to follow. All eight men preceded him, and behind Dramon came the rest of the little men.

The tunnel roof was low enough to force all the Earthmen except Rogofsky to stoop. There was no sound now save the patter of hundreds of feet in soft, powdery soil. The dust rose in a thick pall through which the torches burned feebly. The men coughed as they trudged on, holding bits of rags to their mouths, feeling along the devious turnings of the tunnel. The coughing grew more painful, the dust thicker, like a hot, dry mist.

Once, when the torches ahead disappeared around an abrupt turn, and those behind had not come up quickly enough to break the sudden descent of darkness, Brewster was startled by something that glowed weirdly, swinging near him. It turned out to be the luminous dial of Abbott's watch. The hands said 5:40. Wildly, Brewster thought, *Six hours ago I was home...*

The tunnel straightened and inclined down for a short distance, and Brewster peered ahead and saw the ghostly rows of figures swathed in cloaks, moving forward silently like bleached shadows in a white fog. Though full realization of what had happened to him and his men had not yet come, nor would it for some time, strangely, it seemed to Nick Brewster that of all the things that were going on in his mind, the memory of home was the most unreal...

AN HOUR later the column stopped. Dramon went ahead, returning in ten minutes to ask the Earthmen to follow him forward again. When the group reached the head of the column, they were once more in a cavern. This cavern was very long and narrow, crossing the tunnel at a right angle, like the crossbar of a capital T.

Four other Venusians were there, standing around a jutting stone on which lay a mass of tunics made of the shining armor, which Dramon alone of these five wore. When the Earthmen came into the cavern, the Venusians started to give each of them one of the tunics. Dramon stopped them, speaking to them in a foreign tongue.

Dramon said, "Come with me." The Earthmen followed him into the crossbar for a few hundred feet, swallowed up in darkness. They heard Dramon scratching and digging, then something heavy rolled away from the wall of the crossbar.

They were looking out on a vast plain. It was nightbound, but its face was clearly illumined by what seemed to be great black pots of fire. The fire was unlike any the Earthmen had ever seen. The tongues of flame spread out evenly in all directions, forming a blazing rosette, and what little movement there was in each of these many petals of fire was slow and almost purposeful. The light that came from these pots of fire was white, faintly tinged with amber, and this light too was evenly spread over the plain.

Two hundred yards away, one-third hidden in a pit, though they saw all of it because they were looking down, was a spear-shaped ship. It was like a queer, bright orange fish, with huge, sloping fins, and tiny lighted windows in its head like many sightless eyes. It was about four hundred feet long.

Beyond the ship were other ships, none of them very near. They were of varying shapes and colors and most of them were larger than the orange vessel. In the center of the plain were several low buildings. Most of them were circular and lights blazed in them. People were moving about on the plain, but there were not more than ten near the orange ship. These were all men dressed in black.

From behind the orange ship, a bowl-shaped vehicle rolled away. Far over to the left, a small vessel shot into the sky. It left a trail of glowing cinders behind it. When its roar and sibilant hissing died away it was quiet again.

Dramon pushed the stone back in place and shut off the view. The Earthmen had heard footsteps passing them in the crossbar all this time. One or two torches along the shallow length of the cavern revealed that the little white men had all taken positions parallel to the Earthmen.

"That ship you saw not far away," said Dramon, "was waiting to take you to Mars. The Martians are confused by what has happened. Most of the armed strength of their colonial regiments are scouring the lighted portions of Boron, your moon. At a given signal we will all come out of the mountain and seize that ship. It is a warship, faster than most, and with a good start, it may outdistance all pursuit, or, if overtaken, it will have a good chance of fighting its way out."

"Where do you intend taking us?" Brewster asked.

"I don't know," said Dramon. "My orders will come later."

Brewster asked, "What happens if the attack fails?"

THE other Venusians arrived, carrying the armor tunics. There was a hurried consultation between them and Dramon, and when it was over one of them took all the armor and went back with it. The other three stayed.

Dramon then answered Brewster. "If we fail, death is the best alternative. The worst is capture by the Martians. Remember the bodies of the men from the first ship."

He looked up at Brewster in the gloom. "What you are thinking is correct," he said. "I decided against giving you the armor. Since you will have no part in the fighting, you will be in no danger if we succeed. If we failed, it would only aid in your capture."

Brewster said, "You mean the Martians want us alive, but if you fail it'll be easier for you to kill us this way."

"If you prefer," said Dramon.

He said something to one of the little men, and his words were passed along. In a moment, down the length of the crossbar at intervals of a few feet, the little men pulled away stones that blocked the cavern off from the plain below the mountain slope.

"Stay here until you are told to leave," said Dramon.

He raised an arm quickly and brought it down. A moment later he jumped out of the cavern and started running down the mountainside, and behind him came a wave of the white men, the Borons. Another long row of Borons swept out of the shallow cavern, then a third, a fourth.

The first row was almost halfway down before the group of black-clad Martians saw them coming. They hardly had a chance to do more than that. They dropped to their knees, and scores of thin green lances were already piercing them. One by one they flopped over.

Suddenly the pots of fire nearest the orange ship flared up in streamers of flame. In an instant it had spread over the field. The petals seemed to join hands and form single, immense pyramids of fire that lighted the field with the brilliance of sunlight. From far off a series of chiming, high-pitched notes sounded. And now the pots of fire died down to a dull, eerie glow that seemed darker than night, with one fantastic difference—the Borons were clearly visible in that glow, though nothing else was.

Martians had long since come pouring out of surrounding vessels, meeting the attack. Now they were lost in the darkness. Lines of Borons, gleaming with phosphorescence wherever their skin showed, swept past the place where the orange ship had been, carrying the battle ever deeper into the plain. The Borons covered themselves with their white cloaks, and as long as they remained under them, were as invisible as the Martians. From their weapons came streams of green fire that covered the plain with planned, intricate patterns as delicate as spider webs.

WHERE the green burst against a ship, it spluttered up momentarily in showers of sparks. Where green answered green, other streams of fire, suddenly coming into existence under the level of the patterns, put an end to those answers.

All at once there were lines of liquid fire pouring down from twenty feet above the plain. Again and again a score of green streaks would stab all around it, until the overhead attack would stop, but only from that one spot. The Martians, with strength accustomed to much greater gravities, were leaping high into the air. Their targets were frequently visible, and several Martians had leaped past the fourth line of Borons, to attack them from the rear, from everywhere at once.

The field was a silent chaos of motion, motion that was described only in terms of light. Little by little the Borons edged deeper, cutting a clear path of destruction behind which there was calm and solid darkness. Little by little the green fires died away. Suddenly lights streamed out of the portholes of the orange ship.

"Now!" cried one of the Venusians to the Earthmen. "Run for the ship!"

As the Venusian stooped to go through the hole, Nick Brewster seized him by the neck, swiftly raised him overhead and hurled him at the two remaining Venusians. Instantly, almost before they had hit the opposite wall of the cavern, he smashed into them, his fists flailing like pistons. It was over in seconds. Brewster felt in the darkness for the cone-shaped rods each had carried. He found them and got up.

The other men had sensed and felt, rather than seen, what he had done. Abbott cried out some incoherent query. The sound of the brief scuffle and Abbott's voice brought approaching footsteps.

"Duck outside," Brewster whispered fiercely. He grabbed at the men nearest him and shoved them through the holes. He jumped out after them and waited for the others. He couldn't be sure that they were all there, so he whispered, "Up the mountain. Hold hands and jump." He clutched hands on either side of him, then leaped up as high as he could. He landed sooner than he expected; the slope was very steep at that point, and as the men crashed into it, their line broke. They felt for each other again and jumped once more, unevenly this time.

A pencil of green fire careened over their heads, seeking them out. The men scrambled for shelter, lying flat against the slope. The green came closer. The sound of their breathing was giving them away. Brewster fumbled with the green cones, but nothing happened. A beam of fire bit off pieces of rock near him. A second beam joined it.

BREWSTER crawled away a few feet and got to his knees. He took a deep breath, tensed his muscles as he crouched, and let go. His leap carried him at least fifty feet down the mountainside, behind the origin of the green streaks, and slightly to one side. He edged in closer and judged the distance. Then he threw himself up and forward. He came down on two forms standing close together. His knees hit one in the back, and as he toppled forward, he spread his arms and encircled the other. A violent stab of pain hit his forearm and crept to his shoulder and he rolled over on one side and kicked with his feet. He got up too quickly and overshot his mark and the green flame brushed his throat. Then he jumped almost straight up, and when he landed, immediately dove forward. One of his hands thudded sickeningly against flesh that broke under the force of his blow and fell away.

He lay very still, trying not to breath, waiting. Something scraped less than five feet away, downhill. He rolled over suddenly, and when he got up, he was holding a squirming body high in the air. He swept his arms down and smashed the body in his grip against the rocks. When he opened his hands, the body rolled down the slope.

He stood up, sick with pain. Nausea rolled through his body and he vomited. He felt numbness coming over him, and he staggered as he started back up the slope. "Joe," he called out, weakly. "Joe." He sank down on one knee, then fell. Moments later, he hardly realized that Abbott had found him.

It seemed to him that the world was on fire. Something crashed and roared in his ears. He had no way of knowing that the orange ship had blasted off. The pots of fire had blazed up again, and their light had revealed scores of bowl-shaped vehicles on the plain. From these rolling monsters, which had come up under cover of darkness, jets of green flame spurted. The Borons, helpless now, scattered, falling by tens under the raking fire from the vehicles.

Abbott stared down into the brilliant light of the plain, watching the carnage slowly come to an end. In his arms he held Brewster's head. There was a bewildered light in his eyes as he looked over the field and heard Nick Brewster mutter, with his last conscious breath, "The Martians…will…save…us…"

Brewster's body jerked convulsively and he was still.

TWO sounds marred a depthless quiet. One was a constant, low-pitched humming that was barely audible. The other was sporadic, a hissing noise which lasted for a few seconds at a time. The second sound was made by little bursts of air that came from a tube placed in the center of the fluted ceiling. Nick Brewster had figured it out after staring at it a while, feeling the air around him freshen after the hissing noise.

He rolled over on his side, just a little. A stout, though somewhat flexible, belt pinned him down. Across the small cubicle, one atop the other in a sort of double-decker bunk, lay Paul Stewart and Bucky Callahan. Brewster wondered whether they were dead or asleep. He monkeyed with his belt until he pressed a button that opened it, then he swung his legs over the side of his cot and sat up, his legs dangling some four feet from the floor. He peered down and saw little Rogofsky lying in the cot underneath.

After he eased himself to the floor he tried shaking each of the three men, but nothing happened. Nevertheless, they were alive; he felt their breath against his hands, testing them… then he saw his right arm. The leather sleeve had been cut open and there was a long, pink scar from wrist to elbow. He touched his throat and felt a chunk of knotted flesh. He remembered a little, then gave it up.

He looked over the small, windowless chamber. It, and the furniture, was made of a smooth substance that felt like the ladder the Borons had used. A plastic? Then so was the belt, though it was pliable. The bedding felt like wool, but it was as spongy as rubber. There was a crack along one of the two free walls. When he touched it, it parted and the two sections slid out of sight, forming a door that gave on a narrow passageway.

Brewster walked down the passageway, turned with it, and came to a dead end. Suddenly the small section of the floor on which he was standing began to descend. It went down for about ten feet and fitted into the floor of a large room. It was severely furnished with a few chairs and tables. Along the opposite wall was a series of cots, in each of which lay sleeping Martians.

Brewster spent a long minute looking at the Martians before he resumed his wandering. Individuals though they were, they shared in common their slender, long faces, skin that was a deep, coppery hue…and something more…something unrelaxed about them, though they slept.

The adjoining chamber was divided by a raised platform in its center. The ceiling was a maze of wheels and dials, and the walls were covered with colored panels, each of which bore a different symbol. Four Martians slept in cots below the platform. At the far wall was an open door. Brewster went through it and found himself in a slightly curving passageway again. It was lined with windows.

At first he saw nothing when he looked through. Then the blackness became pierced with points of light. He walked along the passageway from window to window, noticing the different colors of the lights. When he was near the last window, he saw a circle of light, like a diffused corona around a smaller circle of darkness. Beyond it he saw a much larger greenish sphere—then suddenly, for an instant—a relief map of mountains and plains.

NOW he knew where he was. He was in a Martian spaceship. The corona was sunlight, glancing off the Moon; the green ball was Earth. The Martians had come around to the dark side of the Moon.

He went to the end of the corridor and was in another chamber of sleeping Martians. He retraced his steps along the windows, sensing he was going to the bow. He climbed up three stairs, pressed against a door and was in an oval room. There, strapped in a reclining chair, silhouetted against an orange, transparent wall, was a Martian. Brewster walked up to him and saw that on the other side of the chair was an inclined panel of tiny dials and buttons. Through the transparent wall he saw the planets, gleaming like jewels.

As Brewster stood there, the Martian's eyes opened. After a moment, the Martian sighed and said, "Have you been awake long?"

Brewster said, "About ten minutes, if you understand that." The Martian let breath out slowly and nodded. "I've been wandering around the ship," Brewster added. "Everyone's asleep."

"Not asleep," said the Martian. It seemed difficult for him to speak, and he inhaled several long breaths before he said, "They took a drug to avoid the effects of the first few minutes after a take-off. I use less because I am in command of the ship, but the others should soon be awake." He motioned and said, "I should like to talk to you. Sit down, if you will."

"Where?" said Brewster, but as he turned around, he saw that a chair had come up from the deck. He sank into its softness, watching the deck open again as a low table rose up.

Brewster gasped in bewilderment. He looked from what was on the table to the Martian and saw the thinly veiled amusement in the Martian's gray eyes. Brewster said something inaudible and began to open the carton. For on the table was the huge carton that had been the last thing Nick Brewster had taken from the *Trailblazer II*. His hands were trembling. He took out several long envelopes, dug in past the phonograph and the pile of records and other wrapped parcels and brought out one of several dozen cartons of cigarettes.

The Martian smiled as Brewster fumbled in his leather coat for a pack of matches. Brewster struck a light and took a long drag. The Martian's smile deepened as the first grateful plume of smoke blew out.

Brewster said quietly, "You don't know what this means to me."

"But I do," said the Martian. "We were very careful to bring it along after the Borons abandoned it." He let Brewster smoke a while before he resumed what he had been saying. "We didn't drug you because you remained unconscious after our surgeons operated on you."

Brewster touched his throat and said nothing.

THE Martian said, "Your arm was almost burned away, and you had a hole through your throat. Had we found you a little later, possibly not even our surgeons..." He waved a deprecating hand. "But to the point. The Estann-Venusians' plan would have succeeded if you hadn't attacked them. They had to leave without you or fall to us themselves. We found the bodies of two Venusians you killed in enforcing your escape." He paused, then asked directly, "Why did you do it?"

Brewster lit another cigarette. He liked the calm intelligence in the Martian's eyes, the subdued quality of his voice.

He said, "I don't know."

"You didn't believe what the Venusians told you?"

"I wasn't sure."

"You couldn't be sure. But what if you guessed wrong?"

"Did I?"

The Martian's keen eyes flickered. "How strange and varied you Earthmen are," he mused aloud. "We can stand on the plains of Boron and see your world plainly, with the naked eye. If we use our powerful telescopes, we can look down into individual streets of your cities, see your gardens, animals, rivers. We know so much of the externals of your world, and so little of its people..."

He murmured, "What if I were to tell you that the Venusians cannot lie? *Cannot*—if you understand that."

"I don't," Brewster said. "One of them told me the same thing."

"It was true. It is the outstanding characteristic of the Venusian race. An organic impossibility..." he shrugged contemptuously, "...like an animal that must run toward light...a seed that must grow in soil. The one vital flaw in the destiny of Estannar—of Venus. They cannot lie."

Nick Brewster shifted uneasily in his chair and regarded the impassive Martian. He started to say something and stopped as another Martian appeared in the passage leading to the bow. The two Martians exchanged a few words and the second withdrew.

"How fortunate we are," the Martian said, as an aside, adding, "Will you look in your coat pockets, please?"

Brewster felt the pockets of his leather coat, and from one of the inner ones he withdrew a strange, soft sheet of folded paper. He unfolded it and read a dark-inked, neat handwriting.

To Whom This Message Is Delivered:
You have fallen into the hands of madmen. No matter what you see, no matter what you are told, believe only the words of this message, for they may be the last I will ever write. Torture, unbelievable suffering, and eventual death wait for you—and from

these there is no escape unless the Venusians can help you. If they fail you must destroy yourselves, I have no way of knowing how many years separate us, but if you are a human being, believe these words or live to curse the doubt that prevented you.

Dr. John Stevens,
Commander of the Trailblazer I.

"A forgery," said the Martian.

Brewster passed the paper to him. "I know the handwriting," he said, with no particular expression.

The Martian read the paper, and when he had finished, he held it in one hand and struck it gently against the open palm of the other.

"Rather florid," he remarked, coolly. "As a matter of fact, your Dr. Stevens has been in such poor mental health since he survived the wreck of his ship that he could not possibly have written this. Were you friends?"

"I paid for his ship."

"Interesting," the Martian commented, thoughtfully. "I plan to prove that this is a forgery at dinner. It will be a fascinating diversion for you, observing how the Venusians use their extraordinary intelligence in wild, futile attempts to smash our empire. Dramatic as it is, this adventure is less remarkable than many—"

HE BROKE off for some reason, and looking into Brewster's eyes, he allowed himself to smile. "You know," he said, "we Martians fancy ourselves as somewhat clairvoyant. We like to think that we are the forerunners of a telepathic race. But you are an uncommonly enigmatic subject. Tell me, do I bore you with this…this…"

"This information on the Venusians?" Brewster finished, dryly.

"Ah, but now you have quite given yourself away," the Martian reproved him, toying with the paper. "Well then, I was describing the Venusian resourcefulness. They knew as well as we did that someday another ship would come from your world, and they prepared a surprise for us. Realizing that you were our chance to unite our civilizations, the real surprise is the fact that they did not kill you immediately. Certainly their hatred and envy are equal to it. Some plan, which as yet has escaped our vigilance…

"We still do not know," he resumed, after a reflective pause, "how they managed to smuggle themselves to Boron. Without Venusians to guide them, the Borons would be helpless; they have the minds of children. With direction and weapons, they are magnificent fighters. And though there aren't many of them left—we spread a disease among their females—they have made our colonial outposts on Boron pestilential and dangerous, because of the Venusians.

"The Venusians," he repeated slowly, grimly, "and their truths."

He unfolded the paper, and in a lighter tone that pretended not to realize the significance of his words, he reminded himself casually, "Oh, yes, I meant to explain that. Naturally, I meant they always told the truth as they see it. That isn't always the same thing as being unable to lie, is it?"

And now that he had completed the conversational circle, he studied Brewster watchfully, noting Brewster's rigidity relax the least bit, almost measuring the hardly audible sigh that escaped him. Brewster said evenly, "I'll take your word for it. I'll take your word for anything you say because I've a lot to learn. But if you want to tell me—tell me. Don't play cat and mouse with me."

"Cat-and-mouse?"

"It means I don't like being played with."

The Martian nodded. "We all have a lot to learn. For example, the Venusians made a fatal error in assuming they could force you to their will." Slowly, he began to smile again, until his manner was warm and friendly, more so than it had previously approached being. "I like you," he said.

He rose from his chair. "And now," he said, returning the sheet of folded paper to Brewster, "I have my work to do, and you, doubtless, are anxious to see your friends again."

Brewster started, and a quick flush spread over his face. He rose beside the Martian. They were almost the same height.

"You'd quite forgotten to ask about them," the Martian said, with an odd twist to his smile. "The other four were put in a room similar to yours. Any member of the crew will direct you, most of them at least understand your language."

BREWSTER picked up the carton, caught the questioning look on the Martian's face, put the carton down again and began to empty it. "Do you want me to explain these things?" he asked. "There's nothing in here except some pictures, a machine for playing music, cigarettes, and these."

He lifted out two heavy, blue-gleaming automatic pistols.

"Metal. And very handsome," the Martian murmured, appreciatively. "Do you have much ammunition?"

"About five hundred rounds."

"Bullets, that is? Ah, well, when we have more time to continue our discussion, I'll show you some of our weapons. You should enjoy them.

Until dinner, then, Nick." He held out a firm hand, which Brewster took. "Your friends told me your name. I am Captain Akar."

Brewster grinned and observed, "It sounds like a laxative."

He put the guns back and took the carton with him as he left. Retracing his steps, he found activity everywhere—Martians attending the gigantic, complex instruments, repairing, adjusting. Brewster lingered long enough to satisfy himself that he had the freedom of the ship before asking for his companions. When he was directed, without even an escort offered, he felt happier than he had been for…but when he suddenly looked at his watch, it had stopped.

The men were on the upper deck, in a semi-circular observation room, fronted by a concave, transparent wall that revealed the starry void through which the ship silently forged.

When Brewster entered, the talking he had heard stopped so abruptly that first Callahan, then Drake, tried to pretend that nothing untoward had happened. Brewster let the carton down and looked at the men, and though he had not the least idea of what might have been going on among them, one thing he knew as a certainty—it was not his sudden appearance, in itself, that had stopped the talking. He sensed the hostility that lay in the room. The sense of freedom, almost of well being, and of looking forward to the unfolding of events greater than he could yet realize, disappeared.

He said, "You can tell it straight to me."

Joe Abbott walked toward him. "You're right, Nick," he said. "Anything we've got to say we'll say in front of you." He faced the men a moment before continuing. "It's this," he said. He opened his palm and revealed a sheet of folded paper.

BREWSTER knew what it was before he opened it. It was a duplicate of the warning signed by Dr. Stevens. He looked at it without reading it and gave it back to Abbott.

"Stewart found it in his coat," said Abbott.

"In his coat," Brewster repeated. "But there seems to have been a question as to whether you were going to tell me about it."

As Abbott hesitated, Glenn Purdom stood up and said, "You're right, Brewster." It was the first time any of the subordinate crew had refused him the formal *Mister*. "All we know is that something too much for us to understand all at once…anyway, you've taken things in your own hands, and you haven't seen the things we've seen—"

"What things?"

Abbott answered: "You were unconscious. We were on the Moon for more than twenty hours after the Martians got us. We've seen enough of their slave system and their senseless murdering—"

"They've treated you all right, haven't they?"

"So far. But what if the Venusians were right?"

"They *lied*," Brewster snapped.

Peters spoke up. "We'll make up our own minds."

Brewster regarded Peters in mock wonder. "What minds?" He laughed abruptly. "What difference does it make who you believe? What can you do? Take the ship over and head for Venus, you damned idiot?"

Peters took a step forward and Brewster said, "I'll break you in half if you come any closer."

"Stay where you are, Matt," Abbott said.

Brewster took out the warning he had found in his own pocket, and together with the copy Abbott had given him, handed both to Abbott.

"What does this do to your pet theories?" he sneered. "Here's a copy of that paper that the *Martians* gave *me*."

Conscious of the impact of his words, he stood there, savoring the effect as he watched the men. Then, as each came forward to look for himself, he disregarded them, busying himself instead with the carton, from which he broke out a pack of the precious cigarettes. He threw the pack to Drake.

"From our enemies," Brewster said.

Nick Brewster felt he had won a complete victory. The gratitude with which the cigarettes were taken was subordinate only to the shock of his revelation. It seemed to him that the tension vanished with the clouds of smoke. How sweet the tobacco smelled.

Abbott smiled wanly, quoting: "Beware of a Greek bearing gifts."

"What about looking a gift horse in the mouth?" Brewster grinned.

"All right then. Did you find out where we're being taken?"

The question jarred Brewster. "It was a short conversation," he said. "We didn't get to it."

"Strange," Abbott mused. "It was the first thing you asked the Venusian. You insisted on it."

THE thoughts raced swiftly through Brewster's mind. Yes, it was strange. He had forgotten all about it...as he had not long before forgotten to ask about his friends...his crew, at any rate. Why? Was it because he felt a more trusting instinct for the Martians? There was no reason for it. But so too, there was no answer.

"I'll tell you this," Brewster said. "When I do ask I'll get a straight answer—not an 'I don't know.'"

"But the Venusian didn't know!" Abbott exclaimed, and tried to check the exclamation too late.

"Really…" Brewster breathed, somehow aware that he was stumbling into something important, something concealed, and in which every other man in the room shared. "And what makes you so sure, Joe?"

Tight-lipped, Abbott said, "Nothing. I just felt it."

Now Brewster knew that the hostility he had felt when he had first entered the room had never disappeared. He was baffled by the reason for it, enraged as much as mystified. But he had to go easily, to find out what was up without destroying his chances entirely. He took the pack of cigarettes from Drake and lit one, offering another to Abbott, who had not yet taken any.

Abbott shook his head. "No thanks, Nick. I don't want to offend you, but I couldn't smoke one of these without remembering that you chose to take them when instead you might have saved one of the four men left behind in the ship."

Nick Brewster stared into Abbott's eyes. His mouth opened the least bit and he licked his lips as if from a bitter taste. Then, with the hand that held the freshly lighted cigarette, he slapped Abbott viciously across the face. The cigarette flew out in a shower of tiny sparks, leaving a dark smudge over a reddening welt on Abbott's cheek.

Abbott had fallen back a step. He made no move. The other men came up and gathered around him. Brewster picked up the carton and left the room in a deathly silence.

THE silence had persisted until now. Brewster glanced at Captain Akar, noticing how the Martian's unstudied gaze swept the length of the table, at the head of which he sat. The eight Earthmen who were his guests at dinner sat four on either side of him, having seated themselves in such order that Nick Brewster had been left the chair to the Captain's right, seemingly by chance. Below them sat three Martian officers, their rank indicated by the number of black velvet bands on their sleeves, of which Akar wore three.

Brewster knew that the Captain was aware of something irregular. There was little or no conversation. Though the food was strange and excellent, and this was the second meal for the Earthmen in many hours, there was no enthusiasm. The Captain and his junior officers had made efforts to get the men to talk. The Earthmen asked about a fruit or drink, but never touched any of the countless things the Martians might reasonably have expected them to ask about.

But Akar's eyes were too casual, Brewster decided. Probably he knew or had guessed that there had been a falling out. What he was now trying to fathom was the reason for it, and in this he knew no more than Brewster, because, Brewster realized, the wall between the crew and him was there long before he had struck Abbott. The note that Akar had called a forgery was part of it, and Akar had said he would prove his charge at dinner.

The dessert was the most elaborate of all the dishes. It was a huge pastry made of iced fruit that tasted like pineapple. Brewster reflected on the unusually rich food that these stern, stoical militarists ate, and yet the dining hall itself seemed to prepare one for luxury. Of all the ship, this chamber alone was obviously fitted with an eye for comfort; the walls hung with tapestries, the chairs deep and reclining, the lighting soft, the floors smoothly carpeted. It was a contradiction that Brewster was to ponder many times before he came to understand it.

"And now, gentlemen," said Captain Akar, "we have prepared a diversion for you." He said something to one of his officers, who left the room, and added, "I hope it will cement our friendship."

When the officer returned, several members of the Martian crew followed, carrying a heavy chair. It was an odd chair. Each of the arms terminated in a red, translucent ball, and this same gleaming substance formed a hollow headrest on the chair's back. When it was placed on the floor not far from where Akar sat, a small machine was attached to it. One of the Martians tested the machine by throwing in a switch. Its effect was to bring the red substance to startling, gleaming, sparkling life. It shone brilliantly, and crackling noises issued from the little sparks that flew from it.

The demonstration ended, the machine was turned off. Captain Akar rose from the table, and standing beside the chair, began to speak to the Earthmen. "Gentlemen," he said, "because of an organic deficiency—or construction, if you will—the Venusians are the only race in the universe that are unable to speak a falsehood. They cannot lie."

THOUGH his opening sentence was a bombshell, Akar continued without pause, speaking directly and simply, telling them what he had told Brewster some two hours before, including his accusations against the Venusians and their work among the Borons. And though he made no apparent effort to convince the Earthmen that *he* was telling the truth, and his sole intent seemed to be the bare transmission of information,

Brewster knew that his words were more effective than the Martian knew. For all the Earthmen, Brewster realized, thought back to that moment when Dramon, the Venusian, had sadly said, "It is a tragic fact that since I am of Estannar, I always speak the truth. I cannot lie." And here, from the lips of a Martian, was corroboration.

"I intend now to show you," Akar concluded, "that even truth can have several sides, that what is true for a Venusian is not necessarily a truth for all." His face was expressionless.

He pointed to Joe Abbott. "Will you please sit down in this chair, Mr. Abbott?" he requested.

After a moment's hesitation, Abbott got up from the table and crossed over to the chair. The Captain placed Abbott's hands so that his fists closed around the balls on the chair arms, and he adjusted the headrest to suit Abbott's height.

"I'm going to ask you a question, Mr. Abbott," said Akar, quietly. "An unimportant question. I want you to resolve not to make any reply to it."

Abbott said, "I'm to try to say nothing at all?"

"Precisely. Now, Mr. Abbott, how did you like your dinner?"

As Akar spoke, he pressed in the switch. Abbott cried out and leaped out of the chair, and the next instant smiled in chagrin as he rubbed his palms together.

"You found it painful?" the Captain asked, surprised.

"No," Abbott admitted wryly. "Just—well, funny." He sat down again and gripped the balls firmly. "Let's go," he said.

"What do you think of Martian cooking?" said Akar.

Abbott's fists grew white. His clenched hands trembled and his tight lips parted.

"Wonderful!" he blurted. "It's the best…"

And he stopped speaking the instant Captain Akar released the switch.

"You found it impossible to keep from speaking, did you not, Mr. Abbott?" Abbott nodded. "Well," said Akar, with a slight smile, "I am most pleased to learn that you like our food, but I would like to demonstrate that all this clever chair does is to force you to speak, not necessarily to speak the truth. You were caught off guard that time, Mr. Abbott, but now let us try again. And this time, resolve not only to remain silent, but to lie when you answer me.

"Mr. Abbott, how old are you?"

THE Captain threw the switch in again. After a short struggle, Abbott answered, "A hundred and forty-two."

"And your sex, Mr. Abbott?"

"Female, dammit!"

The Captain released the switch again. "Well, gentlemen, unless we are to assume that Mr. Abbott is an old hag, I think we will agree that this amazing chair has no effect on what one says, but merely makes one speak." He matched Abbott's embarrassed smile as he asked, "Do you agree, Mr. Abbott?"

Again Abbott nodded, then he said, "Would you mind turning it on without asking me anything at all?"

Akar again switched the chair on. After a moment's silence, Joe Abbott unaccountably said, "This is a hell of an idea. When I was a kid back in school we had a teacher named Miss Happy. I guess I just feel like babbling. Will you turn it off, please?"

"So you see," said the Captain, "that it makes one speak, if only to talk nonsense. If you sat here long enough, you could talk yourself into exhaustion, and you could tell us anything, lies as well as facts."

He waited for Abbott to get back to his seat at the table before adding, with soft emphasis: "But what if one couldn't speak without speaking the truth?" His eyes searched the men's faces. "This chair would then have a new function and value, would it not? It has that function and that value when we Martians deal with the sworn enemies of our civilization."

At a motion from the Captain a door opened and a Venusian was led in. It was the same Venusian who had been in the caverns—the one who had taken the armor away.

Akar said, "This important capture, together with penetration of secret recesses in the mountain, we owe to Mr. Brewster's aid." The Venusian was seated in the chair, his hands strapped down to force him to hold the ruby balls, his shoulders pinioned until his head fitted into the headrest.

A dramatic hush came over everything. The Earthmen leaned forward in rigid interest. Two of the junior officers left the table and stood close to the chair.

"What is your name?" Akar said to the Venusian.

The Venusian stiffened and remained silent. He betrayed no fear, but rather a grim defiance in the face of inevitability.

Captain Akar threw in the switch. Slivers of sparkling crimson shone through the white of the Venusian's shivering hands.

"What is your name?"

"Pollo," The word was torn from him.

"When did you come to Boron?"

"Since four revolutions of Boron."

"Your capacity?"

"Technical instructor in use of armor."

"Your task?"

"To assist Dramon in the raid. To equip the Earthmen."

"What preparations for the raid were you aware of?"

"That Borons, under our combat instructors—"

"How many combat instructors?" the Captain interrupted.

"I met three. I know of no others."

"Continue."

The Venusian continued exactly where he had been interrupted. "...had carried out systematic attacks on Lightside patrols and captured large numbers of weapons."

"Is that all?"

"Yes."

AKAR'S disappointment was brief. For the first time he faced the intent Earthmen. "You see," he said, "though there are a great many questions we should like to have answered, it is useless to ask. The Venusians, knowing that capture means that we have access to their secrets, protect themselves by limiting their knowledge. If ten men are to go on a mission, only one knows what the mission is, and even then only to a limited extent. Their plans are shared among many of them—"

"For instance," Joe Abbott broke in, "would you say that it was entirely possible that none of the Venusians knew where they were to take us after they had taken us off the—off Boron?"

Captain Akar smiled through a frown. "I see they could not satisfy your curiosity," he said, shrewdly. "Undoubtedly it was true. What they had arranged was a rendezvous at some specific point. Only one of them knew that point, and since this fool was an armor technician he wouldn't even know that point, though we shall examine him minutely later on. They can take advantage of any loophole in a question to evade it without actually lying."

Nick Brewster observed: "What happens if the one man who knows where to go happens to be killed or captured?"

The Martian shrugged. "Failure for all." He waved to the Venusian and said, as if it was self-evident, "Only demons would persist in the face of such tremendous difficulties. These Venusians are as tenacious as plague lice. I have caught Venusians who were at great meetings, only to find that everyone present was blindfolded, to avoid knowledge of their number or identities. For instance, observe how little this one knows."

Switching the machine on again, Akar said, "Do you know anything of the make-up of your new armor?"

"No."

"Where is the armor hidden?"

"I gave it to a friend."

"His name?"

"I don't know."

To the Earthmen, Akar observed, "And if he did know his name, and if we fortunately captured this friend, undoubtedly we should find that this second one had given it to a third, the third to a fourth, until finally it had been given to a Boron to hide."

He asked the Venusian, "How did you know exactly when the Earthmen were coming?"

Captain Akar shrugged and was about to continue questioning when the Venusian answered. "We posted watches on all your gravity cushions. We knew that you would arrest the fall of the next Earth ship, and that if you moved the gravity cushions, the Earthmen were coming."

"And to find out where they would land?"

"We detailed forces to cover all movements of the cushions."

THE Captain nodded and showed slight satisfaction, observing, "This is something our friend here should not have known, though it is common sense enough. Valueless as it is, it tells us something. It tells us that he overheard things he shouldn't have—a condition that was possible only through a relaxation of discipline and order. What is true for him must be true for others, and when our forces have brought in some of those others, they too will know things they shouldn't. Perhaps we may discover what new type of bomb destroyed your ship so effectively. Perhaps another may have a clue to the schedule they use for smuggling Venusians past our space patrols on Boron..."

The Martian Captain paused, as if reflecting, and his flashing eyes swept the room. Brewster had seen him do this more than once, and each time he had felt a vague uneasiness, as if he could fathom the same feeling in the Martian. He wondered why he assumed it at all. Certainly Akar was capable of hiding anything he wanted hidden. His face was an obedient, expressionless mask, altered only when it suited him. Why then did Brewster feel that he understood this being?

Now Akar said, "Has it occurred to you to wonder why this Venusian answered in your language, English? Why did he not speak in Martian, certainly a more natural language for him?"

"Why Martian?" Brewster asked. "Why not Venusian?"

"There have been no other languages but Martian since the spread of our civilization. Ours is the language of the universe."

"Then why did he speak English?" Brewster asked.

Akar said, quietly, "We are dealing with a highly intelligent being, remember, an individual whose brain is capable of many twistings and turnings. To understand his thought processes, let us make one assumption—that he had something to hide both from me and from you. By answering in English, he calculated to make me think that he had nothing to hide from me. As long as he is safe from me, he is safe from you, for only I know how to ferret out his secret."

Brewster shook his head. "I don't see it."

"I know you don't. Not yet. But let us go further. Assuming that he had something to hide from me and from you, he could now choose to answer either in Martian or in English.

"Now, the moment he came in here and saw that I was going to question him before you Earthmen, he guessed that I might have some suspicion, that I was going to try to make him admit something to you that he didn't want to admit. Knowing that, he could have played safe. By answering only in Martian, he could prevent me from getting his answers to you, because I would be forced to translate them..."

"And if you translated?" Brewster asked.

"Would you believe me? Especially if I claimed to be translating an extremely damaging confession?" Akar let himself smile. "I wouldn't expect you to believe me. Neither would this Venusian. But the price of keeping his secret from you would be practical admission to me that he *had* something to hide. And since he wanted to keep this admission from me as well, he answered in English, hoping I would thus assume he had nothing to hide from any of us. Do you see it now?"

"Only partly," said Brewster, thoughtfully. "But suppose we don't assume that he had anything to hide? He might very well have answered in English even in that case. You haven't proved he actually *had* anything to hide."

AKAR NODDED somberly. "Nor could I by reasoning alone. I have tried to trace his thought processes to show you what we are dealing with. Because the fact is that he had something to hide, as I knew all along."

Brewster asked, "And what is he hiding?"

"The fact that he knows the notes hidden in your clothes, supposedly written by Dr. Stevens—are forgeries!"

The effect of these words was tremendous. Even the Martian officers seemed to react. Brewster knew that the accusation itself had stunned the men, but he too felt surprised to learn that Akar had known of the other note and done nothing about it.

Presently, Joe Abbott said, "You haven't proved it yet."

Captain Akar turned to the Venusian, from whose face all blood seemed to have drained. The switch went in with a snap.

"Did Dr. John Stevens write those warning notes?"

The Venusian gasped. "No."

"Did he know anything about them?"

"No."

"Was he capable, as far as you know, of either writing or dictating them?"

"No."

"Are the notes Venusian forgeries?"

"Yes."

The Captain switched off the machine.

As quietly as before, the Captain said, "Shortly after we left Boron, a dispatch came to me with the information that a captive Venusian on Boron knew of certain warning notes intended for the Earthmen in the event that they were rescued by us.

"We had already rescued you. How could the notes now be delivered? Only by a Venusian. Where was there a Venusian close enough to you to hope to deliver such notes? There was a Venusian prisoner on this ship, being taken to Mars for expert questioning. And deliver the notes he did, though how is a small detail to be taken care of yet.

"But consider this important fact, this Venusian was captured by accident. Surely, therefore, he could not be the one originally intended to deliver the notes. The original bearer probably let himself be captured easily, hoping to get aboard this ship. When he didn't he passed the notes on to this one here. That was a great mistake, though probably unavoidable. For while the original bearer probably knew nothing about the notes, this substitute knew too much. He knew enough of their origin to know they were forgeries. That knowledge couldn't be hidden. And that was the knowledge he tried to hide from *you*, by first hiding it from."

Brewster scratched his chin. Somehow he was more troubled than before. The more he thought about it, the less it added up.

"Excuse me," he said, getting up. "Suppose everything you say it true. Why shouldn't he have spoken Martian just the same?"

Akar hesitated. "But I explained—"

"I know, I know," Brewster interrupted. "If he spoke Martian he would give himself away to you. So what? All he cared about was getting the notes, and he had already seen to that. After that, for all you could do about it, he might as well have walked in here and told you he'd given us forged notes...and you could never get him to disprove those notes *as long as he continued to answer in Martian.*"

THE edge of resentment, almost of arrogance, with which Captain Akar had met Brewster's objections, disappeared. He ran a slender finger along the line of his lips. Softly, his voice incisive, he said, "Then perhaps you can infer why he chose to answer in English?"

"I don't know," Brewster mused, "but your assumption that he was hiding *something* is a good one. He may be hiding something—something so important to him that he even took the chance of having to admit the forgeries in an effort to cover up this other thing."

"But what could be that important to him?"

Brewster said, "Ask him."

Thoughtfully, Captain Akar began to speak in Martian, when Brewster hurled himself across the room, his outstretched arms sweeping the Captain off his feet. Two thin lines of green fire hissed in midair over Brewster's head and started slashing down.

They never reached the floor. Lying on his back, Brewster fired his automatics from inside his pockets. Across the room, the two junior officers fell as if they had been smashed down by weight alone. The walls reverberated again and again as the pistols fired. When Brewster got to his feet, the third junior officer was still standing woodenly, his slender weapon halfway out of his tunic, his face blank, seemingly paralyzed by the explosions and their ghastly effect.

Captain Akar rose beside Nick Brewster. A quick glance told him that the Venusian too had escaped assassination. His voice was steady and completely controlled as he said to Brewster, pointing a finger at the third officer: "Kill him."

Brewster brought up one of the automatics and pressed the trigger. Thunder cracked; the officer spun halfway around, went to his knees and died before he had sprawled on the floor...

But for Brewster's incomprehensibly quick action, the green flames would have killed both Akar and the Venusian, but now that it was over, Brewster stood there, unable to understand the event in which he had played the chief role...

The Venusian sat stolidly. The Earthmen, shaken, stared at the single pool of blood that bound the three dead Martians. The doors to the dining hall had opened and black-clad members of the ship's crew waited there.

ONLY Akar moved with assurance. An officer, taller than he and with hard, stony features, came in, and after a brief conversation with Akar, ordered the crew to remove the bodies. After they had left the smell of blood hung oppressively in the room. Akar, still paying no attention to the Earthmen, spoke to the Venusian. Both questions and answers were in Martian, the questions long and thoughtful, and the answers, often no more than a word or two, after long pauses.

Presently Akar walked to Brewster. Stopping before him, the Martian inclined his head and touched his forehead with his hand. He said, "Though I am but a humble servant of my Emperor, I owe you my life. I thank you for it."

To the Earthmen, speaking quietly and without looking at them, he said, "You cannot understand what happened here, I know. Let me then once and for all show you what the Venusians meant by offering you their friendship...

"This Venusian knew from the start that sometime during this voyage my personal enemies would make an attempt on my life. Venusian espionage had so informed him while he was still on Boron, imprisoned there with several others. That was the secret he hoped to keep from me, hoping also that if it were attempted, that you might all be killed in the uprising.

"My junior officers, having questioned this Venusian while we were still on Boron, discovered that he knew of their plot. There was nothing they could do about it, for they were being held responsible for his safety. When they found the forged notes, hidden here—"

Captain Akar tore away the Venusian's tunic, baring his torso. He turned the stolid captive around and showed them his back. There was an imperceptible cut along the lateral surface of the skin. The Captain carefully took hold of the skin and pulled it. It came away—showing a little pocket that had been formed under the skin.

"When they found these notes, they told the Venusian they were going to deliver them for him. In that way, by binding themselves into a secret compact with him, they hoped to secure their own safety, for if he mentioned them at all, sooner or later he would have to tell about the notes he hoped to have delivered..."

At length, Brewster sighed. "I see. They gave him a stake in keeping his mouth shut altogether. And when did they deliver the notes?"

"Sometime before the ship left Boron," Akar said. "They had ample opportunities then—and the note was already in your clothes when you woke up aboard ship before anyone."

In the silence that followed these words, the Venusian sagged forward against the bindings that held his arms. His head slumped against his chest, and his breathing came faintly. Without saying anything further, Captain Akar left the room. Soon, crew members came in and carried out the chair...

LATER, sitting together in the observation room, after each of the men had spoken to Nick Brewster, Abbott sat with him before the huge transparent wall.

"You know, Nick," he said, "I don't have to tell you how sorry I am about this whole crazy mess. The others have told you what they think, but I feel worse than they do because it was my—"

"Forget it."

"It was lousy of me to make that crack about the cigarettes."

"Sure it was." He sat there, watching the plume of smoke rise from the tiny butt he nursed, wondering what unnatural luck had made him watch the Martian officers so carefully. And he had really been right with his guess about Akar's uneasiness. How strange it all was...

"Nick."

Abbott broke in on his thoughts. Brewster met Abbott's eyes momentarily. "Nick, you're still not satisfied, are you?"

Brewster carefully ground out his butt. He played with the tinfoil from the empty pack. "Nope," he said, quietly. He stood against the concave surface of the great window and when Abbott got up beside him he whispered, "Be careful. We're being listened to."

"By the—no—you must mean...Captain Akar?"

Brewster nodded. "How else did he find out we'd quarreled?"

"But why should he spy on us?"

"He didn't explain that when he was being so honest with us."

"You don't trust him?"

Nick Brewster smiled. Through his teeth he said, "Stop being a kid. Did you see that Venusian—the way he never batted an eye when I fired those automatics? And the way he passed out at the end? Why? The Martians had exhausted him before they brought him in. Why? Maybe they just wanted him to answer questions without getting off any speeches on his own hook. That chair forced him to talk, but maybe if he'd had some energy, he could have added interesting facts too."

"Do you think what he did say was the truth?"

"Sure. Only trouble was—the questions weren't the ones I would have asked. And that last conversation in Martian—what really went on between them? Not that I doubt the general story, but why did our host, the Captain, forget to mention the most important fact in that deal of the Venusian and his junior officers?"

"What fact?"

Nick Brewster smiled again. "You better stay close to papa," he said. "The Captain told us all about that deal, except *why* any officers should deliver notes like that. How could the Venusian know whether or not they would deliver the notes? Evidently the Venusian assumed they would. Why?"

Slowly, Abbott asked, "Do you know why?"

"No," Brewster sighed. "But so far it looks like even the Martians are divided. Remember what I said about falling on one side when we might choose the other? If the Martians are divided, how do we know if we want to be on Captain Akar's side?"

Joe Abbott turned and faced the men in the interior of the room. They had cut up sections of paper and made a crude deck of cards and they were playing for imaginary stakes.

Abbott said, in a subdued voice, "Then why did you kill those other Martians, if you weren't sure?"

There was an irritated edge in Brewster's voice as he answered, "I didn't know then what I know now, and I'd have done the same even if I knew. For my money, the Captain's still our man. But just in case I'm wrong…just in case, understand…knowing what I do, and being one step ahead of him…I can still change my mind." And very softly indeed, he added, "As long as I have my wits. And my guns."

"And us?" said Abbott.

"Sure," said Brewster. "Smoke?"

CHAPTER FOUR

AKAR SAID, "The city's name is Ho-Tonda. It means Great Tonda, and since the word Ho is used only for those of the dynasty, in this sense it means also that it is the Emperor's City."

Nick Brewster nodded but made no attempt to keep the conversation going. In this last hour, as they had hovered at space-anchor over Mars, Captain Akar had more than once shown how pre-occupied he was. But he had invited Brewster to his quarters for the landing, and he kept speaking to Brewster, in the midst of his activities, for the sake of politeness.

The city was well named, Brewster thought. Even from their great height—the ship hung almost motionless miles above it—Ho-Tonda seemed vast and sprawling. It had been laid out in interlocking geometric patterns that constantly changed as one's point of view altered. At the center lay a huge hexagon, which Akar said was the walled inner city of the Ho-Ghan Lyric, the Emperor. Ho-Tonda was a maze of colors, of gleaming towers and tinted ribbons of roads, but the inner city was predominantly crimson, with spires and steeples that glistened in the sun and gave the hexagon the effect of an enormous red diamond.

Akar had several times looked below through an instrument that Brewster guessed was a telescope. He had not offered it to Brewster. Something had been bothering him from the time that three escorting warships had appeared, coming up suddenly to meet them. It had happened almost simultaneously with Brewster's entrance to Akar's quarters, and a few minutes after that the Captain had stopped his own ship. He had conferred with two of his officers and spoken heatedly— the first time Brewster had had an indication of Akar's temper—over a small phone attached to the panel at his elbow.

After that he had continued to talk to Brewster, but his mind was elsewhere, and his growing anxiety ill-concealed; there was something in the way he watched the three wheeling warships, the way his eyes narrowed in silent judgment, that indicated a deep hostility. And Brewster had noticed that the hexagonal design emblazoned on the three warships' hulls was a duplicate of the formation of the Inner City.

Suddenly one of the row of buttons on the panel began to flick on and off. Akar reached for the phone, listened briefly and quickly pressed down the flicking button. Across the room, a metal shield imbedded in the deck rose horizontally and tilted at an angle that faced Akar. Its under side held a round screen. A red light flashed across the screen once and then the screen remained blank another moment.

Slowly, the irregular form of a small stone appeared on the screen. It was an ordinary stone, pale-hued and lined with bluish veins. Suddenly, as if from within it, an amber flame burst out, devouring the stone, filling the screen until nothing else was left. When the stone had been burned away, the fire died and the screen was empty again.

Akar let his breath out in satisfaction. He returned the screen to its position in the deck and deliberately pressed several of the panel buttons. Immediately afterward, the ship shivered a little and Brewster felt the slight impact of the rockets starting again.

"We're landing," Akar smiled. He glanced out through the transparent bulkheads of his small oval room and saw the warships lying alongside and one leading the way.

"What was that I saw on the screen?" Brewster said.

Akar's smile remained. "I continue to like your direct manner," he said. He rose, adding, "There was some confusion about the escort. I had not expected it and would not land without direct orders. The orders came through, and what you saw was the sign of Jev Thyle, my lord."

"Sort of a seal or coat-of-arms?"

"Exactly. The five Jevs each have their own, and they cannot be duplicated. The Jevs, you see, are the WarLords of Jegga and the commanders of the five armies. Together with the Regios, who are the civil governors, they are the administrators of the Empire. As a warrior, my allegiance belongs to Jev Thyle, Lord of the Flaming Stone."

"And the Emperor?"

"Naturally. The Imperial hexagon is made up of the five-sided Empire and the Ho-Ghan, who represents the dynasty. Our allegiance to the Ho-Ghan is paramount."

BOTH men stood in silence now as the ship descended, Akar again busy with his thoughts, Brewster subdued in contemplation. Ho-Tonda, as they drew closer to the ground, resembled nothing so much as a dream city, and whatever beauties it had displayed before were multiplied a hundred times by closer scrutiny. Its buildings, varied and arresting, were magnificent affairs of colored stone and glass, massive structures that lost no grace or delicacy. Though each building was in itself a work of art, with pillars and abutments and arches and open walls of glass like lacework, the buildings formed larger groups of unified effect, and the colors spread to complex harmonies.

And on the roofs, and in the windows, and as the streets became evident, there too, tremendous crowds milled. The tiny dots of color that were their clothes were like innumerable bits of confetti, contributing to the holiday effect. The ships, on their way down, had not come near the inner city, but now, passing over what seemed to be the outskirts of Ho-Tonda, Brewster saw a huge canal. He might have thought it a great lake except for its perfectly straight shore; it was many miles across and stretched away to either side until it was lost in distance. Its water was tinted a pale red, and its surface was dotted with numerous craft that moved about with the erratic speed of waterbugs.

The ship's bow swung down sharply and went into a deep glide, and for a moment, flaring bow rockets cut off the view, but when they let up

Brewster saw a great field under them. The field was ringed by small, conical green structures, and as the ship swept by them, they glowed vividly even in the full light of day. A group of small, extremely ornate buildings, like miniature cathedrals, stood in the center of the field. At several places near these buildings, groups of ships sat on the ground with their bows tilted upward. Like the escorting ships, all were crimson and marked with the Imperial hexagon; Akar's ship alone was orange-amber.

"We will be down in a moment," said Akar. "You will want to join your friends again." Brewster nodded and started to leave when Akar added, "We are being received by the Imperial Guard, the Argyres. It would please me greatly if you and your friends made no mention of what happened aboard my ship."

"Meaning what?"

"The Estannar and the—ah—slight case of mutiny."

"Mentioned it to whom?"

"To anyone."

"All right," said Brewster.

"You see," said Akar, "since the Argyres are taking you over, it may be a short while before we meet again. Until then, I should like to feel that our secret remained—"

"All right," said Brewster. "Anything you say."

CHAPTER FIVE

THE Argyres were strange. Brewster first saw them through the transparent wall of the observation deck, when he rejoined his men. As the ship slowly settled down, the Argyres marched to the ship, forming a double-filed lane back to the buildings from which they had come. There were some five hundred of them. By comparison with Akar's crew, they were all exceptionally tall, at least as tall as Akar's second in command, Kaenas. Their uniforms were cut like those of other Jeggite warriors, but their alternating horizontal stripes of black and red gave them a bizarre, harlequin effect, which was heightened by their swift, stiff-jointed gait and the startling unison with which their red peaked helmets bobbed up and down. They were completely expressionless.

By the time Brewster joined his men, the ship had landed and the men went down to the locks. They were dressed in the meager clothes they had salvaged, in grimy coveralls and jackets, not talking much. Once or twice remarks brought laughter, but it was self-conscious and expectant. Yet they had taken on a certain bravado that was close to swaggering, and when Brewster surveyed them, he liked their look.

The Argyres were directly outside. Kaenas supervised the opening of the locks. They opened slowly, and then the Argyres were outside, but none of them came forward, nor did any of them speak; their officers, who seemed to be marked by heavily-jeweled tunics, just looked into the ship and regarded the men.

The pause became awkward, and Brewster said to Kaenas, "We seem to be waiting for something." But the next moment, as Akar came down the corridor toward the locks, not hurrying, Brewster saw that they had been waiting for him. He stood at the entrance of the locks, very erect, and exchanged sharp, silent salutes with the Argyres. Then he turned to one of his crew, who was carrying Brewster's precious carton for him, and said something to him.

The Jeggite went up to the lock, not stepping out, and held the carton out for someone among the Argyres to take. The officers' expressions remained stoic, but none moved. One of the Argyres finally let a bitter grimace cross his face and he cried out something, and far down the line, his words were repeated.

In a few moments, two short, stout little men dressed in spotless white came running up. They took the carton from the Jeggite and ran back with it. Then, smiling, Akar said to the Earthmen, "Goodbye," and as they filed out, he shook hands with each.

Later, remembering the scene, Brewster wondered if the others had understood it, or had shared the sense of isolation he felt after Akar's ship had blasted off. He thought not. They were glad to set foot on land again. The day was warm and clear and invigorating. One of the officers made a short, formal speech, declaring that the Argyres were honored to take the Earthmen to Ho-Tonda...

They rode in vehicles that were transparent tubes, slender as ships, entirely enclosed and kept in balance by some gyroscopic device. Brewster, Abbott, Callahan and Drake went in one of the larger vehicles, together with four Argyre officers, the other four men with four more officers in the one ahead. The two large vehicles were kept in the center of the procession; smaller ones, seating two men, of which there were scores, kept fanning in and out like highly disciplined gnats.

IT WAS a short ride to Ho-Tonda, and a silent one. Once Abbott started to say something about the episode at the locks, but Brewster shook his head. He didn't want to talk just then, but what was more important at the moment, they were already entering the city, and the scene that greeted them needed all their attention.

Their reception was beyond their wildest fancy. It was not so much the fantastic din that the jammed streets of people raised, though their vehicle fairly shivered from its impact, nor was it the dense clouds of streamers and banners and strange, gaily-colored spheres that floated in air and kept exploding, as much as the people themselves that made the scene what it was.

For they seemed to be of every conceivable size and shape and color. There were tall Jeggites in flowing robes, and much taller, brutish people with a green cast to their skin, and short, stout ones such as they had seen at the landing field, and short, thin ones who were very dark, with skins that were oily and purple-black, like eggplants, as Drake remarked. And still there were others, with slender, elongated heads and bright rings on their arms and throats, and some who were as coppery as the Jeggites, but who were small, with thick legs.

But one thing they possessed in common—their resemblance to humans in general, for they were, naturally, much more similar than they were different. And though there was a great variety to their clothes, there seemed to be no recognizable uniformity in what each of the different races wore. Ho-Tonda told its own story eloquently at a glance: it was a melting-pot, the great cosmopolitan capital of the Empire, and it had turned out in force to welcome the men from the world of Kren.

In all that mad ride—several times the Argyre patrols rode into the crowds when they overflowed—Brewster and Abbott spoke once. That was when Brewster pointed out a group of Estannars. Abbott nodded and made no reply when Brewster remarked that they hardly looked like prisoners or rebels, the way they were cheering and waving. Abbott had seen many other Estannars in the streets of Ho-Tonda.

Slowly, the procession wound its way to the heart of the city, and here it stopped before a pink, massive stone wall. Then the wall parted, opening a low, flat panorama of fields and gardens, and hundreds of heralds inside the wall began a mad tooting of horns, all of them in low pitch, like the sound of shell-horns used by primitive fishermen.

The wall itself was some forty feet deep, and from square niches that opened from its inner face, scores of mounted Argyres came riding to join the procession. Their mounts were clean-shaven, coal-black animals that looked like a cross between a horse and an antelope, larger than either, extremely nimble and sure-footed, with double, curved horns that added to their fierce demeanors. And the Argyres who rode them wore instead of the peaked red helmets, masks that were made to duplicate the heads of their mounts, and the masks completely covered them to the neck.

They had left the people of Ho-Tonda behind. Brewster guessed that they had entered the Inner City. But he could see nothing ahead for at least a mile except another wall. The fields on either side were empty. There were strangely beautiful trees and enormous flowerbeds that were riots of color, and pale pink streams that meandered lazily but there were no people. Only the Argyres in their vehicles and those on their mounts were in evidence, and behind them they heard the horns.

THEY reached the second wall and went through, and here were more heralds, in entirely different costumes, and more horns. From the interior of this wall hundreds of vehicles, twenty feet high, came riding on their one wheel. They were like moving pillars, each with a diameter of some five feet, studded with green cones like spikes in the hard, dull red, lustrous substance of which they were made. Their occupants, if there were any, were not visible, and these too joined the procession.

The land that lay between the second and third walls was covered with ridges. The valleys grew tall, blue grass and held ponds like pools of wine, and the hills held small forests that grew in geometric design. And still no people.

By then Brewster had noticed an odd thing. He had seen birds flying about several times, never close enough to make out clearly, but they had passed many dead birds. They lay in the fields, sometimes quite near the straight white road.

It was another mile to the third wall. This wall was shorter than the others, made of a strange substance, its top regularly spaced by small white domes.

As the procession passed through, Brewster let out an involuntary gasp, echoed by the others. For, though they had seen nothing beyond the wall from the other side, as they went through, a great palace seemed to materialize.

Its intricately curving, convoluted walls must have been half a mile in length. It was surrounded by gigantic flowerbeds and orchards, and streams with footbridges. It was made of something that looked like pink alabaster, with archways and windows and columns. Whole expanses of its walls were covered with detailed reliefs, many of them colored, shining like gold and ruby. It had three levels of terraces and great stairways, and innumerable banners hung in the breeze. And everywhere, there were people, dressed in various colors, but all of them with some red in their costumes.

This was a world of almost unimaginable splendor, the product of centuries of might, of rulers with incalculable labor at their disposal, but there was no softness to its luxuriousness. Rather there was a barbaric strength and vigor, a clashing that often bordered on the savage, and this only added to its beauty.

There must have been a thousand heralds in the gardens before the palace, and several times that number of Argyres, differently dressed, carrying strange lances and swords, until the eye lost the capacity for detail. The Argyres lined the paths and footbridges and terraces, and when the heralds stopped, and one could hear the voices of the thousands of people—the Argyres alone were silent—it sounded like the buzzing of all the bees in the universe.

Finally the procession came to halt in a large declivity, like an inverted, colossal mother-of-pearl shell, and the Jeggites opened their vehicles. The Earthmen came out and stood together without speaking until one of the Argyre officers motioned them to follow him. They walked across a stone footbridge and came to an enormous white stairway that led to the lowest terrace.

A LEAN, aged Jeggite dressed in a long robe of red with a great many stripes of different colors along the sleeves, walked down the stairway to meet them. Halfway down he stopped and began to intone a long speech. It was next to impossible to understand him, not only because his pronunciation was terrible and his voice high and cracked, but because no one stopped speaking while he made his speech. But when he was through, he inclined his head and evidently waited for the Earthmen to come up the stairway.

Only Purdom started forward, and then, seeing that the others were all looking at Brewster, and that he had not moved, Purdom came back. Brewster looked at his men. His head was reeling. He felt completely drained of feeling, and the same exhaustion lay on the faces of his men. It had been too much for them.

Brewster took a step forward and shouted, "Did you say you were taking us to a reception?"

As he spoke, a hush fell over the people. They were hearing an Earth man speak. The Jeggite inclined his head and said, "The Ho-Ghan is waiting in his hall."

Brewster shouted back, "We're tired!" His voice was too loud in the new silence, and there was irritation in it that he could not control in spite of himself.

The Jeggite said, in his quavering voice, "The Ho-Ghan is waiting in his hall."

Beside Brewster, Abbott whispered, "Careful, Nick."

Brewster jerked his arm away and shouted, louder than before, "We want time to rest. Tell the Ho-Ghan we'll meet him later."

They could not hear what the Jeggite said; his words were lost in the great flurry of conversation that followed. From the expressions of those he saw, Brewster knew he had shocked them. But he was angry now, and he stood belligerently, his eyes scanning the terraces and balconies, his lips set hard. His men and he were not going to be placed on exhibition to suit anyone's plans, or orders, for that matter. They were tired, and there was an end to it. Somehow he had felt a sense of power, the knowledge that they could assert themselves. But he would have done it no matter what he felt.

The Jeggite had been speaking all this while, but when silence returned again, and the Earthmen remained where they were, he bowed and motioned to an Argyre officer near him. He spoke to the officer, and the Argyre came down the stairs to Brewster.

"You will follow me," he said.

"Where?" asked Brewster.

"One of the palace wings has been reserved for the use of the honored visitors from Kren. You may rest there."

"Thanks," said Brewster.

They walked up the stairway through a dead silence.

*　*　*

"AND you still think so?" said Abbott. "On no evidence?"

Brewster leaned on the balcony and stared into the descending twilight. Everywhere little lights were springing up, like fireflies in a gray woods. Far off he could see the walls of the Inner City outlined by twinkling ruby lights, with quiet pools of gray land between them.

"It depends," Brewster said, reflectively, "on what you call evidence. Take that little episode when we landed. Akar not only took his time coming down to meet the Argyres, but he insulted them by having one of his crew try to give my carton to the Argyres. It was clear enough; the Argyres are above menial work. They sent for porters. But it was a deliberate act on Akar's part..."

The serving girls were returning with more food and drink, and their giggles floated out to the balcony. They were, as they had told the men hours before, from Hruthes, or Uranus, and they were small and round like the porters at the Argyre field, and like them, dressed in white robes trimmed with red. They had first appeared shortly after the men had been ushered into their quarters in the palace wing, and they had brought food and drink and gaiety with them, but the men had been unable to eat or enjoy their rather pretty, silly wholesomeness.

Instead, the men had slept for a few hours. The palace wing, which had been given them, contained twelve rooms, eight of them with huge beds, but the men had slept on couches in one of the four main rooms, preferring to stay together. They had found some rest, but not from the sheer splendor that covered every corner of the palace, from tapestried walls to giant carvings and soft carpets, and elaborate furniture of every conceivable substance, to high, vaulted ceilings and sculptured railings on the balconies of the four main rooms.

It was on one of these balconies that Brewster and Abbott stood. They had awakened almost together, before the others, and they had eaten while the men slept, and then gone out on the balcony to talk and smoke. Soon the Hruthian girls and their giggling had awakened the others, and the men sat down to a strange, wonderful dinner.

Everything here was wonderful. In the settling dusk, the palace had become a fairyland, a world suspended, its boundaries suggested only by myriad lights. Below the jutting balcony lay a portion of the third terrace, its tiled surface bathed in amber light from concealed sources. On three sides, across the gardens and terraces, hung other sections of the palace, and wherever they looked, there were huge, beautiful rooms and people moving about. From everywhere there came laughter and gay voices wafted along with the garden perfumes and the warm night air.

In the midst of all this, Abbott's voice persisted in the conversation that Brewster had ended more than once. "But maybe it was just an incident. You're attaching too much importance to it."

"Maybe," Brewster said. "I suppose in the end it all comes down to a feeling. I felt the hostility there. And," he added, "I'd say it was you who's attaching importance to things. What the hell are you so worried about? Why should you care so much what I thought?"

Abbott stood away from the railing and looked into Brewster's face. The light that came from the room shone on the two men, one with a faint smile on his lips, the other almost grim. "Because, Nick," said the grim-faced man, "I wouldn't want you to make decisions that might affect the rest of us."

BREWSTER turned away without answering. He leaned out over the balcony and smoked reflectively, and when he turned his head back to Abbott, he saw that Abbott had gone back inside. After a few moments he followed, curious about the general laughter that was coming out.

The Argyre officer who had led the men to the wing earlier that day had returned, and with him were two others. Evidently at his suggestion, several of the men had begun to put on the clothes that the Hruthian girls had brought with them, and it was the sight of Drake and Callahan in those clothes that made the others laugh. Heavy, horny-fisted Mike Callahan was strutting about, chest puffed out, crying out in an exaggerated brogue, "If only me father and five brothers were here to see me, dressed in the garments o' the heathen an' lookin' every inch the fine lady!"

Brewster smiled. The clothes were two loose tunics like dresses, one of which reached just under the knees, the other to the waist. Both were a deep crimson, with a large horizontal band of pale green, very light and silky. Over these came a long, flowing cape of lustrous green, fastened at the shoulders and reaching the floor. The shoes were thin-soled, single-strapped, red sandals, sparkling with gems.

Abbott brought Brewster a pile of clothes. "We're going down to a reception after all," he said. "Seems the Ho-Ghan is still waiting."

Slowly, Brewster began to change. Once two of the Hruthian girls started coming into the room and the men howled them out. The wines they had had with their dinner had put them in high spirits. Brewster said quietly to Abbott, "If you get a chance, remind the men that they're to keep their mouths tight about what happened on Akar's ship."

"Why?"

"I promised."

"They didn't," Abbott said, dryly.

Brewster's lips thinned to a narrow line. When he was completely dressed, he stood for a moment feeling the freedom of the clothes. Not for a moment had he relaxed his scrutiny of the three Argyre officers, as they stood near one of the doors, aloof and silent. He felt himself breathing rapidly, as if from some mysterious excitement. Uneasiness swept through him; it had come on him gradually, persistently, a sense of something impending. It was the kind of feeling he had come to know when hunting—the smell or knowledge or intuition of danger...

He could not shake the feeling off. The others were still busy. He ran his hands along his sides, and then he left the room passing through three doors to the third bedroom, which was his. His carton was in a corner of the room. He dug his hands in and pulled out a wide belt with two attached, flap holsters. Then he took out his automatics, put them in the holsters and strapped the belt tightly around his hips, under the outer tunic. The guns didn't show.

He heard the door behind him opening and he whirled. A stout little Hruthian porter stood there, holding out a hand. When Brewster didn't move, the Hruthian threw a folded bit of white paper toward him, closed the door and was gone.

Brewster picked up the paper and unfolded it. It said:

Don't be a sucker, Brewster. There's more to winning bets than playing the odds—find out what you're betting on. Interested in palace revolutions, maybe? It's a juicy two to one, in the bag, and you lose either way…

CAREFULLY, Brewster re-folded the paper, and as he did so, he looked up and saw Captain Akar coming toward him, coming through the rooms from the one where the other men were. Brewster put the folded note into one of the holsters.

Akar wore a new uniform. It was a black, tight-fitting warrior's tunic like his other, but much more richly adorned, with the bands of his rank in encrusted jewels, and a jeweled representation of a flaming stone on his chest. He strode through the intervening rooms so quickly that the long crimson robe he carried over his arm trailed after him. He came into Brewster's room and saw the carton.

"Your guns are missing, aren't they?" he said quietly. "It is nothing. They will be returned to you in a little while. Let us go down together," he finished, holding a hand out to Brewster.

Standing there, Brewster realized what it was that had slowly impressed itself on his mind. It was the silence in the room he had left. The voices had stopped. It was an odd thing that silence near at hand, a still core in a world of noise, like walking into a vacuum. Through the frames of the three doors that separated him from them, he saw two Jeggite officers. They were backing away from something.

Brewster shot a glance at Akar's grim face. He started for the door, but with a quick step Akar backed into the doorway and blocked it. "Your friends," he said, "are waiting for you in the corridor. There is an exit closer at hand the other way."

Brewster backed off a step. The corners of his mouth twitched.

"I don't think you want to go in there," Akar said.

Brewster said, "You're wrong. Don't make me prove it."

Strangely enough, Akar bowed his head and moved aside without a further word. Swiftly Brewster went back through the rooms to the one he had left a few moments before. When he entered, the four Jeggite officers who were there turned to look at him. He stood rooted to the spot, his eyes fixed on the sight on the floor.

The three Argyre officers who had been in the room were lying on the floor, sprawled grotesquely, face down. Something had burned deep, bloodless terrible wounds into the small of their backs just under the shoulder blades, and from these wounds, as in a small fire-pit, tongues of amber flame spread to devour their bodies. They spread evenly, with incredible speed, enlarging the horrible wound and racing along the limbs, and a slight hissing sound, almost the sound of a kiss, came from the flames. The room was filled with a sweet odor.

Over the flames—a little behind them—stood Kaenas and another Jeggite officer. The two Brewster had seen before stood to one side of him, and on the other side Akar stood, intent on the scene. Brewster felt a violent reaction in the pit of his stomach, but he turned back to look again, fascinated.

Now, as the flames destroyed the dead men, they divided the bodies into sections, and as they reached the ends of these sections, the four Jeggite officers bent over quickly and held cupped hands out to the fire. In their hands were gleaming receptacles. The several fires ate the last remaining shreds, flickered an instant as if they were searching for something, and then one after the other they leaped across the intervening inches of space into the waiting receptacles, which received them and were snapped shut. Then the Jeggites put the receptacles back into place. They were the blazing center jewels in the representation of the flaming stone that all of them wore.

SILENTLY Akar picked up a wine flagon and poured Brewster a glass. Brewster shook his head. He fumbled for a cigarette, remembered that he had left them in his trousers, and went to take one. His mind was so far away from what he was doing that he started when his lighter flicked on and the yellow flame danced in his hand. He took a long drag and let the smoke out, and he looked again to the floor where the Argyres had lain. No trace of them remained, not even an ash.

Akar walked over to him. "I told you once that you would be interested in our weapons. I would have preferred another occasion."

"This one was all right," said Brewster. "What was it?"

Akar smiled darkly. "A question of politics, shall we say, and leave it at that for the while?" He had, Brewster thought, a really smooth delivery for understatements. "A complicated question," he added. "I spared your friends this disturbance—perhaps it would be better if you made no mention of it."

"Look," said Brewster, "I don't know what's going on here, and I'm willing to wait on your say-so, but don't get the idea that I'm going to hold out on my friends too."

Akar nodded soberly. "As you wish, then."

A minute later Brewster and the Jeggites joined the Earthmen in the corridor. Three more Jeggites were with them. Following Akar, the entire group walked down the corridor. Suddenly, as they made a turn, a door thirty feet farther down the shining wing opened and six Argyres came out. Following them was a small, thin, very dark man with a nervous step, and behind him came four Hruthian porters. The porters were carrying a rigid stretcher, and on it lay a body.

The first of the Argyres to emerge had tried to go back, but the others had followed too quickly. They remained where they were, exchanging precise formal salutes when the Jeggites passed. As Brewster went by, he looked at the body on the stretcher. It was the corpse of the little Hruthian porter who had brought him the strange note. There was not a mark on him, but where he had had bright, curious eyes there were now empty sockets, gaping at the ornate ceiling.

"Nick, what is it?"

At the moment Abbott spoke, Akar had turned around to look back at the body, and before he turned back he swept Brewster with a long, searching glance which he made no attempt to hide—as if the chance of finding something on Brewster's face was worth the transparency of the effort.

Brewster kept walking without answering Abbott. He had halted involuntarily for an instant when he first caught sight of the Argyres; probably too, he had reacted to the sight of the body. But he was confident he had shown Akar nothing. He wasn't quite sure why, but he felt it was important that Akar should have seen nothing.

CHAPTER SIX

SHE was tall for an Estannar. She was slender as a reed, and her hair fell in a pale golden shower almost to her waist, its sheen soft in the thousand lights. Once, when she danced by near him, Brewster thought he had never seen such flashing eyes. Their bottomless depths were more violet than her robe, and her lips were full and redder than the sandals on her feet.

The sight of her almost made Brewster forget everything else.

The Earthmen were on a slightly raised platform, the lowest of a group of several, in the great hall of the Ho-Ghan. They had entered without causing more than a little ripple of interest, coming in through a side door, but inevitably word of their presence spread among the more than three thousand people there. Yet this great hall, more dazzling than anything the Earthmen had seen, with its glorious sheer white columns rising from a deep ruby floor, its transparent walls through which the surrounding gardens were visible, its shimmering masses of gorgeously costumed, different peoples, its glitter and excitement and noise—all this was lost on Brewster after he first saw that lovely girl.

He might never have seen her if the awaited ceremonies had begun. But they didn't, and except for those who maneuvered into positions where they could get a close look at the Earthmen, whatever had been going on before their arrival continued with no interruption. Hruthian servants, scores of them, scurried about like an army of white ants, carrying enormous trays of food and drink; whole circles of friends stood talking with no regard for the dancers who had to dance right through them, and everywhere people jostled and called and laughed.

It had seemed to Brewster that a squad of Argyres far down the hall, at an enormous entrance, kept milling about and looking toward the platform. Looking about him, Brewster saw that numerous other Jeggite warriors, many of whom wore unfamiliar symbols on their tunics, had congregated in the vicinity of the platform, engaged in casual conversation, leaving occasionally to dance but always returning. But there were a great many Argyres in the hall, and Brewster was watching those nearest him when he saw the girl.

When she moved, a dozen men followed her. When she drank, she had to choose from a score of goblets that flashed before her. When she danced, the men she left took no other partners. Brewster couldn't take his eyes from her.

BESIDE him, Akar was talking about something, but Brewster hadn't heard a word of it. He was watching the girl dance an oddly graceful dance to music from an orchestra of massed strings, coming from some hidden source, and Akar's voice kept droning on. He turned to Akar then with a vacant look on him, and he interrupted:

"How much longer are we going to wait here? Any idea?"

"Until the Ho-Ghan arrives."

"Do we have to stay here on this platform?"

Akar nodded. "Ritual forbids commerce with anyone in this court until you have been presented." As he spoke, the path of his gaze lay beside Brewster's. "Her name," he observed, somewhat absently, "is Suba, of the great Marannes family. Be patient, my friend."

Brewster scowled and turned to see what the others were doing. Callahan was matching Drake and Stewart huge draughts of wine. Purdom and Rogofsky were talking to Kaenas, asking questions and toasting the answers. The holiday mood was stronger than ever. For a brief moment, Brewster felt a twinge of danger. He couldn't place it, but it was there. He didn't like the way they were drinking. Even Abbott, who had been standing with Matt Peters a few feet away, came toward Brewster.

"What's eating you, Nick?" he asked with a loose smile.

Brewster shook his head, looking at his men, and then he took the glass Abbott held out for him and gulped it down. "Wow," he muttered, and when he turned around, the girl was quite near him. He gave Abbott the glass with a grave gesture, and without another word he stepped off the platform and began walking across the floor toward the girl.

The few people in his way stepped aside, so that a path kept opening for him. He walked with an arrogance that perhaps he himself did not realize—a lean, strong man with a face set as if for some perilous undertaking. He knew she had seen him coming, for the path to her had cleared moments before he reached her, as if by magic—or, he realized, as if more people than he expected had noticed the way he had kept his eyes on her, but she gave no sign until the last.

He touched her partner's shoulder and murmured politely, "Thanks, old man," and brushed him aside, and taking the girl's hand, he fell into the rhythm of the strange courtly dance.

She had smiled at him before she began dancing, so he didn't care much about the miserable job he was making of it. The steps were far too complex for him to have mastered from observation. But suddenly the music stopped, and the next moment the soft, gay strains of a Viennese waltz were filling the great hall.

HE STOPPED short. A glance at the platform showed him Joe Abbott and Akar smiling, and Abbott raised a hand and made his fingers do a jig in mid-air. By then Brewster had recognized the music—it was one of the records he had brought with him! At another time, any time but this, the circumstance would have started him to thinking, but now his gratitude asked no questions. It was perfect. He bowed gallantly and swept the girl into his arms. And then, to his added surprise, he saw numerous others in the hall join the dance.

Suba laughed. "We learned your dances in your honor," she said. "We were to have danced them after your presentation to the Ho-Ghan."

Brewster laughed with her. When he looked again to the platform, it was empty. They were all dancing now; even Akar had taken a partner. So Brewster danced as he had never danced before, unthinking, letting the smooth waves of music sweep him along, and Suba Marannes was a magnificent partner. On and on the music went, until the world had become a whirling thing and the smooth floor had ceased existing. When he opened his eyes again, he saw that Suba and he were dancing alone in that vast ballroom.

So he stopped, beautifully poised and not the least whit embarrassed, and with a slight bow, he gave Suba his arm and escorted her off the floor. He led her through a door in one of the transparent walls and found himself in one of the lower gardens. Still holding her hand, he walked with her, saying nothing.

The night was full now, and the sky a dark mystery. There were luminous flowers in the garden, he discovered; but he felt no surprise. He wandered along terraces and up great stairways, until he was lost in the intricate vastness of the palace, and the hall seemed far away, its noise like the distant buzzing of insects. There was confusion in his mind, but somehow he felt strangely happy. It was a long time since he had felt the sense of isolation he loved so well, the feeling of being alone that gave him security and strength.

Yet, after a bit, the isolation itself seemed odd to him, for there were no people about, and they passed sentinel Argyres rarely, so that when he finally spoke—after wondering what he would say to her—it was to remark, simply, "There's no one out here. I wonder why."

"No one must leave the Ho-Ghan's hall when he is expected."

"Then I broke one of the rules?"

"At least one."

"Perhaps I ought to take you back?"

She stopped and looked up at him. "Do you think you could find your way back?" she smiled. "But no, I wanted to get out, and I could never have done it without you." She held his arm tightly and led him on. "Let's go higher, as high up as we can, where we can look down on all the world."

"The world," Brewster echoed, shaking his head, a curious smile on his lips. "Maybe I'd better not start thinking about that again…"

UPSTAIRS they went, past terraces piled on each other, past huge hanging gardens, past dark halls and great chambers, climbing up and up until before them there loomed an enormous circular structure with no openings in its deeply fluted walls. It was like the topmost tower of some immense building, but its roots were lost in the architectural masses that led to it. A long, sloping walk led to it, curling upward from its base like a thin serpent, reaching the very top.

There they went, climbing the walk, and when they had reached the summit, they stood at the edge of an alabaster bowl. A few feet away from the interior of the circular wall were columns that rose for more than forty feet, supporting a slender balcony that went all the way around the rim of the bowl. Except for this balcony, which was perhaps six feet wide, there was nothing over the bowl, and its only roof was the still night sky, and the bright winking stars.

Here, at the very top of the palace, they felt the vigor of the wind. Brewster leaned over the balcony, looking down at the darkly glistening floor of the great bowl, and then he turned to Suba. She stood holding the balcony rail, her face lifted up to the sky, beautiful and strong. The wind played with her hair and caught her robe, pressing it to her body until it revealed every delicate line, the fullness of her breasts, the soft suppleness of her thighs. Standing there she might have been made of the same material as the stone balcony, until she turned her face to Brewster, and then she was too alive and vibrant for him just to keep looking at her, and he felt that if he didn't speak he would let the moment carry him too far.

But even while he was wondering about it he knew that he had waited too long and that he had lost and couldn't help himself. Later, he didn't remember how it happened. The intervening moments were gone, and she was in his arms and he had kissed her. He didn't know how much like a dream it was then, until it had ended, but while it lasted it was like nothing he had ever known.

Fragments of thoughts drifted through his mind, images like the swift review of life before the eyes of a drowning man. He knew again the intolerable cold brightness of the Moon before the crash, the amber fire burning the dead Argyres, the weary Estannar gasping an answer in the chair of truth, the myriad faces in the streets of Ho-Tonda, the first cigarette Akar had given him, the laughter of a Hruthian girl...they passed through his mind without apparent meaning...

Or was it that in less than four days he had lived a lifetime? It was a dream, unsubstantial and chimera-like, filled with fantasy and half-truths. But this he knew to be true—this woman in his arms, soft against his throat, and the sky and the wind and the stars, and nothing else, not even, finally, his thoughts.

BUT suddenly her hands were pressing into his arms pulling him down. He dropped to his knees beside her. Through the hewn fretwork of the inner balcony rail he saw a white light moving over the floor far below them. It came from a long, taper-like object in the hands of a Jeggite, its nimbus so small that it illuminated only the upper half of his body, so that he had the appearance of a disembodied trunk floating erratically in the hemming gloom.

Erratically, because he was running, but never quickly. As he moved across the floor he changed directions again and again, and each time one of the columns near him glowed with a weird, white, opaque glow and opened like a tubular shell, and from its interior a Jeggite warrior would step out to stand in his path. Retreating then, he would take a few steps in another direction only to be confronted by new warriors, until finally he stopped and stood quite still, satisfied that there was nowhere he could go anymore. Yet the remaining columns—there must have been fifty or more—kept coming alive in the darkness and opening up and releasing warriors like black moths from cocoons, until they had formed a large circle around him.

Gradually also, these columns had spilled their light into the bowl, so that its interior was filled with a shallow, diffuse light, and this together with a line of slowly moving lights that now appeared, as if from over an invisible horizon at the far end of the bowl, provided enough light for Brewster to see everything.

He was a middle-aged man, dressed in a full robe of deepest crimson, with a stern though reposed face and long iron-gray hair. He stood in the center of the circle, turning from one warrior to the next with an expression that seemed merely curious, and this curiosity he turned on the advancing lights when they broke through the circle and came towards him, for they were long tapers such as he held, in the hands of five masked Jeggite warriors, and they formed a smaller circle around him, but none were closer to him than fifteen foot.

Though they wore masks, Brewster knew their identity was plain, and was meant to be, for these were no ordinary warrior officers, both by their manner and their dress. The emblazoned insignias they wore were so splendid and large that they covered the upper half of their black-sleeved, red tunics. One wore three bolts like unfeathered arrows of emerald jewels. The second displayed a fiery red streak like the wake of a rocket. The third bore the amber flaming stone, and the fourth carried an ensign that might have been the amorphous, quivering mass of some protozoid, its body blue and its many eyes a deeper blue-black. On the tunic of the fifth was a pattern of diamonds, like a field of well-ordered stars. And all the other Jeggite warriors in the larger, still circle, and all Brewster had previously seen, wore one or another of those blazing heraldic symbols, though smaller ones.

IN THE hush that held the three-score men below, the central Jeggite suddenly spoke out. Though Brewster could not understand a word of what he heard, the deep acrimony in the voice and the casual imperiousness with which they were delivered impressed him, as courage and contempt for fate always did. And there was courage in the man, unmannered, insolent, controlled. He made only one gesture, and that was to thrust a finger at the one who wore the flaming stone, his robe whipping around him in great folds, his forearm muscular and knotted, and then he was through. He had spoken for less than a minute.

Still no one moved, and the center Jeggite laughed and threw his taper to the floor where it exploded with a tremendous white flash, and nothing of it remained. Then the five warriors moved in on him, their tapers held high, and one after another plunged the feebly glowing points into his body. He gave them no resistance, standing with his hand at his sides, and even after the five white shafts had sunk deep into his body, in his breast and his back, he stood there swaying, looking at them, the shafts moving with the effort of his breathing, until he sank to his knees, then to his hands, and then quietly, so quietly, he rolled over, as far as the shafts would allow him on his back.

Within a minute of the time of passing, the floor of the great bowl was empty—but strangely, though everything that had occurred until then had been precisely arranged, and the assassination had been accomplished with the simplicity and inevitability of a drama, its end was chaotic; it disintegrated rather than ended. The five warriors stepped back, their eyes for a time still on the dead man, and one by one they left the bowl in the direction from which they had come, hurriedly, not speaking to each other, some attended by officers who joined them, some alone. And those officers who remained went back to their columns and they too were gone, quickly, as though none wanted to be the last to leave.

But even after they were gone, the graceful columns retained much of their light, losing it so slowly that for several minutes the floor shone with the reflection of their luminous pallor. Gradually the light grew more faint, and the spaces between the columns were the first to return to darkness, so that the light formed fingers that pointed to the dead man, and the fingers shrank away until the body was alone in the darkness and silence. Only then did the dead body begin to glow weirdly, with an inner radiance the color of blood, and the focus of the light came from five tangential points—and so bright did this light become that at one point Brewster could see that the dead man had worn only one sandal, as if he had not had time to put on the other.

That was the end, though none had stayed to see it. Soon there was darkness again.

NICK BREWSTER got up. He looked over the balcony to the floor below but he could see nothing. He closed his eyes momentarily, and the scene came alive again for him, though with the distant quality of unreality. It had come at such a moment that it might have been a dream, but what he felt within him was real. He met Suba's steady eyes for a moment before she turned away, and though he had already guessed the answer, he said to her, "What did it mean?"

Facing away from him, she stretched out an arm and pointed to the surrounding fields, to the walls that protected the inner city. Far away there were occasional flashes of light in the fields, streaks of livid green and once the sudden flare of amber.

"They are destroying the loyal Argyres," she said softly. "The War Lords have killed the Ho-Ghan. The dynasty has been overthrown. It has not happened in a great many years."

"But why did they do it?"

She made no answer, and when he turned her to him, her face was weary, drained of feeling. Again he asked her. "But you know," she said wearily. "You must know. It was because of you."

"What are you saying? What do you mean because of me?"

"I meant all of you—the Earthmen. They wanted to receive you quietly. They wanted the arrival of the Earthmen to remain a secret, so that they could use it to ferret out the members of the Estannar underground, for all who knew would be traitors. And they had quarreled with the Ho-Ghan until they knew there could be no retreat..."

"Who do you mean by *they?*"

"The Jevs, the War Lords. The Ho-Ghan had killed two of them secretly as soon as you landed on Boron. The Jevs were determined that your oath of fealty would be to one of their choosing. They took no chances on which side you would pick."

It was her last words that stopped Brewster cold. He still did not understand her, but there was something in her phrasing—and as he thought of it, in the other things she had said.

"Because of us, you say?" he repeated, slowly. "Then you knew this was going to happen? You led me here so that I could see it. That's it, isn't it?"

She remained silent and he gripped her arms, holding her close to him. "Answer me!" he demanded. "You led me to see it!"

"Yes."

"And these other things you know, you've no business knowing them, have you? How do you know about these quarrels? How do you know what the War Lords wanted? How do you know so much unless you...you..."

"Yes."

"But why?" Brewster cried. "Tell me why!"

"I'll tell you why."

BREWSTER whirled around as he heard a hard, incisive voice behind him speak these words. He was face to face with Kaenas. The Jeggite had silently come up behind them. He stood there, inches taller than Brewster, a dark figure with a darker face, so still that the dull gleam of his jeweled tunic did not waver, the wind whipping his cloak around him.

"Because the Estannars sent her to poison you against us, to use her beauty to blind you and make you believe the lies she—"

At that moment Brewster struck. All the strength in him lashed out behind that blow, and his fist smashed squarely into Kaenas' face and sent him staggering against the outer balcony rail. There he braced himself for an instant and Brewster was upon him, raining blows on his face, hammering his fists into the Jeggite's body, until he doubled and fell forward. And then, before he could think about it—though of course he had thought about it already, thought it through to the end—he lifted Kaenas high over his head and threw him out over the rail into space, down the precipitous drop from the tower's summit. For an instant his figure seemed to hang in air, shrouded by his cloak, and then he was gone, lost in the night.

Brewster stood at the rail, steadying himself, and Suba came to stand beside him. He took her hand away from him. "Let's go down," he said. "Let's get away from here."

"You believe me," she said.

Brewster looked out across the slender rail. Whatever had been happening in the fields of the inner city had long since stopped. From far off, welling up from below, he heard the muffled roar of drums, and he looked down toward the sound trying to create some meaningful form out of the confusion of lights. His hands trembled as he held the rail and his breath was still shallow and rapid.

"You were sent to get at me," he said.

"Let me tell you in my own way. It isn't—"

"Answer me my way. I want to know."

"But you knew it your way before you killed a man to save me."

As her hand touched him he turned and seized her wrist and flung it away. "Get this and get it straight," he said, a soft, sullen fury in his voice. "What I did I did for myself, for my own reasons."

"And not because you love me?"

Her words stopped Brewster short. For a long moment he looked at her, and then he said, "You've got to understand that you've failed, if that's what you wanted. Don't make any mistakes—I don't want any part of this fight between you and them."

"Even before you're sure you know what it's about?"

"That's it. And you can get that simple message to your friends."

She stood before him defiantly, her eyes flashing, but when she spoke there was only sadness in her voice. "What you want doesn't matter. You're in this whether you want to be or not, and blind and vicious and selfish though you are, we need you. And we will have you. You've killed for me and you'll lie for me and kill for me again."

Brewster shook his head and sighed. "That makes two things you shouldn't have said," he said, softly. "Now get me the hell out of here before I say something I shouldn't."

But before he followed her, Brewster had to take a last look around again. The lingering sensations of a man waking from a dream were still with him. He could not believe that he had felt the things he remembered feeling, nor what he had seen...or done. When finally he looked down into the bowl he saw nothing, but he knew that somewhere in the darkness a body was lying propped against strange white shafts that would not let it rest. Two murders had been done up there, and the reasons for either were not clear in his mind...

WHEN they had almost reached the lower gardens, Akar came racing across a terrace towards them. All the way down they had kept picking up an escort of Jeggite warriors—the sentinel Argyres had vanished—and some of these had run ahead, evidently to where Akar had been waiting for word of them. He ran up to them, his usually impassive face torn between relief and smoldering irritation, and he addressed a terse, irate remark to the girl in his own language and then to Brewster, "Quickly! Follow me—there is still time for you to be last in line."

As Brewster left the girl—she silently waving him to go—and ran along with Akar, he started to say, "It was all my fault. She didn't want to..." But he didn't finish. He was startled at the realization that he was lying for Suba Marannes!

For some minutes before he had heard repeated blaring of horns and ruffling drums, but in his state of mind he had scarcely wondered what they might mean, aside from some kind of pageantry. For after what he had seen, he knew that the awaited presentation of the Earthmen to the Ho-Ghan would not take place, so that his first view of the court in its formal arrangement, glimpsed through the transparent walls, puzzled him.

When they came into view of that glistening facade, Akar stopped running and continued the rest of the way at a decorous pace, leading Brewster into the great hall through the side door they had first used. And here Brewster stepped behind Matt Peters and Tom Drake, who were standing apart from the rest of the Earthmen, while Sam Rogofsky stood before the lowest platform, between both groups.

The hall was arranged in masses of color, with the thousands of people in the court separated according to their races, making perhaps a dozen fan-shaped formations, which faced three central, ascending platforms. On the lowest platform stood five men, all Jeggites, their robes red and their sleeves striped with many colors. One of them, Brewster saw, was the aged man who had addressed the speech of welcome outside the palace. Above and behind them were some forty Jeggite warrior officers—among them Akar, though Brewster couldn't see how he had gotten there—dressed as Akar was dressed, each with the sign of his Jev.

On the highest platform, and Brewster's breath escaped in a sigh when he saw them, were the five Jevs, the chief protagonists in the drama he had so recently witnessed.

They were unmasked now and he could study their faces, but there seemed to be little difference among them save in age. Resplendent in their tunics, cold-eyed, dispassionate, they seemed characterless except for their extreme military bearing and the might that lay on them. The eldest, his granitic face lined with age, was the one who bore the flaming stone; the youngest, who seemed no older than Akar, with a heavily scarred cheek that did not detract from his insolent handsomeness, was the one who wore what Brewster thought of as a protozoid.

Flanking the platforms were rows of drummers and trumpeters and dozens of robed officials, one of whom stood beside Rogofsky and spoke his name toward the platforms. Rogofsky bowed his head, accepted an enormous volume from the official and crossed over, very unsteady on his feet and smirking, to where his friends waited. At a sign from the official, the drums and trumpets went off again and Peters stepped forward to have the brief ceremony repeated.

WAITING his turn, Brewster glanced around. The atmosphere of the court had changed tremendously; he had not thought this gay, almost frivolous court capable of such restraint. But it was more than restraint. When be looked at the faces of the people nearest him, they seemed dull and stupefied, as people look when they are drunk…or very frightened. Was it possible for an Emperor so mighty as the Ho-Ghan to have gone to his death so easily? Had there been none to fight for him? Were there none to mourn him? Was there not even to be a semblance of tribute, however mocking, to the memory of the ruler of so great an empire? But the drums were rolling for him and he went forward to receive the heavy volume, to stand with his companions.

He had no sooner taken his position when the entire court bowed their heads. A hundred men rapped their staffs like the crack of lightning. All who stood on the three platforms turned so that their backs were to the court. A single herald blew on a deep horn, a low, majestic, melancholy note, and all the lights in the great hall faded to darkness. And then, from behind the other platforms, rising so that it was higher than they when it stopped, a fourth platform rose up, illuminated by a soft, blood red glow, the only light in the hall. On it, in a great, gleaming throne that seemed to have been carved from a single, unbelievably enormous ruby, sat a man whose face was covered by a silken veil that hung down from a pointed hood.

He was dressed in a robe of purest red, exactly as the man Brewster had seen in the tower had been dressed, and he was built the same way. His hands were clasped in his lap.

He nodded once, and lights sprang to life at the feet of those who stood on the platforms facing him. He nodded again and lights went on under the feet of the Earthmen. He nodded a third time, and officials ran behind the Earthmen, always facing the throne, and they hung something heavy and gleaming around the necks of the Earthmen. Then the throne began descending and the horn blew again, and when all the lights went on the throne was gone.

Still in silence, the five Jevs left the platform and walked slowly through the length of the hall and disappeared. The instant the last one was gone, the formations broke and everyone seemed to be talking at once. The presentation was over.

"Well," Abbott breathed, evidently moved, "that was something."

BREWSTER watched Akar coming towards them. He fingered the pendant that had been placed around his neck. It was an uncut, jagged emerald hung on a silk green and red cord. The volume in his hand was bound in green leather. The first page bore Brewster's name written in gold script. The next page held the legend: *An Introduction to the Civilization of the Empire of Jegga.*

"For you," said Akar, beside him. "It will tell you much of what you will need to know of the interstellar worlds. They were prepared especially for you and inscribed by the Ho-Ghan."

"That was the Ho-Ghan we saw?"

"Yes. These jewels he presented you are the sign of his friendship and benevolence. Did you enjoy the ceremony?"

"A great deal." Brewster beckoned a porter and took a goblet off the proffered tray, Akar and Abbott doing the same. "Why does everyone seem so excited?" he asked. "No one's bothering to dance."

Akar sipped his drink and nodded. "I imagine they were confused by the new order of precedence," he said. "You see, caste and rank are very important among us, and the order in which the ranks were placed tonight were quite different from previous ones."

"How so?"

"Excuse me," Abbott said. "I see a young lady I greatly admire."

"Your interest in us seems unique," Akar observed with a slight smile, indicating the other Earthmen who were all scattering, some to take partners, some to talk to other officers. "As I was saying, the old order held only three ranks. The bottom platform was for Jevs, the one above them for Regios, and the third for the Ho-Ghan. Tonight, due to the Ho-Ghan's gracious command, the Regios were lowest, and a new caste, the warriors of Jegga, were placed over them, followed by the Jevs and the Ho-Ghan."

Brewster waved his glass. "From the commotion it caused, it seems to have been quite a change."

"It was," Akar acknowledged.

"What about the Argyres? There were a lot of them around."

"You're very observant."

"I'm more accustomed to drinking than my friends."

"Or perhaps the night air helped," said Akar. "The Argyres represent the Regios, the civil governors, forming a sort of civil police. In Ho-Tonda, the Imperial City, they were, naturally, the Imperial Guard, but with the elevation of the Jevs and the warrior caste, many of their functions will fall to others. I trust you understand?"

"Everything except that remark about the night air."

"Your pardon. I have no wish to intrude. I merely meant to comment on the change that appears to have come over you since you left the hall with Suba Marannes."

"I didn't think it showed," said Brewster. "Tell me about her. Who is she? What does she do? I can't make her out." He had been looking for her all this time without being able to find her.

"HER family has lived on Jegga for many centuries. They are very wealthy and influential people, merchant princes. Her grandfather is a widely respected man, having twice been decorated by the Jeggian Regio for service to the Empire. She herself is—how shall I put it?—occupied chiefly with the social world, with travel and sport and with whatever man seems to suit her at the moment."

"She's had a lot of men?"

"She has been married five or six times."

"What?" said Brewster, considerably surprised. "It's incredible!"

"But true. If you get to know her, you may understand, though I doubt if she will remain in Ho-Tonda much longer. One doesn't enjoy seeing one's friends fall from power. Like most Estannars, she generally moves in circles close to the Regios—a natural enough preference since Estannars dislike the inflexibility with which we warriors handle their venomous rebels. After tonight, Ho-Tonda may not suit her tastes."

"I see. It's all very complicated. I thought at first that all Estannars were rebels, but of course I was quite wrong."

"Quite," Akar agreed, "though there are several schools of divergent thought on the matter. It is an age-old question."

Brewster was silent then, leaning against a nearby pillar as he sipped his drink and looked on thoughtfully. Had the tension he had felt before been the work of his imagination? There was noise and gaiety again, and drinking everywhere. Glenn Purdom whirled by, dancing, calling out something that was lost in the confusion and Brewster absently waved to him. His mind was a seething turmoil, filled with countless questions, and a heavy weight lay on his heart. Suba was nowhere to be seen...

Presently he turned to Akar and bade him good night.

BUT there was no sleep for Nick Brewster. Several times he had dozed off, only to toss fitfully and awake again, to hear the music from below still going on, hearing the laughter, the luxury of his bed strange and oppressive. Now it was quiet. He listened to his own breathing, unable to understand why it was so quick and troubled. A heavy smell of smoke seemed to lay in his lungs.

He sat up and flicked a button, which turned on a soft night lamp. A thin veil of smoke hung in midair, passing slowly to the next room. Beside him lay his guns and a pack of cigarettes. He took a cigarette and lit it, then he put on a robe and went through the adjoining rooms to the central ones that had balconies. The other beds were empty, but on the balcony he found Joe Abbott, still dressed. The horizon was lit up luridly by a great fire in the distance, smudged by clouds of smoke.

"I thought you were asleep," said Abbott. "I sneaked into your room before and helped myself to some cigarettes. Felt like talking. What do you think that fire is? It's tremendous."

"Be damned if I know. Where is everybody?"

"Gone, by now. They left almost half an hour ago."

"Who left? What are you talking about?"

"Don't you know?" said Abbott. "I thought you knew. The officers said you did. They've gone away—Stewart, Peters, Callahan, all of them. Funny your not knowing."

"Where did they go?"

"To a city named Lacus. It's not far from here."

"But what the hell for?"

"Some of the Jeggite officers invited them. There's some sort of party going on there and, well, they'd been drinking and they had women with them and," Abbott shrugged, "they just went, that's all."

"Why didn't you stop them?"

"What for? They wanted to go." He looked at Brewster, adding, "Don't you see yet, Nick? No one's giving anyone orders anymore."

Brewster kept looking at the fire, not saying anything. When Abbott struck a match to light a cigarette, Brewster saw that Abbott was still regarding him. "What the hell are you looking at?" said Brewster.

"A guy with something on his mind, I think. That's why I stayed behind. I thought maybe you'd want to talk it out. It's time, I think."

Presently Brewster said, "Maybe it is, Joe." He exhaled a long, thoughtful drag on his cigarette. "Joe, have you thought much about what's happened to us? What are we going to do here? All right, we're pioneers and great explorers, and we've come into something that...that..." he cast about for words, and not finding them, he said, almost angrily, "We're in a world that can't take us back to our world. Where do we go from here? What happens tomorrow, the next day? Where do we go from here? Have you thought about that, Joe?"

"A little," said Abbott, slowly, "if I understand you. You can't mean that there's no way for us to get back. There are at least four of us who know enough about metallurgy—but hell, it's not the chemicals and blast furnaces and converters you're talking about. We know we can build a ship capable of taking us back...so what *are* you talking about?"

"About the things I saw tonight," Brewster began, but he stopped there. He had been on the verge of telling Abbott everything, but something stopped him. He had never confided in anyone, and he could not now. He had started something he had no desire to finish; he had already said too much. He ground his cigarette out, looking at the fire in the distance, then he turned to Abbott and said, "I'm sorry, Joe. I don't feel much like talking anymore. I'm very tired."

HE LEFT then, and returned to his room, surprised to find it in darkness, for he seemed to remember that he had left the light on. But when he turned the lamp on, he saw Akar sitting in a chair near his bed.

"I am very pleased that you didn't continue your conversation," said Akar, quietly. "I like a man who has the strength to stand alone." He nodded, adding, "I came here to tell you that I will be away for a few days. While I am gone, you may do whatever you like. I took the liberty of arranging for you to visit Dr. John Stevens. For the rest, I wish you a pleasant holiday." He rose to go, then, as an afterthought, he picked up the tunic Brewster had worn and turned it in his hands. He found a slight tear in the fabric of the green stripe, where part of the cloth was missing. From a pocket of his own tunic he took out a small piece of torn cloth and fitted it to the tear. It matched perfectly.

"Where did you get that?" said Brewster.

"The fragment? It was in Kaenas' hand when we found him. I took it before anyone saw. It might have been difficult to explain, though you are Kaenas' superior."

"Then you know I killed him?" said Brewster, slowly.

"Yes, I know."

"And you're not going to do anything about it?"

"But what can I do?"

"It was murder," said Brewster. Akar shook his head. "One cannot murder one's inferior. One may take life away, but that is quite a different thing, the privilege of a superior. Kaenas' life belonged to the Jev Thyle, and he could punish you if he chose—but how can he learn of it unless I tell him? And how can I tell him, who owe you my life, my elevation from a lowly Captain of a warship to full nobility as Lanae, and the honors heaped on me because of the ring of conspirators you discovered."

He paused at the threshold and said, "If you leave the inner city within the next few days, you will be well guarded, but be careful. We are striking at the Estannars, and they may try anything in desperation."

"That fire outside?" asked Brewster.

"We are burning their quarter," said Akar, and he left.

It was very early in the morning by the time Nick Brewster fell asleep...

CHAPTER SEVEN

THE days that followed were tranquil, but none was without some event that wove an inner meaning in Brewster's life. From the day that he first saw the ruins of the fire in the Estannar quarter, to the time that he witnessed the capture and execution of a small cell of rebels, to his meeting with the mysterious, beautiful Vrita, to his visit to Dr. Stevens, to his unspoken quarrel with Joe Abbott—but it was an endless list, for each day brought something new, often strange, and Nick Brewster found himself in a life that fascinated him, a life in which time slowly ceased to have its old meaning.

From the very beginning, the volume that had been given him was an amazing storehouse, filled with fact and theory, stimulating him as nothing had in years.** (see page 189 for Raymond A. Palmer's notes on *The Introduction to the Civilization of the Empire of Jegga*) He read and re-read it, familiarizing himself with this strange world in which he found himself. Its frankness, both in what it said and what it left out through ignorance, surprised and pleased him, and it brought him to begin learning the Jeggite language, to which he devoted an hour each day. He roamed the palace from one end to another, except for the Ho-Ghan's own palace. Comparing what he had read of the inviolability of the Ho-Ghan's life and what he had seen, he felt a cynical amusement and nothing more, and if he wondered who was now occupying the Ho-Ghan's palace, it did not trouble him.

Whatever doubts and misgivings he had had faded away. As he had admired the discipline of the Jeggites, and been overwhelmed by their achievements, he discovered he liked the way they lived. If he did not believe everything he read, if their stands occasionally dismayed him, if new events came along to worry him, they were unimportant beside the good he found. Brewster had lived dangerously, frequently in self-imposed hardship and deprivation, whether on his wanderings or his hunting and exploration trips, and he thus placed a high value on will and the ability and strength to live severely, but his wealth had taught him to enjoy luxury whole-heartedly. Luxury for him meant the time to read, to play, to understand people and life and the world, and it was a sort of state to which he felt true civilization aspired. But he did not worry if it would ever come. He already had it. He was a civilized man.

Still, once or twice, observing the Jeggite warriors, he wondered that they did not relax more often, and he remembered that seeing Akar in the luxuriousness of his wardroom aboard ship had seemed to him to be a contradiction. It was an interesting notion, but it passed. He found his every want anticipated, and because it was so much like the life he had known, there were times when he felt almost at home.

BUT there were shadows, too, and disturbances. The men who had gone to Lacus did not return. Tom Drake came back for a day and then went to rejoin the others. They were making a grand tour of Jegga, going from city to city, accompanied by Jeggite officers and women and hosts of servants. Once or twice, Brewster and Abbott spoke to some of them through Sinju, and their smiling faces were beginning to look worn from too much drinking and dissipation. On the fifth day of their absence, Brewster spoke to Rogofsky in the distant city of Chorcha and learned that he and Steward were taking a spaceship to Hruthes. At first inclined to order them both not to leave Jegga, Brewster ended by wishing them a pleasant voyage.

But he didn't like it, and later that day when Abbott put in one of his increasingly rare appearances, Brewster spoke about it. "I don't like it," he said, soberly. "I didn't like the idea of their going in the first place and I don't like their splitting up this way."

"Why not?" said Abbott, disinterestedly. "Afraid they're not in good hands? Seems to me you're doing what you want to do." He paused in his packing and asked, "Got a carton of cigarettes you can spare?"

"In my room," said Brewster, and when Abbott returned: "Going somewhere in particular?"

"Let's not get nosy," said Abbott.

"Still mad because I wouldn't talk that night?"

"Not at all. I don't give a damn, really."

"Listen, Joe, I'm going to see Dr. Stevens today. Why don't you postpone whatever you're doing and come with me?"

"Your first invitation is a little late. I saw Stevens two days ago." He stopped on his way out. "Just one thing, Nick. I caught the word going around that that dame you're playing with is too much dynamite. I don't know anything, but it sounded bad. Maybe you ought to layoff."

"Let's not get nosy," said Brewster. "So long."

After Abbott had gone, Brewster wondered whether Abbott had meant Suba Marannes or Vrita. He had been seeing them both. But it didn't seem likely that they could mean Vrita, though he knew nothing about her, not even her full name, because his meetings with her had been secret. The mystery about her spiced their visits.

He had met her two days before, toward evening. He had spent part of the afternoon at the Sinju, tuning in Jeggian cities and places of interest on its broad screen, fascinated by its range and full color. He had only to call to a central switchboard to be transported to the cloth mills of Bundokari, the great plastic foundries of Jesudar, the farms that stretched for miles in the agrarian Toctai province, or the bustling canalport of Kardandan, transferring to the waterways the products of the System, newly landed at the Kael spaceport.

LATER in the day he had left the palace, changing his clothes to a gray civilian Jeggite robe and looking very much like a Jeggite in it, and eluding the nuisance of his ever-present bodyguards by a series of quick shifts through the connected balconies of the palace wing. He had left the inner city and hired a tyar, a two-wheeled vehicle similar to the ones the Argyres used, but which could unfold wings and blades and become a helicopter plane for longer distances. In the tyar he had gone to the uncultivated plains and woods some miles from Ho-Tonda.

The day before, Abbott had attempted to tell him of the samples of limestone and ore he had taken from the soil, for already Abbott had started thinking of the possibilities of producing steel, the first step toward getting back to Earth. But Brewster, busy with his thoughts, had been inattentive, and now he was checking up for himself. He had been unable to find Abbott that day.

He was walking about, climbing rolling ridges on the edge of a woods, when he first saw the second tyar appear overhead. For a moment he gave no thought to it. In his mind he was already seeing the construction of vast steel mills. He knew, and had known before, that every element needed was to be found within the System; he saw the buried coal mines, the limestone and iron ore pits, the flaming converters and open-hearth furnaces, the yellow molten rivers of steel, the bright hell of the ingot soaking pits, the gigantic blooming mills—all of it he saw in his mind's eye, done as it had never been done before, using the far advanced science of the Jeggites to build his dream...

But then it suddenly occurred to him that it must be Abbott in that other tyar, Abbott seeking him out. Before he could remember that Abbott could not have known where he had gone, he had run toward where the tyar was landing. It was already dusk and the sun was behind him, so that by the time he saw that it was a woman who had gotten out of the tyar, he was already upon it. He stopped then, and would have turned back except for the way she stood there, seeming to wait for him to come closer, her face tilted curiously at him.

So he came forward to explain, searching his memory for the few Jeggian words he had learned, hoping they might add up to an explanation. *"O morra...bahazrad...o igon,"* he faltered, confused because he realized he was saying *"I am always wrong,"* and more confused by her beauty. For she was tall, very tall, and her black, lustrous, large eyes reflected the glorious fire of the setting sun, her soft olive skin glowing in that radiance, her long, slender mouth parted in a half smile and the teeth so very white against the red lips, her hair thick and braided, framing the straight forehead and the chiseled long oval face like a portrait of some Egyptian queen. She wore a gray silken robe like his, her waist shaped by a broad jeweled belt, her hips easy and angular, her hands crossed over her breast.

HOW expectant she seemed, how her eyes carefully scrutinized him from head to foot. And when she spoke, that same expectancy was in her voice, in the deep, husky voice that made Brewster think of velvet rubbed against the nap.

"O morra ezad bahazrad," she said. "I am seldom wrong."

"You—you speak English?" Brewster blurted.

"It would appear so, would it not?" she asked, her eyes never stopping their examination. "I caught a glimpse of you at the reception of the Ho-Ghan," she said, after a moment. "You were leaving. But now I see *O morra ezad bahazrad.* You are indeed a very attractive man."

"Thank you," said Brewster. He had regained his composure by then; a large portion of his twenty-seven years had been devoted to the quest and conquering of feminine beauty, and if he had never lost the ability to react freshly to the stimulus, he had learned to control it. He was proud of the fact that he could think on his feet, that his judgments were as instantaneous as they were accurate, and these and other talents were seldom used so well as they were on women. It had once been said of him that if he were dying of thirst and a beautiful woman brought him water, he would first concentrate on the woman.

"You know," said the woman, "I like that speculative gleam in your eye. I hoped you'd have a gleam like that."

"You almost sound as if you came here to meet me," said Brewster.

"Ah, I like that. You've been around women. I had you followed after I saw you leaving the inner city, and then I came here. I thought you might enjoy a quiet dinner in the country."

"You have a secluded little lodge not too far away," said Brewster. "We'll be quite alone and we can talk."

"Rather a large lodge, but quite right otherwise. Tell your tyar you won't need him. Make sure to get his number."

When Brewster returned a few minutes later he said, "I'm considered rather a fast worker in my country, so my only request is have a little respect for my reputation. So far this is wonderful and terrible. What's your name?"

"Vrita," she said. "We'll let it go at that."

And as far as talking went, they had let it go at that, and it continued rather more wonderful than terrible. That night, far away in the still fastness of the forest in the Paipurth Mountains, had been everything Brewster could have wanted. He had known several women whom Vrita brought to mind, fiery, extremely intelligent, restrained and passionate by turns, mysterious, but Vrita was the synthesis of all and something more, something elusive.

SHE had returned him to the outskirts of Ho-Tonda the next day, and that night, after he had fallen asleep, he woke up to find her in his room. Fatigued as he was, his mind filled with the things he had seen that day in Ho-Tonda, he was glad to see her. She refreshed him, she soothed and calmed him, and when for a little while he was able to forget what he had seen, it was easier to forget entirely.

He had gone to Ho-Tonda that day dressed in the civilian robe, for it avoided curiosity and crowds and so made his bodyguards' task easier. He had not attempted to evade his guards that day; he had found new ones that morning, and upon inquiring after the others, he was told that they had been executed for failure in duty.

It had shocked him at first, learning that what had been a light-hearted maneuver for him had cost two men their lives, and then it had infuriated him. He sought out the Jeggite officer, a Lanae, who was responsible for his safety and told him in measured tones that he refused to have bodyguards. The Lunae, old enough to be Brewster's father, told him that his own life depended on Brewster's safety, and that since he valued it, he would not hesitate to execute as many bodyguards as he had to, until this process of elimination would finally furnish bodyguards who could not be eluded.

"That's a damned cold-blooded thing to say," Brewster had said. He found his rage useless against the man's calmness. "That's the—"

"But reflect a moment," said the Lanae. "It is you who is being cold-blooded. The lives of these men now depend upon you."

So that in the end, when Brewster went to Ho-Tonda, he was accompanied by some six or seven Jeggites; he wasn't sure how many there were because he wouldn't let them get too close and they were dressed in civilian clothes, but he had agreed not to attempt to get away. He took a tyar to the city itself and there walked toward the Estannar quarter.

The fire that had raged for four days had finally burned itself out, though black columns of smoke still spiraled into the sky from smoldering areas. There were dense crowds for blocks around the ruined quarter, milling against the cordons of Argyres and Jeggite warriors, and Brewster found himself unable to get closer than two blocks to the edge of the quarter. But even from where he stood, jostled on all sides, he could see gaunt, charred skeletons of stone buildings and hear the roar of a fresh fire springing to life among the embers. He listened to the conversations on all sides, not because he could understand them, but because he understood enough from their intonations and actions.

WAS there no sympathy for the Estannars among all these people? Vrita had told him the night before, when he spoke to her of the fire that was then still raging, what had happened to the Estannars. She had spoken vaguely, not wanting to talk of it, and he had not pursued it, but he had heard enough to prepare him for something bad. He looked about him, trying to understand.

Here and there would be a sad-eyed Phyladian, towering even over the Jeggites, their brutish faces impassive and tragic as they gazed at the ruins, but they were the only ones who seemed affected. The others, the shifty Usuaus, laughed uneasily, exchanging rapid comments with the curious Anaians, the slow-talking Darzizts, and once, when a group of Argyres came charging through the crowds, chasing an Ermosian and hitting him over the head with long pikestaffs—for Jeggian law forbade Ermosians from public gatherings because of their ugliness—even the dour Phyladians joined the laughter.

They were no different, Brewster realized, from comparable mobs he had seen at such occasions; they were vultures, gawking and gossiping and titillating their nerves with the view of disaster, and they disgusted him no less than other crowds he remembered. He had many times had reason to hate mobs.

His revulsion made him impatient and careless. He began pushing through the people, elbowing them aside. They cried out at him, hurling insults at him, and one stout Phyladian put a hand against Brewster's chest and pushed him back some five feet with a gentle shove. And Brewster, already simmering, boiled over. He surged back at the giant Phyladian, and instantly, where a moment before there had not been room enough for him to pass, there was now a cleared area. The giant saw Brewster coming toward him and came to meet him, his enormous arms stretched out before him as if to seize Brewster and throw him somewhere.

Brewster stood there until the last instant, then he suddenly ducked under the extended arms and buried his left fist in the Phyladian's belly, then his right, then his left again, short, murderous blows that hit like hammers. Then he backed away, and as the giant's head came down, Brewster landed his right fist on the side of the man's face with such a furious, full-bodied smash that the giant literally flew off his feet, landing at the edge of the cleared area. And then, before the Phyladian could get to his feet—for he was rising, though he swayed like a dying ox, one eye closed tight—and, while Brewster waited ready to hack him to bits, over the screams and yells, sharp whistles blew on all sides and Brewster's bodyguards surged through the crowds.

In a moment they were joined by Argyres. They would have killed the Phyladian if Brewster had not stopped them. But stop them he did, and then, when they were taking the bloody brute away, he remembered the fate of his bodyguards and he said, "Don't do anything to him. I want him brought to my quarters this evening. That's an order, and if it's violated, I'll have a new set of bodyguards in the morning."

The strange language he had spoken, as well as the perplexing circumstance of this apparent Jeggite being so well attended, so inflamed the curiosity of the crowd that Brewster's bodyguards had to get him away before his identity might be guessed, for then, they told him, it would take an army to clear them. So they hustled him down into the cleared area of the ruins, where he had wanted to go anyway, and there he saw the capture of several Estannars, and there too he met Suba Marannes again.

IN THE company of his guards and Argyres, Brewster walked through the devastated blocks. It stretched for perhaps a quarter of a mile, two or three blocks deep, paralleling a series of branch canals. Everything, docks, warehouses, piers, had burned to the water's edge, and though from the rubble and charred remains Brewster knew it had been a natural fire and not the work of the Jev Thyle's flame, the destruction had been almost as complete.

Patrols of Argyres and warriors were everywhere, poking about in the ruins, but when Brewster had been there no more than a few minutes, he saw patrols running toward a point some distance away where official tyars, the only ones allowed over the area, were dropping. By the time he reached the fire-blackened pier that had become the center of much activity, the place was filled with warriors and officials and a sprinkling of civilians, several of whom were Estannars—the first he had seen that day. There was a good deal of commotion, with the Argyres spreading out in a large semi-circle around the pier, and it was impossible to see what was going on.

Suddenly everyone began moving back. Warriors came up from under the jutting skeleton of the pier, carrying the bodies of five men whom Brewster saw were Estannars. They had been hiding under the ruins, breathing through hollow reeds like the ones that lined the canals, and they were so utterly exhausted that they could not move. All young men, they lay where they fell on the sandy beach, their clothes in seared tatters except for thin belts that hung heavily around the waists, holding several bulky pockets.

Warriors carefully removed these belts, and then a Jeggite officer went among them, examining their faces patiently. After a moment he stood up and pointed to one of the men. A murmur ran through the people near the pier. Looking closely, Brewster saw that the man who had been singled out was odd-looking for an Estannar, with the wiry smallness of a Usau and somewhat darker hair than the others.

They killed that man where he lay. The others were dragged erect and half-carried to a waiting tyar. They were taken directly past where Brewster stood, and as he studied their faces, seeing that they were already half dead from fatigue and exposure, he backed into the assemblage of officials and civilians. Then he felt a hand close on his.

SO TAUT was he, and so swiftly had he turned around that he saw the fleeting change of expression on Suba's face before she had had time to adjust herself, for evidently she had touched his hand the moment she recognized him standing just before her. For a brief instant he caught her surprise and fright—or had it been fright?—but it disappeared immediately and she said something to him in Jeggian, pleasantly, quietly. He understood only one word: "hello."

If it had not been for the constant pressure of her hand on his, he might have spoken. As it was, she had inconspicuously taken him off to one side. "What are you doing here?" she asked, her voice barely audible. "What made you come here?"

"I don't understand," said Brewster. "I'd heard about this—the fire, I mean. I thought I'd look around. What's the matter?"

A cloud had spread over her face. "These men near you are your guards?" she said quietly. By then her quick eyes had seen the guards hovering closely, and her intelligence had organized everything. The cloud was gone and she was smiling, chattering very casually. "I think you've seen everything," she said. "I'll go back to the city with you."

He hadn't wanted to go with her. He didn't know whether it was because he wanted to stay or to avoid her. At any rate, he got no chance to answer, for she walked away quickly. A few yards away several Estannars and Argyres were waiting before an official tyar. She spoke to them and they all looked curiously toward Brewster. They left without her, she waving to the ascending tyar, and then returned to Brewster.

"It's impossible for anyone except officials to get tyars here," she said, "but I'm sure you can get one. Tell your guards to ask a Jeggite officer for one."

Brewster looked at her and saved his curiosity, but he asked for two tyars; he wanted to talk to her alone. The request produced the expected stir. A guard of honor formed and a Lanae who was present introduced himself and provided the tyars with a graciousness that scarcely hid his inquisitiveness. Brewster stood there politely ducking questions until they left.

The moment they were alone Suba's cheerfulness collapsed. Her smile fell off unnaturally and she sat pressed in a corner of the tyar without saying a word until the retreating ruins were out of sight, and then she quietly said, "Your being in our quarter this afternoon was an unfortunate coincidence, but I am greatly obliged for your kindness."

When she didn't say anything after that, Brewster let his impatience out. "I think I deserve at least a rudimentary explanation."

"Yes," she agreed, but several moments more went by before she spoke. "Those men who were waiting for me were my father and two of my uncles. The Jeggites have been pretending to think my family had a hand in hiding those rebels. Your presence there, where they might infer you had been led, was most unfortunate under the circumstances. They might have said you were led there to give rebels a chance to kill you. As it is, they may still say it, but you have been very kind."

"Kill me?" said Brewster, confused. "They wanted to kill me?"

"I don't know. I think they were meant for you."

WHEN she said nothing else, Brewster said, "I don't think I've understood a single thing you said. Not one thing."

She turned to him. "You haven't heard about Chorcha?"

"I don't even know what it is."

"And you don't understand about the fire?"

"I'm not sure. I thought I did."

"What did you think the fire was? Why was it set?"

Brewster hesitated. "I thought it was…well, I thought it was a general punitive measure against the Estannars. I imagine they cleared out the inhabitants and burned down the quarter to force the Estannars to leave Ho-Tonda."

"You think the entire Estannar quarter was burned down?"

"Yes," said Brewster, "though it seems like a fairly small—"

She interrupted. "The Jeggites burned down only that part known as the Marannes quarter, my family's docks and warehouses, and the homes of the people who worked in them."

"I don't understand. Why only that quarter?"

"They had found out that a rebel cell was hidden there."

"You mean," said Brewster slowly, "that an entire section of the city was razed just to get at those five rebels I saw caught?"

"Yes."

"But surely the Jeggites could have found them some other way?" said Brewster. "I know something of their capabilities."

"Yes," said Suba, softly. "They are very capable monsters."

"Look here!" Brewster exploded. "Suppose you stop giving me these half answers and vague hints and questions that lead nowhere! Or if you don't want to talk, say so and…" His anger subsided before her suddenly taut face. It was as if he couldn't hurt such loveliness, he thought, annoyed with himself. He couldn't hurt her and that was that.

But then she began speaking, her voice still soft, and she never looked at him but kept her eyes on the horizon, and he felt that she was very distant from him all the time she spoke.

"Two hours before dawn, on the first night of your arrival in Ho-Tonda, thousands of warriors encircled the entire Marannes waterfront. The warriors had already seized power from the Argyres. The Jevs sanctioned an act that even the Regios would never have allowed. They gave no warning to the hundreds of people who lived and worked in our quarter. A score of fires started simultaneously throughout the quarter. Less than half the people trapped there escaped with their lives, and they ran into waiting cordons of warriors. When the rebels they sought were not found among them, they waited for the fire to subside and then searched the ruins until they discovered them under the pier…"

FOR a moment she turned to Brewster, her eyes savage with dark purple light. "You say there must have been other ways to find the men they sought—but there was no better way for their purposes. The Jevs could hardly have thought of anything better to demonstrate their ascendancy. They killed hundreds of Estannars and struck a public blow at the Marannes family, not only by their wanton destruction, for we are wealthy enough not to feel even such a loss, but by showing that Marannes property had been used to shelter enemies of the Empire."

Brewster was thoughtful for a moment after she finished speaking, and then he said, "But they were right, weren't they?"

She turned on him, fury in her. "Right? Right to kill—"

"I mean they were right in believing you had sheltered rebels."

"No," she said. "None of my family could possibly have done it."

"I'm not talking about your family. I meant you."

"I had nothing to do with it."

"You didn't know they were there?"

"No."

"Then it was just a coincidence that rebels were found in the property of a family that has a rebel member?"

She flushed, but her lips were steady. "Yes. I am not lying."

Her words brought Brewster up sharply. He had been about to say that the responsibility for the terrible loss of life, no matter how cruel the Jeggites were, was actually hers. But now he remembered with a recurrence of that queer sensation that he was talking to someone who could not lie—that if she gave him an unqualified denial, he had no choice but to believe her.

He shrugged. "Then how did you know those rebels were here to kill me?"

"I didn't say I knew," she said. "I only think so." She looked down at the city hundreds of feet below them, the hum and bustle of its life a steady sound in the silence.

"I thought at first the Jevs had fired our quarter to injure us, on the pretext of hunting rebels. Today Argyres from Chorcha reported to the Regio. Rebel cells had been discovered in every city your friends went, this morning even in Chorcha where they were expected. The Regio informed my father, knowing how bad it would be for us if they actually did find rebels in our quarter. When they found them I saw it could not be an accident that they were everywhere you Earthmen were—they are special agents called Konos, assassins, sent here from Estannar itself."

"Have you any idea why they chose your quarter to hide?"

"It was clever of them. The Marannes family's position and well known loyalty would make our quarter an ideal hiding place ordinarily."

Brewster could not help the trace of a sarcastic grin, but he forbore comment. Still, something was definitely wrong with the story as it unfolded. He pursued it. "It seems," he said, "that these Konos were trapped here in the fire the first night we arrived. If they came to kill us, why weren't your orders in line with that? Or were they?"

"No!" she said, sharply. "My orders were to conciliate you, to win your friendship and trust until you would believe us."

"But that same night there were already men in Ho-Tonda who were here to kill us? Doesn't that seem wrong to you? Isn't it possible that you're mistaken in your analysis?"

"The analysis is not mine. The Konos they found in Chorcha and the other places all told the same story. They had come to kill you."

"It still doesn't make sense," Brewster pointed out.

"I know," she said, meeting his glance. "It will when I have found out."

BREWSTER doubted it. "Do you know what happened when we landed on Boron, or in the ship that brought us to Ho-Tonda from Boron?"

"No," she said very slowly and quite puzzled.

That was it, of course. After the break on Boron, and after the mutiny on Akar's ship had failed, the rebels had decided their only answer was to kill the Earthmen. Acting independently, as they had to for safety, they dispatched killers to Jegga. Meanwhile, those who still operated under the previous orders were trying to conciliate the—

What nonsense! Even that neat theory had a tremendous flaw in it. The rebels had planned to prevent the Earthmen's falling into the hands of the Jeggites—Dramon the Estannar himself had admitted that he would sooner have seen them dead than taken by the Jeggites. The failure of those plans had decided them to kill the Earthmen. Fine, as far as it went. But—*the very fact that Suba had been ordered to win Brewster over already presupposed that he was in the hands of the Jeggites...*

What did it mean? Had the rebel chief first sent Konos, then changed their minds and been unable to call their killers off? The ones trapped in Ho-Tonda, perhaps—but what of the ones in the other cities? Was there no communication among them? Or was there more than one source of orders? In any case, the rebels were a badly muddled lot and he pitied their puerile attempts at revolution.

But what of the Jeggites, he asked himself, irritably. Did he yet understand what the mutiny aboard Akar's ship was all a bout? Did he yet know why Jeggite should have been pitted against Jeggite? Even if he assumed that the mutinous officers had been Argyres—in disguise, say— how did that explain their connivance with rebel Estannars? Then he dismissed it, temporarily. At least there was sufficient order and intelligence among them to have uncovered these rebels. He was grateful for that, though he felt contempt for these confused plotters. When Akar returned, he would have it out with him. It could wait.

He said, "Well, now I understand why you were so upset when you found me at that pier. First you thought I was alone, so you tried to pass me off as a Jeggite before I could spoil it by speaking English. When you saw my bodyguards, you realized it was no use trying to conceal the fact that I had been there. But you might have tried getting me out of there without stirring up that fuss. You wanted everyone to know I was there, didn't you?"

She nodded. "I capitalized on it. I demonstrated we were good enough friends to leave together. If matters grow worse we may need even the suggestion of powerful friends—and you are powerful, make no mistake. The Regio is a figurehead now, and the Argyres quickly made their peace with the Jevs when enough of the loyal officers were killed off. You'd think life was valueless to them," she added softly, "but it isn't so...not their lives."

"And your life? Aren't you ever afraid they might seize you and...and, well, make you answer some questions?"

"A silly girl like me?" Her laughter was gentle, bitter mockery. "They'd never suspect me. Why should they bother with someone whose only interests in life are foolish rounds of fun? I travel and hunt and dance and have picnics and little else."

Little else except get married, Brewster wanted to say, but he said, "What if any of your family knew about you? What if they were to be questioned?" He couldn't understand the irritation he felt.

"No one knows. And my family is too powerful, too famous. They wouldn't dare," she said. She said it again, as if to reassure herself. "They wouldn't dare. They never have dared...until now..."

BREWSTER thought she was going to cry. "I meant to ask you," he said quickly. "When they found those five rebels under the pier, they killed one of them immediately, an odd-looking fellow. Why was that?"

She hadn't cried, after all. She turned to him, seemingly surprised that he had asked that question. "But he was a Bheynor," she said. "He was the offspring of an Estannar and another race, a Usau, I think."

"Is that forbidden? I don't understand."

She looked at him. "Have the Jeggites told you nothing?" she said, unbelieving. "Don't you know that the punishment for intermarriage between Estannars and other races is death for all concerned?"

"I didn't know. Why is that?"

"Why?" Suba echoed. There was a distant look in her eyes when she spoke again, a kind of nonsensical visionary look, as Brewster mentally characterized it, and her voice held a sort of cold passion, more in her words than anything else, for her voice remained quite soft.

"Because sometimes the offspring of such a marriage looks like an Estannar without inheriting the curse of our race—sometimes it can lie. It can go among the Jeggites and confound them, and so they call these invaluable allies Bheynors, which means: able to resist. But they are wrong, for in that sense their malevolent empire is filled with Bheynors. We are all able to resist, each in our own way…"

Brewster let the ensuing silence remain unbroken. He was tired of her little orations. They only provoked his impatience. When the tyar landed not far from one of the gates to the inner city, Brewster quickly said his goodbye. "If you can use my help," he offered, "don't hesitate to call on me."

After he had left he was sorry he had offered his help. He had no interest in helping her or any of her cohorts. She was a beautiful woman, but why in hell should that make any difference? When he compared her to Vrita, he wondered which of them he would sooner have taken to the mountain lodge, given his choice and other things equal. Not that Vrita was…hell, no, but there was a kind of innocence about Suba that had a tremendous appeal for him. Strange, that innocence, in a woman who had been married six times. Or five times. Probably an invaluable quality in a spy that ability to appear innocent.

He had been suddenly stirred for a moment when she told him about the Bheynors. A wild idea had flashed through his mind…something about her marrying so often as a trick, to bear those curious hybrids for her cause…absurd, of course, because her marriages were only too well known. She might, though, marry an Estannar as a blind for mating with someone of another race. Then where were the children—surely so well known a person couldn't hide a brood? If anything, this new aspect that had at first excited him and why?—only galled him more when he examined it.

HE HAD been in a bad mood when he returned to the palace, and the Phyladian who was waiting for him hadn't helped any. He had completely forgotten about him until one of the guards asked if Brewster wanted to see him. They brought in the giant, his huge skull bandaged and his greenish skin discolored and bruised, and Brewster had nodded and told the guards to let him go peacefully.

But then the Phyladian had refused to go, and his deep voice had rumbled on in a distressed monotone, and the guards were preparing to use force when Brewster stopped them. "What does he say?" Brewster said.

"He thanks you very kindly for your mercy, O Fyavo."*

So Brewster had nodded and tried to send the Phyladian away, but the giant had still refused to go, and he had made violent gestures with his hands, pointing to the guards. When Brewstar again asked what the giant was saying, the guard said, "He is grateful also because you saved him from injury at our hands, O Fyavo."

"Fine. Now tell him to go."

"He is very dull-witted and does not understand that you cannot grant him leave in the Jeggian tongue, O Fyavo."

Brewster's enormous *Introduction* was lying nearby, so he had shrugged and picked it up, opening to the appendix. He read three different phrases aloud, combining them: *"O gahy ortram jhaba miratro O igo; haftgi; O brui mettaz."* "I wish you the very best fortune for the future; I go now; I bid you farewell."

The Phyladian's objections had only increased, until Brewster caught one word, then another, then a phrase, tracing them all. Then he had risen and stood before the guard who had done the translating. "Tell me again what he says," Brewster said in an even voice.

The guard's brown face blanched.

"Your indulgence, Fyavo, for not listening carefully. He says he fears we will kill him when he goes from here. He has seen you are merciful and wishes to remain here as your bondsman. He says his life is yours."

Brewster slapped the guard across the mouth. "He stays, and I'll expect to see him every day. If you ever try this on me again, I'll break you apart." He pieced together a few reassuring syllables that he spoke to the Phyladian and retired to his room.

And here again Brewster was uncertain about his motives. Why had he bothered about that stupid brute? Was it merely his anger at the guard's effort to deceive him? He was sure they had meant to kill the giant. And the brute had said his life was Brewster's. Great. He was getting to be a collector of lives. First Akar, a noble, now this green-headed brute. He remembered suddenly Suba's saying: "You'd think life was valueless to them, but it isn't—not their lives." How true was it? They seemed to have a sliding scale for the value of life, like their tables of rank and law and ethics.

---

*Fyavo—word meaning honored visitor, but carrying with it the connotation of princely position and power, conferred by the Ho-Ghan's gift of the emerald. –ED.

Before he went to bed, he tried to contact his friends. An officer appeared on the Sinju and said he would pass the message to Chorcha, where the Earthmen were expected the next day. Abbott was nowhere to be found. He had lain awake, falling now and then into a shallow, restless slumber, and then suddenly Vrita had appeared. He hadn't known where she had come from and he asked no questions, taking the silken loveliness of her body in his arms.

SHE was gone when he awoke, and then Rogofsky had called in from Chorcha, saying that he and Stewart were going to Hruthes by spaceship. He had not told them what he felt, and he had avoided it when he saw Joe Abbott later in the day, before he went to see Dr. Stevens. A call came in from Suba Marannes when he was leaving; he didn't take it. And not because Abbott had just told him there was talk about him and a woman who could only be Suba, but because she had plagued him and given him a bad day the day before.

Not that this day started out much better. His escort was a taciturn medical officer who spoke less than a dozen words all the way to the hospital where Stevens lay. When he took Brewster into the large room, he jerked his head toward the bed and said, "Hopeless. Spinal injuries and shock. Dying slowly." It was a long speech for him.

When Brewster had last seen Stevens almost a year before, Stevens had been a man some fifty years old, with a finely molded face and keen, intelligent eyes and a firm, vigorous step. The man who lay in bed with jaundiced, tearing eyes still retained some of the cast of Stevens' features, but nothing more. A dozen scars had disfigured him. The hair on the right side of his head had fallen out, the rest was thin and white as snow. His cheekbones were large and prominent in his wasted skull, his hands gnarled and bony and trembling. Though his tear-filled eyes were open, there was no sign of recognition in their vacant yellow pools, nor did he seem to hear the few words Brewster spoke...

When Brewster returned to the palace, he dug into his carton and took out a pack of cigarettes. He emptied the pack and took out the last cigarette. Instead of tobacco it held a rolled up bit of paper.

Don't be a sucker, Brewster. There's more to winning bets than playing the odds—find out what you're betting on. Interested in palace revolutions, maybe? It's a juicy two to one, in the bag, and you lose either way...

He realized then, reading and rereading it, that he had stored the question of the existence of this note in some far recess of his mind, as he had stored the note itself. Now it was out again and Brewster had no answer. He realized that he had retained some vagrant idea that Stevens had written it...*maybe, for some reason I will learn, it was Stevens:* that was the way he had stored it in his mind. But now he knew it wasn't Stevens.

Then who was there among these people who could write in slang?

He replaced the note in its hiding place, and the questions in a little receptacle in his mind marked: To Be Opened When Akar Returns. So secure and satisfactory a place was it that he smiled when he held his two automatics in his hands. He had not touched them since the second day. He blew the dust off the guns and put them away.

IT WAS as if someone had been watching him. There had been only that one note in five days, but after the fifth day there was a new note every day. He found them in his food, in his bed, once in a half empty pack of cigarettes. Only the first of this new series disturbed him to the extent that he did something about it.

Get it, Brewster? One by one they're gradually going to separate your whole outfit. Let them. Keep your eyes peeled and your mouth shut, and maybe you'll wind up in the bed next to Doc Stevens. Maybe all of you will.

He called on the Sinju and found that all except Rogofsky and Stewart were together in the Nogansi province, and even those two were on their way back. And Abbott called him briefly to inquire what he was doing. Abbott was in work clothes, making metallurgical surveys in the Totamangu mountains, surrounded by troublesome bodyguards.

After that he ignored the notes, even when one of them referred to Vrita, calling her the first self-appointed satellite of the coming star. For all her secrecy and care in meeting him, he knew that sooner or later their meetings would become known, but he was angry at this spying. It was not difficult to deliver such notes, he knew. The palace teemed with servants and attendants, and even the watchfulness of the Argyres and warriors was not enough—that much he knew from their constant nervousness in challenging even casual passersby, from sudden hurried searches he would see conducted at all hours.

He could have stopped it easily enough. Because of Vrita, he had reduced his guards' functions to merely straggling behind him, and there were times when they would wait for him at appointed places far from where he was meeting Vrita. It was an unspoken agreement between them; he made life comfortable for them, and they stayed out of sight if he required it. Thus, Vrita felt at ease in the mysterious role she still kept up and which still intrigued him. Having pushed his guards into the background, he was reluctant to ask them to watch for the note-bearer.

Not that they mattered, except for irking him. The notes had failed in their primary purpose, he knew. Because they had waited until he re-examined the first one, they had probably inferred that he was ripe for their war of nerves. The opposite was true, because he understood their motives. He completely gave up calling the others on the Sinju. He relaxed entirely, forgetting the passage of time so well that he had to consult the calendar he kept to remember.

Afternoons he spent watching the warriors drill or go through complicated maneuvers in spaceships, even in tyars. Evenings he was with Lanae and officers, dining with them, present at their entertainments. He was invited everywhere in the palace, until he felt he was one of the great number of nobles who had lived there for years. And always adding a welcome element of excitement was his relationship with Vrita, her sudden appearances, her notes marked with a large, flowing symbol that she would not explain. Trying to understand her became his pastime; he had never met her at any of the palace functions, yet she seemed to be in the palace quite frequently.

Suba Marannes called twice and he refused to answer both times, and then he heard no more from her. One night he overheard the name Marannes mentioned by several people, but it stopped when he came closer and he asked no questions. Once Abbott called in and left word from the Nogansi province. Brewster was too busy trying to arrange seeing Vrita to call back. The next day no one in Nogansi could locate Abbott.

So it went on easily, pleasantly, for days…

Twelve days after the Earthmen had first landed on Jegga, everything exploded.

THE first gray light of dawn was lying on the open terrace when Brewster woke. Because his head was still heavy from the wine he had had the night before, and because the sudden noise in the darkness had startled him, at first he could not understand what Abbott was saying. His eyes focused slowly on Abbott's form sitting on his bed, and he listened, then suddenly he sat up and turned on his night lamp. Abbott emerged from the gloom, his face grim and hard.

"Do you understand, Nick? Rogofsky and Stewart are dead! The others are scattered all over this planet. I can't find any of them."

Brewster said, thickly, "How do you know?"

Abbott opened a little bag and took out his *Introduction* book. He had pasted the flyleaf to the inside cover and formed a pocket. From this pocket he took out a handful of small, wrinkled sheets of paper and thrust the papers into Brewster's hand. "I've had a special courier service for the past few days," he said, grimly.

Brewster knew what they were the moment Abbott took them out. He went through them carefully. They had been written in the same stiff, heavy handwriting that he had found on his own notes. But they were a good deal more specific in what they said. They gave information and had none of the sarcastic lines he had received. One of them read:

Who are you making these surveys for? Why don't you wait until you find out? Find out what the Jeggites intend doing with the metal you hope to make. If you want to see how heavily they're banking on you, get to a Sinju alone at the 95th hour. Tune in to 80-77-15.

"This was the first one I got," said Abbott. "I couldn't get to a Sinju right on time. When I dialed it later, a Jeggite came on and asked what I wanted. I said I was fiddling around and stopped trying. The next day I got this long note, telling me what they had wanted to show me on the Sinju."

Brewster took the paper from Abbott's fingers, lifted his brows at the length of the written message. It was the longest of all.

The second note told Abbott that the Jeggites had long before prepared everything needed for the manufacture of metal. They had laid out the sites of mines of every description, needing only the techniques and methods to put them into operation. It listed some ten different places on Jegga, Usau, Darziz and Ania where everything was waiting. It ended by saying that it had cost the lives of hundreds of men to get that list, and that it might cost his to be found holding it.

There was a note similar to one Brewster had received, warning Abbott that they were all being separated, but it went on to say that the reason for this was because the Jeggites feared if they were kept together, they might combine what they were learning and unite against the Jeggites.

"I checked on that one," said Abbott. "I tried to call the men, but all I could get was that they had been in Nogansi. I called you that night but you didn't call back. I went to Nogansi. The men had been there and gone, some to one place, some to another. They had split up in groups of two. Purdom and Callahan, they said, were in Ulatai. I went there and stayed on their trail until I caught up with them in Pingui. They were all right, but they had a lot of women with them and they were having a fine time. I stayed all day with them trying to get them to come back. When they wouldn't, I tried to get to Casia, where I learned Drake and Peters were. On the way there I got this last note."

Don't bother going to Casia. You're on a wild goose chase. While you're scuttling back and forth, Rogofsky and Stewart are taking a little trip from which they won't return. They were on the Hruthian ship Mowhana *yesterday. Better go back and see what's happening to Brewster.*

BREWSTER put the note down and reached for a cigarette. "How do you know Stewart and Rogofsky are dead?" he asked.

"I kept trying to trace them. Finally somebody told me they had taken passage from Hruthes. I checked all their ship lists and saw that the *Mowhana* hadn't come in to Jegga. They told me the ship had had to turn back to Hruthes, I called Hruthes on their Tonju*—that ether telegraph of theirs—but they wouldn't say anything about Stewart or Rogofsky being there. They just said they didn't know."

"So that made you decide they were dead?"

"Not that alone. I took a tip from you and put on a civilian robe and ducked my guards. That was in Lucansor, where they told me the *Mowhana* had turned back. I went back to the ship offices and hung about the place. There were crowds there all afternoon, so I knew something was up. Later that day there was an announcement over the Borju that had dozens of people screaming and crying. Then they hung up some kind of announcement. I couldn't try deciphering it there, so I began to copy it down word for word.

---

* The word Tonju, like Sinju and Borju, derive from the same root: Ju, or news. Their uses, however, encompassed a good deal more than that. The Sinju was a colored screen capable of reproducing images in natural color for vast distances, but not through space. At the same time, the images, which could be magnified to any size depending upon the receiving screen, were accompanied by voice or natural noises. Such natural noises could be toned down or magnified.

The Tonju was more or less what Abbott called it—an ether telegraph. It was used when communication was wanted between planets, or from ship to ship in space. Once through the atmosphere of a planet, it became possible to use the Sinju. The Tonju did not reproduce voices, but only impulses of some electrical nature, working on the principle of light beams and bent by electricity. There were several regular Tonju codes, and the various Jevs each used their own military codes.

The Borju corresponds to Earthly radio. It reproduced voices, and was able to penetrate some distance into space, though it was seldom used for that except in emergencies.

There was also a device called a Sorju, though none of the Earthmen had seen it. This was a device of limited range, combining the uses of the Sinju and Borju—that is, capable of projecting images and voice or natural noises, but able to perform in space. There were not many of these and were chiefly used on warships, where they could, without any receiving operator, by themselves tune in on images in space, and thus were extremely valuable to warships in battle, since even their limited range outdistanced any other form of vision. -ED.

"I'd just about finished when some Argyres arrested me. They thought I was an Estannar and wanted to know what I was copying the list for. Not that I understood them, or they me, but when I ended up in the Lucansor prison, there were my bodyguards. So they arrested my guards and gave me a new set and I started back to Ho-Tonda. I wouldn't explain and I still had the stuff I had copied. When I deciphered it with the stuff in my book, I saw it was an announcement that the *Mowhana* had been lost in space. The rest of it was a list of passengers."

"Did you find Stewart and Rogofsky listed?"

"No, but would they have put their names on it?"

Brewster took a long drag and smiled at Abbott. "Then all you have to go by is this note saying they were on the ship. What makes you believe this note so implicitly? Have you any idea who's sending these notes to you?"

"It's not just the note, I tell you! Why can't I get through to either Rogofsky or Stewart if they're alive? And since then I haven't been able to locate any of the others."

"But what about the notes themselves? Any ideas?"

"Yes," said Abbott, evenly. "I don't know if you've noticed, but these notes are written in slangy expressions, and to me that means that there are…" He took a cigarette and waited until he had lit it. "It means that someone in concert with the rebel Estannars knows our language very intimately…"

BREWSTER grinned at him. "Joe, you're a laugh. Why don't you say it? You're remembering what that half-witted little Boron told us about survivors from the first *Trailblazer*, and you're sure these notes not only prove there were—at least one—but also that they joined the side of the Estannar rebels."

"Then you knew?"

"Sure I knew. I've thought the same thing for days." His grin widened. "I had my own little courier and my own little notes."

"Then what do you think it means?"

"Means?" Brewster shrugged expressively. "Just what it is. We have one or more of us playing the rebels' game. It's a surprise, sure it is, but there's a logical answer and we'll get it."

Abbott regarded him steadily. "And Rogofsky and Stewart?"

"One gets you five they're perfectly all right. They've just gone off somewhere and these fools are trying to break you down with their notes."

"And the others? Peters? Callahan? Drake?"

"You left out Purdom. What are you worrying about? You said yourself they were having a whale of a time. It's just tough to get in touch with them sometimes. I gave up a few days ago," he added.

Abbott got up, facing the terrace. The sky was beginning to show pale red streaks through its gray-blue. "And the general idea of there being men from the *Trailblazer I* here on Jegga, siding with the rebels—and our not being told a word of it—all this just means what it seems on the surface and nothing more? It doesn't make you wonder a little? It doesn't stir you in any way?"

"Hold on now. In the first place, we don't know that there are men from the *Trailblazer* here. I mean, it might just be one man. It might be someone with the kind of intelligence that Mike Callahan has. He might have been taken in by the rebels' big talk. Or he might even be a prisoner among them, forced to write these notes. As for our not having been told—maybe even the Jeggites didn't know about it. Or if they did, maybe there's an excellent reason for their not telling us. I know this is a surprise, a shock, finding it out this way, but there's no sense letting yourself get carried away by it."

Abbott seemed to calm down, but after a moment he shook his head and said, "You may be right about some of this, but not about the *Mowhana.* If they expected to build any sort of confidence in us with these notes, they'd be crazy to say something they knew we'd find out was wrong."

Brewster grinned again. "Maybe they had other reasons than just building your confidence. Maybe they wanted to get you in certain places at certain times—so they could take a crack at you, for instance?"

"Then why didn't they? I went."

"Sure you did, but our Jeggite friends were a little too smart for them." He laughed at the way Abbott looked at him and got out of bed. "Okay, okay, I know something, and I'm going to spill it. But we might as well have breakfast. I can see I'm not getting back to bed."

SO, WHILE the dawn gently flooded the sky, Brewster and Abbott sat out on the terrace under brilliant streamers of sunlight, having a breakfast that Brewster ordered by name, dish for dish, grinning at Joe Abbott. He had even concocted a palatable substitute for coffee, and all this, combined with the really serene morning, finally had its effect on Abbott. He listened attentively while Brewster told him everything he knew. Or so he thought, but there were some things Brewster held back. The thing with Vrita, for instance, and his short-lived romance with Suba Marannes, or the killing of his guards.

But he did tell him about the slaughter of the Argyres, and the assassination of the Ho-Ghan, and the burning of the Marannes quarter, and then everything Suba had told him. He cautioned Abbott very grimly about ever revealing the source of the information that Suba had given him, but he weighed all of it against a lively skepticism. In the end, Abbott was very quiet. He had hardly interrupted, once asking why Brewster had been worried about the men that day when he, Abbott, had left, and the answer that Brewster had known of the planned rebel ambushes had seemingly satisfied him.

Still, when Brewster had finished, Abbott insisted that they try getting in touch with the men. Brewster had gotten dressed and joined him at the Sinju. When he came into the main room of their wing, Abbott had looked at him peculiarly. Brewster was wearing one of several new tunics he had gotten some days before, a handsome tan and green thing, with a jeweled belt.

"You know," Abbott said slowly, "with that heavy suntan and the clothes you're wearing...I don't know, maybe it's the way you carry them, but I don't think I could tell you apart from a Jeggite if I didn't know you."

"Comes in handy," Brewster grinned. "You should hear me spill the lingo. Not just ordering dishes, either."

They spent two hours at the Sinju in fruitless efforts to reach any of the men. Official after official appeared on the screen, all of them professing ignorance, all accepting messages for relay. When Brewster saw that it was beginning to wear Abbott down, he took him for a walk through the palace gardens as a native might escort a visitor. He remained cheerful to the last. The last was when Captain Akar came.

THE news that Akar was back reached them in the gardens, and from the very way it was delivered, it smelled of bad news. The messenger who came for them almost lost his life doing it. Evidently he had seen the two Earthmen on one of the upper terraces, and feeling the urgency of his mission, he had forgotten elementary caution and come dashing at the two men. He was one of a score of Hruthians who were searching the grounds for them.

He came running up a flight of stairs, but he was still twenty yards from them when suddenly the otherwise deserted gardens became alive with armed guards who sprang from nowhere. They might have killed the messenger in his tracks if he hadn't been knocked down when he reached the top of the stairs. In a twinkling the guards were swarming all over him, and Brewster and Abbott came running.

Five minutes later they were ushered into a spacious room where Akar awaited them. "Sit down, gentlemen, both of you," he said quietly, but he remained standing. When the attending warriors closed the doors behind them, he stood a few feet away from both men.

"I have distressing tidings for you," he said. "Two of your men, the ones named Sam and Paul, or Rogofsky and Stewart, as you call them, are in the hands of the rebels. They were taken when the ship on which they were returning from Hruthes was attacked and captured by a rebel warship. The few survivors of the attack told us that your men were taken alive. We do not know where they now are."

He paused a moment, then said, "I see that this news is not as much a shock as it might have been. That is why I wanted you both here. I had information that led me to believe that both of you either already knew or expected this news. The rebels seem to have picked you two out as their main targets for the notes they have sent you. They, as we do, believe in the principle of leadership, and they, again like us, seem to have decided that you two are the leaders of your group.

"I regret that necessity forced me so long to secrecy about matters which I know must have aroused your curiosity. Undoubtedly we were at fault in believing you could be kept in total ignorance until it suited our convenience; for our enemy is, as you know, extremely resourceful. But matters have now come to a pass where you must be told everything, if we are to retain your trust. Since I am uncertain as to what you already know, I will answer whatever questions you put to me."

"All right," said Abbott, "suppose you tell us why the rebels took Rogofsky and Stewart, and what you think they'll do to them."

Brewster said, "No, we'll get to it. I think it would be better to go about this in an orderly way, taking first things first."

Akar nodded. "And first you would ask..."

"About the mutiny aboard your ship. Why should some Jeggites have been involved in a deal with rebel Estannars—unless you Jeggites are divided among yourselves?"

AKAR remained thoughtful a moment before he answered. "There is some truth in what you say. Not that we Jeggites are divided in our opposition to the rebels, or in our determination to keep our civilization dominant and our Empire intact. But, as always, there are varying opinions as to how any ideal should be preserved and furthered, and these differences of opinion have in the past divided us on the questions of method. You would like a complete answer, I imagine?"

"As complete as possible," said Abbott. "It sounds complicated."

"It is," Akar said, with a slight smile. "Everything, as you know from reading the volumes we presented to you, revolves around the Ho-Ghan. From time immemorial his position, his dynasty, his very person, has been something sacred. The Ho-Ghan combined civil and military law, ruling Jev and Regio alike, but the Ho-Ghan's power was originally a military one. The first Ho-Ghan was a Jev more powerful than the rest, and nothing more, but in time he took on new attributes. In a growing empire someone had to, and so he became the repository of all civil law as well as military law.

"But here a strange thing developed. In time this military ruler attained such power that he was able to appoint Regios and declare that since they represented him, their power was greater than that of the Jev. From time to time the Jevs rose and overthrew the Ho-Ghan. A new one took his place, but inevitably the new Ho-Ghan followed the path of the others. Since only the Lyrio family knew the secret of the forcewall, only Lyrios became Ho-Ghans, and thus, unassailable, they soon, within a generation or two, elevated the Regios above the Jevs. For generations more the Jevs would endure it, busy with conquests, building the Empire, until they too rose, each time hoping that with the exile of this Ho-Ghan they would permanently resume their rightful position.

"It was always a vain hope, and continued so to this day, but in the lines of this struggle we see the lines that have divided all Jeggite power through history. As there was enmity between Regio and Jev, so was there enmity between Argyre and warrior, and this enmity existed through all their relations. Because the warriors were primarily responsible for the subjugation of the Estannars, the Estannars sought power and influence and friends among Regio and Argyre. And found them, for the Estannars are intellectually gifted, and even their rebellious elements have never been enough to stop the rise of loyal Estannars to all sorts of positions of wealth and power.

"In many ways this friendship has benefited the rebels too. We warriors have always felt the subtle hand of the Regios in our dealings with them. Not that they were traitorous, for as I say, no Jeggite is a traitor to his race, but their caution and regard for the Estannars had many times stopped drastic action where only such action could succeed."

Here Akar paused for some reason, but after a moment he went on.

"WE JEGGITES have waited centuries for men from your world to break through to us—and when you came, you arrived at a time when the Jevs were restless. The arrival of your first ship was unexpected, but it presaged the coming of a second. Waiting for that day, every rivalry became more bitter, every question of policy became a major issue. The Jevs ruled Boron with martial law, but the Regio of Estannar wanted to have Argyres take over and be the first to greet you. The Jevs realized, after your arrival and after the Estannars had made an attempt to seize you, that knowledge of your arrival would establish guilt among Estannars if your arrival was kept secret. The Regios refused. It was more important to them that you be received in great style.

"The final outcome of this struggle was in doubt all the time you were on Boron, after we had gotten you back. We didn't know it then, but when word of your arrival reached Jegga, the Ho-Ghan acted swiftly. He executed two of the Jevs who happened to be in the inner city and ended the struggle. The other Jevs gave up, and acting on orders of the Ho-Ghan, made changes in the personnel of all ships. We waited twenty-two hours until word came to proceed. I still knew nothing.

"I left with several new officers aboard. They were Argyres, dressed in our tunics, sent to make certain there was no trickery by the Jevs. As officers they had the run of the ship, and they quickly examined the captive Estannar aboard, eager to discover if there was anything they didn't know. As you know, among other things they found out that the rebel somehow knew of their plot to mutiny and kill me if necessary. But they had also found the notes he had to deliver to you. To bind him to silence, they proved to him that they had delivered his notes for him, and he could not reveal one without revealing the other. It was a difficult choice for them, but the success of their mission depended on it, and they paid the price.

"We later discovered that the Estannars had ships out after us, and this spy hoped a mutiny might play into their hands—or it might result in the death of everyone aboard, which suited him as well."

Akar smiled grimly at the memory and regarded Brewster. "You saved us for the second time then," he continued. "But when we reached Jegga, an Argyre escort came up and Jev Thyle ordered me to obey them. The Regios had won. But there never was any question of cooperation with the rebels. It was a continuation of the struggle between the Jevs and Regios, or the Jevs and the Ho-Ghan."

Brewster said, "But that same night the Ho-Ghan placed the Jevs over the Regios and elevated the class of Lanae over them as well."

"Ah," breathed Akar, "but that was not the same Ho-Ghan—and for that we have you to thank. That was the third time you saved us."

"Me to thank?"

"Yes, for had you obeyed the wishes of the Ho-Ghan and appeared at his reception that afternoon, it would have been over. We were too disorganized to attempt anything then. Your refusal gave us several hours of grace, hours during which the assembled Regios and high Argyres tried to calm the Ho-Ghan. He was in a wild rage at your insolence. He blamed the Regios for the great public reception they had given you, saying it had given you too great a sense of your importance. He finally threw them all out, in a tantrum all that afternoon.

"THAT was our chance. We brought in thousands of our warriors. When the reception started, the Ho-Ghan was already on his way to exile at a secret destination. The Jevs made the Ho-Ghan's brother the new Ho-Ghan, and he issued the new laws elevating the Jevs and Lanae. The Regios were ready to believe anything at the time, and by the time they manifested doubt, the Jevs already ruled the inner city. They were ready to use force against the Regios themselves, as they had on the Argyres.

"So the Regios gave in. Since then they have tried to see the Ho-Ghan but the Jevs have refused, and the Ho-Ghan sends out word that he will not see them. Meanwhile the vast armies of the Regios are being disbanded, and edict after edict cuts their power. The secret of the Ho-Ghan's overthrow will be kept until it is safe to reveal it. Less than a hundred people know that the Ho-Ghan who received you that night was a new Ho-Ghan."

Brewster nodded to indicate his satisfaction with the answer, but more for Abbott than Akar. To forestall the possibility of Abbott pursuing the subject of the Ho-Ghan's exile—for Brewster had told him of the assassination, Brewster quickly said, "Suppose you tell us what happened to Rogofsky and Stewart?"

"I have already told you what I know."

"I mean about the notes Abbott and I have been receiving." He added, very casually, "Why didn't you tell us that there were other survivors from the first ship besides Dr. Stevens?"

Akar didn't move a muscle. "There was an excellent chance that we might rescue them from the Estannars. I had hoped to return with at least one of them. To have told you beforehand might have further confused an already bad situation."

"How do you mean *rescue* them?" said Abbott.

"I think I am using the correct term. You see your contact with them, brief as it was, still breeds doubt in your minds. They can be very convincing. I say rescue because it hardly seems likely they went willingly with the rebels. They had been on Jegga less than three weeks when they were taken, most of that time in a hospital."

"How many of them are there?" said Brewster.

"Suppose I tell you the whole story," said Akar, watching Brewster light a cigarette. "You'll have to teach me to do that sooner or later," he smiled. Then he resumed: "There were six survivors from the crash. Two men died on Boron the first day, but their bodies were stolen by the Borons. The others were taken to Jegga. Dr. Stevens steadily deteriorated in spite of everything we could do, but the other three, Harper, Crane and Burke, recovered under our care.

"Possibly all three are still alive. All we know is that one day there was a magnificently coordinated rebel raid and they were all taken. Dr. Stevens was in the hospital, and was thus saved. We turned the System over without finding a trace of the three men. We never again heard anything of them. Until the day you landed on Jegga, it was thought the Estannars might have killed them.

"OUR first information that at least one of them was still alive came from that Estannar we brought back from Boron in my ship. Expert questioning brought out an amazing number of things, among them the fact that the Estannars were bringing one of the three to Jegga. We also learned that there were already dangerous agents called Konos in Ho-Tonda itself, hidden in the Marannes quarter."

"And that's why you burned the quarter down?" said Brewster.

"As soon as we knew. The Konos are trained killers, and it could only mean that they were going to make an attempt on your lives. To decrease the danger, we removed most of your men from Ho-Tonda, inviting them on a tour of our cities and provinces, and putting small armies of bodyguards around all of you. Then Argyres discovered that the rebels were following the tour, and in one instance at least, the Estannar espionage was so good that they anticipated a visit to the city of Chorcha itself.

"By that time it was too late to stop Rogofsky and Stewart from their journey to Hruthes, but on their return trip we sent an escort of two squadrons of warships. We still have not received all the details of the attack the rebels made, but it was a characteristically excellent one, planned and executed to perfection. It became apparent that the rebels were expending their full resources in their efforts to get you.

"We didn't want to alarm your men, but the danger of a successful raid was too great. To minimize the danger of losing them all in one huge attack, we encouraged them to keep separating and kept their whereabouts a secret even from both of you, for the enemy might have been listening at any time. But from the way Mr. Abbott here began trailing first one group, then another, we surmised that the rebels had found a means of alarming him.

"We followed Mr. Abbott everywhere, intercepting all the notes the rebels sent him from Ulatai on, but letting him receive them to encourage the rebels to send more. We knew we could disprove what they told him, and it was imperative to try finding the man who wrote them. For we then knew that one of the three was on Jegga, and that he was writing these notes. I imagine you guessed there were survivors in the same way?"

Brewster nodded. "From the kind of expressions we found in the notes. It was what we call a dead giveaway. But you didn't get him?"

"No. We caught four messengers, but they knew nothing. We knew the other men weren't being sent these notes, but we were sure you must have gotten some, Mr. Brewster. We tried to find out, but our men here said you wouldn't even let your own guards near you half the time, and it was impossible to know."

"Oh, I got them, all right," Brewster grinned. He unbuckled the belt he was wearing and took out a small roll of papers. "I got the first one the first night we were here. A Hruthian porter just walked in and handed it to me. Ten minutes later we passed that porter in the corridor. The Argyres were carrying him on a slab, dead."

AKAR'S jaw tightened. Half to himself, he said softly, "Then that was how the Argyres found out there were rebel cells on Jegga. The first clue must have come from that porter, and they killed him after he told them to keep us from finding out. You see," he added, turning to the two men, "the struggle between the Argyres and us affected even your safety sometimes. Both factions were jealous of the privilege of safeguarding you."

Brewster drawled, "I don't care who saved us, as long as somebody did. And a pretty fair job, too, from what I've heard." He tossed the roll of papers to Akar. "Some of these notes get pretty personal, if you'll notice."

Akar quickly ran through the notes. Once he observed, "We could never duplicate this use of your language. We learned it chiefly from your men while they were here, and from the many books we were able to save from their ship. But the rebel Estanners learn it from these men and pass it on, and one of the ways we trap rebels of other races is by finding out that they speak your language but cannot honestly tell us where they learned it."

Abbott asked, "Then there are other rebels besides Estannars?"

Akar looked up at him. "Not many," he said. One of the notes seemed to make him pause. "This reference to a woman called Vrita," he said presently. "Is she a very beautiful woman? A Jeggian? With large eyes and braided hair? Quite a beautiful woman?"

"It sounds like her," said Brewster. "You seem to know her."

"I do know her, slightly," said Akar. He rose from his chair, and it seemed to Brewster that he had put on what Brewster thought of as his impassive expression, not an expression at all, but the too careful avoidance of any expression.

"Well, tell me about her," he pursued. "I hardly know a thing about her. She's a complete mystery to me."

"Another time, perhaps. I must go now. We still have ships out searching for your friends. Perhaps something has happened."

Abbott said, "You don't seem to think there's much hope."

"It would be foolish to hope. We have had extraordinary success against the rebels in the time that you have been here, and yet we have failed. Not only have we lost two of your men, but we have been unable to find one of the three they took away a year ago. And the danger is still as great as it ever was, if it has not increased."

"I had no idea the rebels were so powerful," said Abbott.

"That is our fault. We seldom underestimate them, but we did not wish to alarm you as long as the situation was under control. Not that we are unduly alarmed even now; we have been their masters for too long not to know how to handle them eventually. As for your other men, you can look forward to their return shortly. The inner city is quite impregnable, and Jegga will be cleared of the rebels in due time."

BREWSTER and Abbott rose to go, but Brewster stopped halfway across the room and turned back to Akar. "By the way," he said slowly, "if you don't want to continue underestimating your Estannars, you might do worse than have a conversation with Suba Marannes…"

Akar nodded imperceptibly. "Thank you," he said, quietly. "You evidently do not know that she left Jegga for Estannar several days ago. It is to be hoped that her welcome on Estannar will be warm indeed. We had quite the same idea, but your frankness and trust in us will not be forgotten. Our debt to you grows daily." And he touched his forehead in formal salute…

Abbott waited until he was alone with Brewster before he spoke. He might have said anything then if Brewster hadn't quietly asked, "Well, Joe, are you satisfied?"

Abbott turned on him, his eyes blazing, his voice filled with scorn. "What do you mean am I satisfied?" he ground out. "You're the one who ought to be satisfied! You deliberately turned that girl over to them! You told me to be careful about revealing anything she had told you and then you turn around and dump her into their—"

"But you don't understand—"

"I understand only too damn well. That Vrita, whoever she is—that's the reason. You've got your hands so full with one woman that you can afford to sacrifice another for the sake of a lousy gesture... For a compliment and a salute you turn spy for them!"

"Not at all," said Brewster evenly. "These people are our friends. The rebels are our enemies. It's as simple as that."

"Is it?" said Abbott, his voice growing very quiet. "Are you so sure it's as simple as that?" He looked at Brewster and there was an odd light in his eyes. "Yes," he said, quietly. "You've made your decision at last. You've picked your team."

"And you?"

Abbott didn't answer, and for a long time the silence lay in the room, heavy and oppressive. When finally the Hruthian girls brought in the mid-day meal, Abbott walked out and left Brewster alone. Brewster, however, did ample justice to the excellent food, and later he whistled a tune as he stood on the balcony, smoking and watching several platoons of warriors go through drill on a nearby field.

CHAPTER EIGHT

AN HOUR or so later when Brewster left the balcony, he found Abbott sitting alone before the Sinju. The shades were drawn against the warm afternoon sun and the great central room was cool and dark and faintly astir with the sounds that accompanied the projections on the large Sinju-screen. Brewster sank down on the couch beside Abbott and looked on as Abbott took the controls.

The green hills of Jegga kept re-appearing and blurring as the Sinju tried to bring them into detailed focus. Again and again the Sinju circled the hills and tried to close in from a new vantagepoint but always the image blurred.

"What are you looking for?" Brewster asked.

Abbott gave no sign that he had heard Brewster, and under his direction the screen blotted out and then came to life again high above a canalport that Brewster recognized as Kardandan. Far below moved many small boats and barges and lines of squat vehicles ran swiftly along single rails that fed into the port from the hills in the distance. The Sinju went along the canal for miles until it came to a great concentration of the boats that moved to it from Kardandan. Along the canal shore at this point there seemed to be a harbor, but here again, when the Sinju descended for closer focus the screen lost the image.

Brewster grunted and was about to speak when, from across the room, a voice called, "The Fyavo Brewster."

Brewster got up and saw two warrior officers standing under one of the arched entrances. Seeing him, the officers came forward and met Brewster halfway and one of them handed Brewster a black scroll. Brewster broke the hexagonal seal, opened the scroll and studied the large red letters. He frowned, then nodded to the officers and said, *"O igo miratro,"* to them and walked to his room.

He was dressing in his red and green ceremonial robe when Abbott came in. "Where are you going, Nick?" Abbott asked quietly.

"The council of Jevs wants to see me."

Abbott looked down at the scroll that lay on the bed and observed, "You really do speak their language, don't you?"

"When in Rome," said Brewster. He put on a broad green belt.

"Nick, you know what I was looking for on the Sinju."

"Yes?"

"I saw you did. That's why I didn't answer. You think you're the only one who knows what's doing here."

"All right, I'm not."

Abbott studied him, then said, "I saw a lot in the Totamangu mountains. The Jeggites have been mining ore and transporting it to Kardandan and then up the canals. They censor the Sinju from coming too close but it's evident they've got everything ready to start manufacturing steel and every other metal they need—if someone who knows enough to fill in the gaps will show them."

Brewster put his feet into green sandals and picked up the scroll and started out of the room. He turned at the door and said, "I'm way ahead of you, Joe," and went out.

In the central chamber he joined the officers. In the corridor they picked up a guard of some fifty warriors and together left the wing and started for the council-room of the Jevs. Halfway there, from the direction of their steady ascent, Brewster knew that the council room would prove to be the great columned bowl where twelve days before Suba Marannes had led him to witness the assassination of the Ho-Ghan Lyrio.

WHEN they reached the tower, Brewster was led into a lower story as huge as the bowl above it. In the darkness of this empty chamber the roots of columns which ascended through the floor to the bowl were alive with a strange glow. The floor was marked with various glowing symbols and to one of these, a circle in the center of the room, the officers led Brewster.

The moment Brewster stepped on the circle, it detached itself from the floor and began to raise him. Simultaneously, a similar circle appeared in the ceiling above, sliding open to allow sunlight to pour into the gloomy chamber. A moment more and Brewster had been lifted up through this second circle to find himself standing on the floor in the center of the bowl.

But he was also enclosed within the loose center of a great pentagonal table around which sat the five Jevs. Each facet of the table was perhaps twenty feet long and a Jev sat alone at one of these facets, the surface of which was marked with his oriflamme. Standing there, Brewster could not face more than three of the Jevs at anyone time, and he turned slowly until he had seen them all.

The Jevs regarded him impassively. Overhead the afternoon sun shone down on the alabaster columns and the black-gleaming floor, its rays like fire in the jeweled symbols and the wind ran through the open bowl and fluttered the red ceremonial robes.

Still no one spoke. Then the white columns that rose forty feet to the sky turned a pale crimson and opened and a host of officials came out of them and took their places around the Jevs. Now, though they still seemed to be ignoring Brewster, the officials began to talk to one another in low tones, consulting with the Jevs from time to time, and the bowl was filled with the sounds of their voices.

Brewster took out a cigarette and lit it, his lips tight, a thin scowl on his face. When he blew out smoke, every eye was on him and a deep hush descended, magnifying the loudness with which Brewster said in an irritated voice, "Well?"

The silence became meaningful.

Presently the Lord of the Flaming Stone, Jev Thyle, said, "We have summoned you here to discuss with you some way of returning you to your world of Kren." There was no emotion on his aged, granitic face. "We know you would like to return. Is that not so?"

Brewster started to say, "I'm not—" when one of the officials, evidently for the benefit of the attentive Jev Nastrond, began to speak in Jeggian, and Brewster knew he was translating what Thyle had said. At the conclusion, the official nodded to Brewster.

Brewster said, "Eventually, but neither I nor, as far as I know, any of my friends feel any great urgency."

Behind Brewster, Jev Ahriman asked, "Why?"

Brewster turned to him. "Your hospitality, among other things. Jegga is quite a wonderful world, and we have scarcely begun to see it."

Jev Thyle said, "But you will wish to return eventually?"

Brewster turned again and said, "Of course."

At this there was a new flurry of discussion among the officials and Nastrond, oldest of the Jevs, a rather sleepy and somewhat feeble old man, nodded stonily as the translator summed up the exchange for him. Finally Jev Eblis, he of the red rocket streak, spoke up.

"You are aware, Fyavo, that we know little of metals and that if a vessel capable of returning you to Kren is to be built, you men of Kren will have to teach our smiths your metal-science?"

"Possibly," Brewster said.

"What?" cried Ahriman.

Brewster half-turned to him and said in a louder voice, "Possibly, I said. There's more than one way of looking at it."

THYLE said moodily, "Cease your riddles, Fyavo." He waved an imperious bejeweled hand. "Will you teach our smiths or not? Answer forthrightly and at once."

Brewster's scowl lay undisturbed. He took a thoughtful drag on his cigarette and blew out smoke slowly, then pointed his cigarette at Thyle and said, "Will you give me your flaming stone?"

Ahriman shouted, "Remember your position here!"

Brewster spun around and said in a level tone, "I intend to—as soon as I've established it." He stared at Ahriman and the young Jev paled with a rage that turned the scar across his cheek to a livid line. Before Ahriman could speak, Brewster jabbed his cigarette at him and said of the blue-black many-eyed Anzus on Ahriman's robe, "Give me that creature of yours with the eyes!" and turning on his heel he said to Eblis, "And your rocket!" and to Nastrond, "And your green heat!" and to Azevedo, "And your navigation board!"

In the ensuing silence Brewster addressed Thyle again. "Have I made myself sufficiently clear, mighty Jev?"

Jev Eblis got up. In one of his hands he held a small red ball. He opened his palm and let the ball drop to the table. It rolled along the smooth black surface until it fell off to the black floor where it smashed into a hundred fragments. Without a word Eblis turned and walked across the open chamber down a flight of stairs. His expression had never altered from its impassive cast, but there was dismay on the faces of the group of officials who followed him out.

Thyle sat with both hands flat on the table before him, his eyes searching Brewster's lean, hard face. Azevedo watched Thyle and Nastrond was still looking at the red fragments like rubies on the floor. But Ahriman too had risen and in his hand he held a red ball. His voice came softly and venomously:

"The Fyavo would be a Jev?"

Brewster nodded reflectively.

Ahriman raised his hand furiously and flung the red ball to the floor at Brewster's feet and several of the shattered particles fell on Brewster's sandals. Brewster's dull, gleaming eyes traveled from Ahriman to the sandals and back to Ahriman and his lips parted to show his teeth in a wolfish, mirthless grin. He exhaled smoke and turned his back on Ahriman and faced the other three Jevs.

Thyle had not stirred and now both Nastrond and Azevedo regarded him as if waiting to follow his lead. In the hands of each, Brewster saw one of the red balls. Finally Thyle spoke, his gruff voice still calm.

"You believe your knowledge is worth so much to us?"

"Isn't it?"

Thyle's cruel eyes blinked. "Why should it be?"

"I don't know, but this is one way to find out if it is."

"Then you believe what the Estannars told you?"

Brewster shook his head. "No," he said and smiled a little and added, "Is it strange that I should try to sell my knowledge dearly?"

Thyle's lips moved before he spoke.

"Not unless your price is so high that purchase becomes impossible." He paused. "Once you give us your knowledge," he asked, "what assurance have you that the power so easily won will not more easily be taken away?"

Brewster sighed and said, almost pleasantly, "I thought I'd give you that problem," and smiled again. "I felt you could work out suitable guarantees if you wanted to strike a bargain."

Again Ahriman broke in, but now he spoke Jeggian and addressed Thyle in a contemptuous tirade. Brewster moved back in the circle to avoid standing along the diametrical line between the Jevs and leaned against the table. Though Ahriman's flood of language was beyond Brewster's ability to understand, there was an element of bitter hostility between these two Jevs that was self-evident.

AS THE younger Jev poured out his acrimony, Thyle made no answer nor any effort to interrupt. He stared stonily at Ahriman, his aging features dull with controlled anger and at length, when Ahriman stopped speaking, Thyle rose from his massive chair. Nastrond and Azevedo rose with him. For a moment it appeared as if Thyle would speak to Ahriman, who seemed to be expecting an answer. Instead Thyle ignored him entirely and turned to Brewster.

"Fyavo, know that in the Empire of Jegga power is not won by bargaining. Think a little longer and weigh your conclusions carefully. We will send for you again."

Then he left the table and walked quickly across the black floor to the stairs, Nastrond and Azevedo following and behind them their coteries of officials. But Ahriman was the last to go, remaining even after Brewster vaulted the table and walked out. He could almost feel the hatred that followed him, not only in Ahriman's eyes, but in the eyes of the jeweled representation of the Anzus he wore, as if it were alive.

Brewster couldn't understand it...

*   *   *

FOR the first time since his arrival in Ho-Tonda, Brewster felt a weariness that was more than ennui. It was not a physical sensation, but it expressed itself in a restlessness that almost wore him out. For the first time he felt the weight of passing hours...and something missing...something he couldn't quite touch.

Abbott was gone again when Brewster returned from the council of Jevs. There was no sign of Akar, nor could he be reached through the offices of the Lanae of the palace, who should have known. Brewster sat at the Sinju and tried to locate Drake and Matt Peters, but their trail ended in Casia, as Abbott had told him. Glenn Purdom and Bucky Callahan had vanished shortly after reaching Pingui.

At twilight, Brewster sat down alone to dinner, but couldn't eat and gave up. He stood on the balcony wondering what it was that had taken possession of him. It was not loneliness, for Brewster had never felt the need of another human, but at the same time he had a sense of isolation, of being cut off from the main stream. He stood there and watched the lights come on all through the Inner City. He clutched the balcony rail with a tightness that numbed his hands, staring into a twilight as gray as the civilian tunic he had put on. The image kept turning over in his mind. To lose himself in that twilight as gray as the civilian tunic he had in the doing...without thinking, without plan...

Silently he climbed over the rail and dropped to the terrace fifteen feet below. He walked swiftly down a flight of stairs, through a landscaped plaza, and now he was running from the sounds of voices and music that were everywhere in the palace. He leaped across a shallow pond and came to another rail and dropped down again until he was on the lowest level.

Before one of the Palace wings he found an area filled with waiting tyars, their drivers lounging nearby in an arbor. He got into one and began to fumble with the controls, trying to remember what he had noticed of the operation of the simple mechanism. He had switched on the murmurous motor and unfolded the helicopter wings when one of the drivers ran out of the arbor toward the tyar.

The driver reached the tyar just as the blades began to revolve. He reached a hand in, crying out something, and tried to touch the motor switch. With a sudden burst of inexplicable anger, Brewster smashed a fist into the driver's face and knocked him down. Then he got out of the tyar and waited for the driver to get up, his knotted muscles trembling with eagerness to hit the Darzizt again. But the driver lay there afraid to move and Brewster got into the tyar.

Playing with the controls, he got it off the ground, lowered it again—for nothing was allowed to fly within the Inner City—and drove it to one of the roads. Speeding along, he was soon through the guarded walls and in Ho-Tonda itself. Here he went aloft and headed the tyar toward the dark fastness of Paipurth Mountains.

He knew that his sudden, successful disappearance would mean the lives of his bodyguards, but somehow it had stopped mattering to him. A strange fever was running through him.

ONLY when he was almost there did Nick Brewster realize that he had gone to Vrita's lodge, and then he saw that he might never have found it if there had not been lights on within. Not many lights—one or two, perhaps, but in the nightbound forest they were lonely beacons.

Then Vrita was there. For once their meeting would not be her doing, the result of a note, tender or curt, coy or demanding. He felt his pulse quicken as he maneuvered the tyar into a soft, gentle landing in a clearing near the lodge. Then he walked the slope of the hill, trying to decide how he would make his entrance.

The lodge was a medium-sized house with two main rooms comprising the lower story and four in the upper. It was made of rough green plastic and stone and wood, a rustic house, but one, which bore evidence of its owner's great wealth from the skill and warm charm of its architecture to its furnishings. Its rugs and couches and curtains were all bright, lovely things, its lamps soft and cheerful. Perhaps it was this almost alive warmth of the lodge itself that had drawn Brewster there as much as its associations.

When Brewster reached the low-based veranda he saw that a single lamp was lit within. The front of the lodge was set with a great oval window. By day its curtains were parted to allow a view of the enveloping woods but at night they were drawn to keep light from showing. Now they were only partly drawn, which explained the light Brewster had seen from miles away. But when he looked in through the window there was no one to be seen in the dimly lighted room.

The door slid open at his touch, but without his finding it necessary to arrange the symbols on the lock as Vrita had taught him. He went inside and the door closed behind him. From where he stood, in a sort of foyer that was also the connecting gallery between the two main rooms, he could see that both were empty. Or, if there was anyone in the lower story, they were in the second, dark room.

Brewster called, "Vrita!"

Silence. Once again he called, and suddenly something happened.

He didn't know why he had done it, but he found his hands tearing at his chest, gripping his tunic. It was as if his hands were looking for something, searching frantically—but his brain didn't know what his hands wanted.

"Selon tikka O jon trucam...selon trucam...trucam..."

It was like a voice, his own voice, whispering in his ear, telling him to do something he didn't understand. Over and over he heard the strange Jeggian words. His hands grew wilder in their fruitless search and his head was filled with the irresistible words and he felt unable to move from where he stood. And now swiftly the turmoil in his brain increased.

He bowed his head and concentrated the remnants of his will on moving away from where he stood, as if from some dim realization that he had to. Slowly, agonizingly, he advanced first one foot, then another, and began a labored walk toward the room with the light. Sweat stood in huge droplets on his face and his eyes were half closed with pain. He watched his legs moving slowly, so slowly, as if they and their movement were part of a dream.

But when he had taken the first step, the second was easier, and the third correspondingly easier, until little by little, some of the pain was lost and his head cleared a little. But still the voice in his inner mind repeated the strange words, and still his hands worked.

Step by step he left the foyer and walked toward the light, and then he was able to raise his head and gulp in a long grateful breath of air. His mouth was dry, his pulse hammered in his veins, but his brain was becoming his own again. And now suddenly he became aware—but only by its growing weaker—of an odor so insidious and yet so overwhelming that its presence had been unnoticed until now. So completely and immediately had his olfactory sense been saturated that the odor was indistinguishable until it weakened.

"Selon tikka O jon trucam...trucam...trucam...trucam..."

FAINTER and fainter now with distance, but still there. He sank down on a couch exhausted, feeling that he had won some terrible fight...or its first round, for it was not over yet. But now he could think and his mind was gripping the edges of the mystery, examining it. There was an unseen presence in this house. He lay back, getting his breath and waiting for strength to return to him, for enough confidence in his will to overcome the whispering influence.

After a little while he got up, his face set in grim hard lines, and started slowly back to the foyer. And the voice and the odor grew more powerful again, increasing in direct ratio with his advance back to the foyer. He stopped and drew back, then suddenly ran into the foyer and ran out again. When he returned to the room with the light he fell to the floor before he could reach the couch, holding his head, and a low moan escaped him.

Again he waited and got up. He stared into the foyer, gathered himself and with a quick lunge dashed through the foyer into the adjoining dark room. With the same movement his hand brushed a lightswitch on the wall. A soft amber light suffused the room and Brewster cried out in pain and hurled himself across the room to a small object he saw on the floor.

It was a cone-shaped glistening mass of substance, some two feet wide at its irregularly circular base and two feet high. Three large indigo eyes studded the apex of its cone, unwinking eyes with evil black pupils, staring at Brewster with horrible intensity.

It was on this creature—an Anzus, as Brewster had realized—that he hurled himself, his fingers tearing into its jelly-like flesh. He fought it without thinking, without knowing what he was doing. He had made his plan of action before he entered the mind-paralyzing sphere of its influence. His brain was twisted by cruel, invisible fingers and he wept aloud with pain. He had succeeded in sinking his hands into the Anzus and now the terrible energy that had been driven to random searching movements was redirected to the struggle.

His hands, imbedded in the viscous substance to his wrists, felt as if they were immersed in hot oil. But he was as senseless to pain as to everything else now and he lay on the floor, crying and kicking out violently, clutching at the Anzus' eyes. His seared palms closed around one and he tore it out and flung it across the room, and then he ripped the second eye out. He could not budge the small fleshy body but now he withdrew both hands and closed them around the third eye and pulled it out with a great backward lunge of his body.

Suddenly a great stillness came over everything. He lay on his back, his arms flung out, feeling the waves of pain in his hands. But he could think again and he knew he had won and he lay there breathing in great gasps, his eyes closed in utter exhaustion.

Though he heard someone enter the lodge and heard, distantly, a voice cry out, he could do nothing. He continued to lay there, hearing the footsteps recede and then come back, and he felt someone lifting his hands and the pain leaving.

Then he opened his eyes and saw Vrita on her knees beside him.

"Nick," she was saying softly, fearfully, over and over. "Nick, speak to me," and her hands moving over him tenderly. "Nick, Nick..."

"It's all right...now," Brewster whispered. "It's...fine..."

Vrita continued bathing his hands in the dark fluid she had brought in a vessel, looking at him. She was dressed in the red and black striped robe of the high warrior nobility. Her long black hair hung down over her shoulders in wild disorder and her olive skin was deeply flushed. Her black eyes were fixed on him.

SLOWLY, Brewster's strength returned and his hands felt soothed. After what seemed to him an interminable time, he tried to sit up and succeeded with Vrita's help. He leaned against her for a few moments as he looked at the remains of the Anzus. The conic form had collapsed to a shapeless oozing mass, its three eyes scattered around the room, dead and lusterless. What little odor of the Anzus persisted was a faintly oppressive perfume. A long weary sigh escaped Brewster.

Vrita asked softly, "What happened?"

He told her, but he remembered only the word *trucam*. It seemed to be enough for her, for she repeated the five words in proper order. The expression on her face was one Brewster had never seen there before, a sort of calm, deeply intelligent, directed fury that reminded him of the way

Ahriman had looked at him. Because of this Brewster began to speak of Ahriman, but Vrita quietly interrupted him.

"I know everything that happened at the council today."

Brewster studied her and when she remained silent he said, getting up slowly, "What I meant to say was that Ahriman—assuming the Anzus is his?—couldn't have known I was coming here because I came here on the sheerest impulse." He paused, looking down at her, then added, "And even that's assuming he'd know about my coming here."

She looked up at him quickly. "The Anzus was not meant for you."

Brewster said in an interested voice, "No?"

But her eyes were distant again and she seemed lost in thought. Presently she started to get up from the floor and Brewster helped her. He took her face in his palms and captured her eyes.

"Don't you think you ought to tell me, Vrita?"

She asked huskily, "Tell you what?"

"Everything. I surprised you here tonight and find you wearing the robe of nobility. And you tell me you know about the council and that the Anzus wasn't meant for me..."

He thought he detected relief in her manner but he couldn't be sure. He dropped his hands and waited for her to speak.

"Of course," she said. "I obviously meant to tell you or I would not have said what I did."

She had left a large drawbag lying on the floor at her feet and now as she made a motion to get it, Brewster stooped to pick it up for her. With a sudden deft motion her hand was under his and she retrieved the black velvety bag herself. Brewster could not help the surprise in his eyes as they rose together.

She stepped back a few feet and drew apart the silk thongs of the bag's mouth. From it she drew out a roughly corrugated case of some strange black substance, fashioned in a crude oval the large diameter of which was perhaps three inches. Her body seemed to tense and she stared at the case for a long moment, holding it in a cupped palm, her hand extended before her. Her eyes, clouded now, flashed to Brewster and back to the case. Her breathing was shallow and audible.

Then she dropped the drawbag and brought her free hand up to touch the top of the case. It swung open slowly. The atmosphere around the interior of the case sparkled with topaz brilliance, shimmering as if from a great heat emanating from a large, blue-veined yellow stone. Brewster could not determine its shape beyond guessing it was a spheroid because its outlines were blurred and vibrating with an incredibly swift ictus.

STARING at the stone, Vrita walked—her movement was more a long swift glide—to the decomposing Anzus and bent over it. She put four fingertips to the stone, not touching it, and four slender amber flames came to life on her fingers. Lightly she waved her hand over the Anzus and the flames leaped—like tiny, airy dancers of living flame—to the Anzus. They had barely touched it when three of the flames rose slowly into the air and moved, one each, to each of the three eyes of the Anzus, floating through the air in a straight line to their quarry. They burned for no more than an instant, then returned to Vrita's fingers and she held them over the stone and they were gone. No sign nor vestige of the Anzus remained.

Then Vrita closed the case, picked up the drawbag and carefully deposited the case in it. She walked back to Brewster, her eyes gleaming in triumph and looked at him. He had not moved and his face was ghastly pale even in the amber light.

"You wonder at the stone?" she asked quietly and shook her head. "The wonder is you—that you fought an Anzus and stand here alive and possessor of your reason."

Brewster looked down at his hands. The palms were wrinkled and dry but there was no pain. "What was that Anzus here for?" he asked.

She waited until Brewster's eyes lifted to her.

"Ahriman decided to kill Thyle," she said slowly. "Today after the council meeting when Thyle would not force your obedience, Ahriman was helpless. Before you came to Jegga the Ho-Ghan executed the Jevs Nastrond and Azevedo; the ones who bear the name today are their successors. They look to Thyle for guidance and as long as the three stood together, Ahriman could not have his way."

"His way?"

"To put you to torture, if necessary."

Brewster shrugged. "How can they, when I have the protection of the Ho-Ghan himself?"

She was silent for a moment, then said, "I thought you understood there is no protection in Jegga except one's own might." Softly she added, "It was one of your most admirable qualities—you, a Krennian, to be so much like our ideals."

Brewster grunted, struck by her words yet trying to get at an undercurrent. From the beginning, from the night he had seen the Ho-Ghan assassinated, he had played the game steadily, keeping his knowledge to himself except for Joe Abbott—and he had more than once regretted the impulse that had prompted him to confide even in Abbott. What it was he didn't know, but always there were hints and suggestions and half-formed ideas in his mind that told him there was a much greater importance to the event than even Suba Marannes had mentioned.

Now as he thought of it, his earlier melancholy returned and, as it mingled with his weariness and confusion, it resulted in a sullen and growing—though still hidden—pointless anger.

"Go on," he said.

She nodded. "The words *selon tikka o jon trucam* are part of an ancient ritual for those of dead nobility who have died by their own hand. The Anzus was placed here to waylay and compel such an action—"

"You mean the Anzus actually hypnotized me though I couldn't understand the words?" He looked at her. "Do you know what I mean? Do you know what the word hypnotize means?"

"Exactly. Our identical word for it is the word *Anzus*, which means: *another's thought*. The words were only words, but the thought impulses applied to you just as well. The movements of your hands you spoke of—you could not resist them. You kept searching the tunic on your chest for something that was not there." She paused. "But suppose that something had been there? You would not have had time to recover, to think, to be able to fight the Anzus. You would never have known an Anzus was there at all, and death would have come quickly. As it was, a less strongly willed person would have lost his sanity—"

He interrupted, frowning. "You said the Anzus wasn't meant for me, so you must know for whom it was meant—someone who wore something on his chest capable of killing him..."

SHE met his gaze and nodded. "But I've already told you it was here to kill Thyle, and only Ahriman could have placed it here."

"Here? Thyle here?" Brewster asked, puzzled. "Why should Ahriman expect to find Thyle here?"

"Because Thyle came here tonight. I was Thyle's wife."

Brewster took the blow without a sign. After a moment he let his breath out and said, "Past tense?"

She spoke the words softly, "By half an hour. I killed Thyle a little while ago. He had found out about us. It was your life or his."

Brewster's eyes blazed. Through tight lips he said, "Did you consider I might have preferred something to save my life myself without resorting to murder?"

A surprised look crossed her face. "Do you object to murder? Don't talk like a fool, Nick. You would have been dead by morning."

"Maybe and maybe not. But if what you said about Nastrond and Azevedo depending on Thyle is true, then you've practically delivered me to Ahriman and I'm no better off—"

But seeing the shocked look in her eyes as she stared past him, he had broken off and whirled around to find himself standing ten feet from the Jev Ahriman who had silently entered the foyer. Tall and overbearing, his black robe whipped around his shoulders, features twisted in an evil smile, he surveyed Vrita and Brewster.

"Tell him the truth, my darling," he mocked. "These Krennians, these precious Aaxians of ours, have a high regard for the truth, so let him know you planned to deliver him to me." His smile grew bitterly contorted. "But I did you an injustice, my darling. I did not realize how great the cost was to you—not only Thyle, but him. Not for the sake of our own—"

As Vrita's hands fumbled with the opening of the drawbag, Ahriman took three swift steps forward and struck the bag from her hands and with a smashing blow knocked her to the floor. But always one of his hands faced Brewster, and in it he held a slender green tube. He bent down and picked up the drawbag and when he rose he looked at Brewster's solemn face. He turned the tube around in his long fingers.

"Not now," Ahriman said softly. "First we must talk."

He nodded and motioned Brewster to the door. Brewster started walking and said, "You can't do this. I'm under the Ho-Ghan's protection and if anything…" He didn't finish, nor had he meant to. The words, couched in a slight whine, tinged with fear, were meant to distract for a brief instant and that instant arrived when Brewster reached the door. As the door slid open, Brewster started through, then with a single move stretched his long arms out so that each of his hands were braced against the sides of the doorway. The pressure he applied through his hands was enough to support his body as he suddenly swung off the floor and kicked both legs behind him.

His feet struck Ahriman squarely on the chest. Before the Jev had staggered back more than two or three feet, Brewster had already landed, spun about and dived at him. His outstretched arms caught around Ahriman's thighs. They hit the floor together but Brewster had unlocked his grip, so that when his open palms hit the floor they acted as a lever and swiftly pushed him up. In an instant he was standing over Ahriman. As the Jev's hand swung upward, Brewster kicked it aside and his foot went on in and smashed down heavily on Ahriman's face.

The short-lived struggle was over. Ahriman lay unconscious, his nose broken in a bloody smear, the blood flowing into the hollows of his eyes. His body shivered convulsively and he was still.

Brewster walked unsteadily to where Vrita had started to get up from the floor. He tried to help her but she brushed him aside. Her slender face was grim with purposefulness. She picked up her bag from where Ahriman's fall had thrown it, took out the black case and opened it and started toward Ahriman's inert body when Brewster quickly got in her way.

"What are you going to do?"

HER laughter was short and forced. She made no answer but held a hand over the shimmering stone. Her fingers caught in flame and she held her hand up. "For Ahriman," she said, and swept around Brewster to the Jev. Before he could stop her—he wasn't sure that he wanted to— she had knelt and touched the flames to Ahriman.

The fire caught with a prolonged hiss and began to spread over the Jev's form, racing quickly...

Brewster stood beside Vrita until the end, until not an ash of the once mighty Jev Ahriman remained. But one thing resisted the fires, emerging, as it seemed, from the consuming flame, until when the long lifeless body had vanished, it alone lay on the floor, bright and hard and enduring. And when Vrita bent over to recapture the flame and restore it to its stone, she picked this thing up.

It was a thin, iridescent blue disc an inch in diameter. It had been the central jewel in the representation of the Anzus Ahriman had worn, but it had been covered with brilliant thread and jewels brighter than itself. Everything around it had burned but this remained. It lay in Vrita's quivering palm like a thing alive, and indeed, as she held it a darker black inner circle appeared and contracted to a pinpoint, like an eye's pupil in intense light.

"The Anzus' central eye," Vrita breathed. She looked up at Nick Brewster's impassive face. "Do you understand?" she asked him.

Brewster wasn't sure that he did. There was too much here for him to grasp all at once. His quick brain had encompassed the larger aspects, but the details resisted him until the puzzle was like a newer, more deadly fire within his mind. He shook himself and said nothing, waiting for her to go on. A plan was forming in his mind but he delayed its execution.

As if some understanding of his thoughts had come to her, Vrita stepped away from him, her eyes clouding.

"What did Ahriman mean?" Brewster asked quietly.

Her eyes kept searching him until he turned and walked away, his back to her. He lit a cigarette and smoked. Her voice came to him, a soft, conciliatory voice.

"I used Ahriman to help me overcome Thyle. I knew he hated Thyle and after today their enmity was open. I saw that if Ahriman should prove the victor that it might mean your life—"

Brewster spun around. "You used Ahriman to kill Thyle and all the while you planned eventually to get rid of Ahriman?"

She shook her head. "It would not have been necessary. Ahriman had brought three *tor** Anzus as close to Ho-Tonda as he could. My part of the plan was to place them where they might enthrall Thyle. It happened in Thyle's own home on the Yassidi canal—I was there when Thyle tore the stone from his robe and burned himself alive. Then I came to destroy the Anzus I knew was here—"

"You hadn't planned to meet Ahriman here?"

"No. He must have guessed my fears and followed from—"

"Your fears? Then you do have—"

She cried out angrily, "Listen and try to understand this thing I have done for you!" She waited and calmed, then said, "When Thyle was gone I seized the amber stone. I had reason to fear Ahriman—for if Thyle had no heirs, whoever gained and claimed before the council of Jevs would be sustained in his claim. Tomorrow the possessor could summon the council—tonight Ahriman knew I had it. I knew I had to destroy all three Anzus before Ahriman could use them to force me to surrender the stone to him."

SHE waited for a sign from Brewster but it did not come. "Alone I was powerless against Thyle," she said, "but without my aid Ahriman could not place his Anzus, for there were guards and warriors and elaborate warning systems that I alone could overcome."

"And which Ahriman trusted you to do for him?"

"Yes."

"But why should he have trusted you?"

"He knew I hated Thyle."

---

*Tor—from *torgho,* or school; roughly translated, tor would mean instructed or orientated. In this particular application, i.e., the *tor* Anzus, it meant *activated.* An Anzus could be made *tor* only by Ahriman or one of his warriors with a *torman,* or power-grant, from the central eye. An Anzus could be made *tor* from a considerable distance by virtue of the central eye, offering a safe, sort of remote control-ED.

Brewster nodded and said, "But there was more than that. There'd been enough between you for Ahriman to feel sure you'd do it. Right?"

"It was before I met you. There has been no one else since."

Brewster grinned dryly. "I'm not complaining—I just want to get this straight. It needs a little straightening, don't you think?"

"What do you mean?"

"When did you find out Thyle knew about us?"

She hesitated. "This afternoon…after the council meeting."

"Takes thought to keep it straight, huh?" Brewster's grin came back hollowly. "If Thyle knew before the meeting, I think you'll agree he'd not only have voted with Ahriman—if I'd lived long enough to get to the meeting—but he'd have taken a hand in the torture you mentioned. But if, as you say, he found out after the meeting, where did you get time to plan this affair with Ahriman?"

"It needed little—"

"Save it. I know the Jeggian Code.* Getting one Anzus, let alone three, near a Jev was a difficult business. So I'd say you'd planned it some time in advance—and your killing him today had nothing to do with saving my life, whether or not it's true that Thyle found out about us. In other words, you had an immediate reason—but it wasn't me or my life. What was it?"

"What do you think it was?"

Brewster took a step forward. As he did so, Vrita moved farther away, increasing the distance between them. Brewster was still grinning as he said, "We understand each other, don't we? You'd planned to give Ahriman the stone, but something happened today that made you change your mind and decide to keep it yourself."

She kept looking at him, then spoke slowly. "Yes," she said, her eyes gleaming. "You are right in most things. Even at this moment you are ready to seize the opportunity to leap at me and take away the stone. If you were sure you knew how to handle it, you would do it now…"

Brewster sighed. *"Right,"* he agreed.

"And here again you prove my love for you is not misguided."

Before Brewster had recovered from his astonishment at her quiet declaration, she had run to him and thrown her arms around him. He held

---

*The Code strictly forbade transportation of an Anzus within 500 *onum* (miles) of Ho-Tonda, or within 300 *onum* of any Jev or Lanae, nor could any Anzus be moved from Ahriman's compounds unless couriers proceeded with due warning. By order of the *Jevro,* laws for the Jevs.-ED.

her close, feeling her body tremble. His mind in a whirl. The plan he had formed and admitted to her was shattered by his confusion.

Presently she released him and stood before him and held out the drawbag and the Anzus eye for him to take.

"For you, my own," she said. "The one thing you did not guess."

Brewster stared at her and wearily ran his hands over his face, his eyes dull and puzzled. "Vrita...I...I..." He stopped trying.

"I understand," she soothed him. "There was so much you could not know." She smiled at him tenderly. "Shall I tell you? Does that sharp-edged mind of yours still reach out to grasp nothing but air?"

He nodded slowly.

"You were right, she said softly. "The plan was formed when the Ho-Ghan killed the Jevs. When the new Jevs Azevedo and Nastrond fell under Thyle's influence, Ahriman knew he would never, so long as it persisted, have a voice in the council. For the sake of our relationship, I consented to his plan. But before I could carry it out, I had met you, and from then on I delayed...because a plan of my own had come to me. I needed time to find out if I was right.

"TODAY I knew. When Thyle told me what you demanded of the assembled Jevs, I decided to carry out Ahriman's plan for my own purpose. I brought Thyle here, but the Anzus had not yet been placed in readiness. While we were here, a private call came through for Thyle on the Sinju. I didn't know what it was at the time, but it was the information that you and I..." Her voice became hard. "He came storming out of that room and seized me and took me to his home at Yassidi, evidently waiting for someone to arrive. It was while he waited that the Anzus there became *tor* and he destroyed himself before my eyes.

"I knew Ahriman was nearby and I had to act quickly. I took the amber stone and destroyed the Anzus. Then I went to Thyle's villa near Ujannor where his heirs lived, and where Ahriman had placed the second Anzus. Last of all I returned here. I found the lights still on, as I remembered Thyle had left them, but the shock of finding you here, in agony on the floor, drove the Anzus from my mind until you spoke. Then I realized that Ahriman must have come here later and left the Anzus *tor* and you had walked into its active field.

"But Ahriman evidently followed us to Kardandan. Perhaps it was there, or more likely in Ujannor that he divined my plan. When he heard us speaking here, then surely he must have known that I myself had decided who would succeed Thyle..."

Brewster looked at the drawbag she had offered him and which he had not taken. He said in a quiet, troubled voice, "You mean me?"

"Yes, my love," she whispered. "Though you are not born of our race you are one of us in mind and spirit and being. These things I know as only a woman can know." She looked into his eyes. "The gods of Jegga are with us. I planned only for you to succeed Thyle, but now with Ahriman gone, you will go to the council to assume the mantle of the mightiest Jev of all: the Lord Thyle-Ahriman..."

"But what of Thyle's heirs? First you said there were none—then you said they lived in Ujannor." He kept staring at her.

Poised and serene and lovely, she smiled at him. "There were heirs," she nodded. "I removed them, for how else could you become the Jev Thyle while they lived?" In the silence she added, "The knowledge that there no longer were heirs, more than my destruction of his three Anzus, told Ahriman what I was doing—for when he seized the stone he gave evidence that he knew it was for him who could take it."

Brewster said thinly, "And Ahriman's heirs?"

"There is but one confirmed, his brother. Before word of the passing of Ahriman is common, we will have removed him." She swept her arms up on his shoulders and pressed her cheek to his. "Shall I let so trifling a matter stand in our way?" she asked. "I, who for your love, this night killed the two sons and heirs I bore Thyle?"

Long minutes passed and then Brewster gently separated himself and took the drawbag and the central eye in his hands. He kept looking at them, and when he raised his eyes to Vrita, they were thoughtful and overcast and he didn't seem to see Vrita at all.

"Nick, my love, you haven't told me you're happy."

It was as if he heard her moments later. He nodded then and his voice was quiet, and somehow had the quality of a sigh, when he spoke to her. "Vrita, I thank your gods and mine I met you. I am happy, my dear, very happy..."

He took her in his arms and kissed her.

CHAPTER NINE

IT WAS a simple note. It had been placed, as usual, in a pack of Brewster's cigarettes.

Before it's too late, before the ascension, go to the Imperial library and get hold of Descoru es Jegga jon Jev, volume II, and read pages 60-62. Even for a big shot like you it won't be easy to get into the library if you announce it, so you'd better wander into the vicinity accidentally and bluff your way in before you can be stopped. Here's a map of the palate wing you want, beyond the Ho-Ghan's gardens—the library is marked X.

But there was more information than was contained in the note to be found among Brewster's cigarettes, for he discovered that three cartons had been taken from his supply. It was rather a definite answer to Abbott's latest disappearance. It looked as if this one was meant to be final—and said so.

As to when Abbott had pulled out, no one knew. Brewster had not returned to the Inner City for two days after he left so suddenly that fateful night. The intervening days he had spent with Vrita, locked in the security of Thyle's castle more than a thousand onum from Ho-Tonda, working to arrange the innumerable pre-ascensional details that claimed his attention. Through *Jev-korman* and *ohfran* and *kotai,* * through these ceremonies and dozens more, Brewster gave his energy. And though he had counted each precious, passing hour, a strange patience had settled over him. He could afford his duties time now because time had already run out on him, and he knew it...

When he returned to the Inner City, to the now empty Krennian wing, he came as heir-apparent, and with him all the trappings and fanfare of the rank he was to assume that day...and he was weary. The day before he had appeared time and time again on the Sinju while numerous commentators explained to Jegga—and others on the Tonju gave the news to the Empire—how the Ho-Ghan had elevated the leader of the Krennian Fyavos to Jev, Lord of the Flaming Stone. It was a symbol of unity between the Empire and the world of Kren, which would soon be opened to enlist under the Ho-Ghan's banner. And, so the news went, the opportunity for all this had been given the Ho-Ghan when Jev Thyle and both his heirs had perished in an accident, the details of which were not yet to be given out.

The story was necessary, Tubal, Lunae of the Censorship, assured Brewster, to preserve balance through the Empire. It was not yet known

---

Jev-korman—grants of power by the Jev to the members of his army, or the ceremony by which such grants were given, including also oaths of fealty by various Lanae, *Ovis* (captains) and other officers. *Ohfran*—a wide category, meaning generally: indulgence. It included property arrangements, granting of pardons and boons, promotions and rewards. *Kotai*—pre-ascensional ceremony of pledging fealty to the four other Jevs and the Ho-Ghan, and the declaring of heirs in their order. Also the submission of new names if the Jev was of a different family than a predecessor—this last an antiquated feudal custom—ED.

what Jev Ahriman would do, Tubal had pointed out soberly, and the wiser course was not to infuriate him unnecessarily—for already he had withdrawn and refused to answer the summons to the council meeting. Brewster agreed to everything, to each request at *ohfran,* exercising no initiative at *Jev-korman,* listening to Vrita and Tubal and to Iga, Lanae representing the council. As he was patient, he was almost docile…

But in one thing he had been adamant—his solitude when he returned to the Inner City. He dismissed his servants and attendants, his Lanae and officers—he scarcely knew half a dozen of them by name—and he had come alone to the quarters he had lived in, to find in their peaceful desolation a few hours in which he could think. There had been a forlorn hope in the back of his mind that he might find Abbott waiting there, but it had vanished when he found the note.

It was odd, that note. Undoubtedly the rooms and all the effects in them had been thoroughly searched and by more than one interested party—yet here was this note. Brewster knew, of course, that it had not eluded detection because it had not been there to detect. It had been placed in the cigarette perhaps minutes after Brewster arrived in the Krennian wing.

Brewster had quickly walked through the wing. It was, as he had ordered, empty, except that out on the central terrace, he found Poro, the Phyladian whose life he had saved. The green-skinned brute had often been found by Brewster, sitting thus, his great cloudy eyes scanning the horizon, his strong face relaxed and calm. He had become a fixture in the wing, a silent figure whose presence or absence was scarcely noticed by Brewster. He had looked at Brewster then and bowed obediently.

AFTER that Brewster had gone, as the note directed, to the palace wing beyond the Ho-Ghan's gardens. Wearing his gray civilian tunic and sneaking out through a side door, once he dispersed the guard he found even there, he was able to lose himself in the thronged, bustling halls of the palace. But as it had not been difficult to cast aside his now celebrated identity for a little while, this same anonymity was a hindrance when he reached the site of the Imperial library. The great marble doors facing down an empty gallery lined with Argyres bore the legend *Coru Es Ho-Ghan* on its massive hexagonal seals. Brewster, instantly conspicuous because he was alone, had wandered to the door, but as he had come up to it the guards had planted themselves in front of him. Several officers had come running down the corridor. Until that moment Brewster had shown only desultory interest in the doors, but then, as the officers had shouted at him and been about to lay their hands on him, he had stepped back, his face the picture of so cold a fury that it stopped them. And his voice, quiet and controlled, somehow more audible because of their shouting, had sounded deadly.

*"Ento o brui. O dej-Jev Thyle."**

When he started forward again, they melted out of his path. He had acted, as he had planned, as if these warriors were stable boys back home, refusing the owner entry to his own premises. It was a part that came easily and naturally to him, and though he was now long past being able to feel the sting of the thought, there was still a vestigial bitterness to his easy success. He had entered the *Coru*, the library or repository of histories, searched the elaborate archives for the title, and though he had been able to translate *Descoru es Jegga jon Jev* as History of Jegga and Jev, he knew the language would prove too much for him. So, finding Volume II, he had slipped it under his robe and gone out of the library shortly after entering. Ostensibly he had gone in to humble the guard; the point made, he had left.

And then, back in his own quarters, the *Introduction* to guide him, he had read pages sixty through sixty-two.

Now, the bulk of it translated, he re-read its most salient—from the point of view of the writer of the note—parts, marking here and there a still elusive word. But it was clear...

"...Thus, when Jev had reached the age of thirty and one winters, he had led the armies of Lyrio to their final sytemal victory. Behind him lay ten and four winters of campaigning, which had added to the young Empire not only the recalcitrant empire of Ermos and the kingdoms of Ania and Darziz and Phylades, but hundreds of smaller dependencies. In honor, therefore, of the most ruthless and cruel soldier in the history of Jegga, the Ho-Ghan Lyrio gave voice to the first of the later laws of Jevro:

"From this day forward, saving only the Ho-Ghan, the mighty of the mighty shall be known as Jev. The name Jev shall become a title bestowed by the Ho-Ghan upon the WarLords of the Empire first created by the first Jev. So long as the Empire shall persist, so too shall the name and title Jev...

"...and in the time of his fifty and sixth winter, great Jev, who for twenty winters had lived in Boron, the small moon of green Kren, knew that within his lifetime he would not see the conquering of this most beautiful of the inner worlds. The secret that had countless centuries before enabled the men of Jegga to penetrate the atmosphere of Kren, had gone with them. For twenty long winters Jev had sent his warships, of such construction and such another and yet another, to essay the journey, and he had seen all turn to flame. There was no way. There was no way ...

Dej-Jev—literally, Jev-to-be, or heir apparent. (What Brewster said was: "Stand aside, I bid. I am Jev-to-be Thyle.") -ED.

"…and so Jev wept, and his eyes were not dry so long as he gazed upon Kren, nor would he leave Boron. It is written in the hand of Proh, who lived with him that last winter of his life, that Jev knew no peace, knowing the world of Kren to be beyond his grasp…

"…at length, weary and weakened by sorrow, and, so says Proh, often given to talking aloud when none were present to listen, Jev wandered naked across the barren face of Boron to stand on its higher-most peak. And there he stood for the time of a full revolving of Boron around Kren, and he would not sleep nor take food nor water, nor speak to any man, but he stood there and wept as he looked down at the green fields of Kren. And the revolving done, Jev permitted himself to die, but before he died he spoke for the last time.

" 'O Kren, O Aaxia, thou most prized of all, thou hast been given to out-live Jev, but there will be a day when another Jev shall hold thy green throat until all who livest in thy quiet fields shall remember to curse the time in which the dream of Jev came to naught…'

"…and until that day none who spoke the tongue of Jegga or Estannar, or the tongues of any of the empires or kingdoms or dependencies that Jev had conquered, in none of these tongues was there to be found the word Aaxia. *So writ Proh. But from that day on the word* Aaxia *came to mean* most prized, *the name by which Kren was henceforth known, to keep imperishable the dream of Jev and to serve as reminder that the vengeance of Jev would one day be visited on Kren…"*

HAVING read and re-read these paragraphs, Brewster put away the *Introduction* and the *Descoru*—or meant to, when he looked up and saw Poro, the Phyladian, standing on the threshold of the balcony, looking into the large central chamber where Brewster had sat reading.

It was the first time Brewster had ever seen Poro watching him, and the silent scrutiny brought an imperceptible, thoughtful frown to Brewster, where the reading of the *Descoru* had not changed his expression at all. He returned Poro's gaze, who stood there like a dumb, faithful dog waiting its master's call, and seemed about to speak to the Phyladian when he saw the shadow of someone entering the chamber from the corridor. With a swift movement Brewster slid the heavy, gilded volume under the low couch. Poro, who had seen the action, now saw Akar coming in just as Brewster did, and he silently turned away and went back out on the balcony.

Brewster had not seen Akar since the morning after Thyle's death and then but briefly, for Akar immediately appointed to ranking Lanae by Brewster, had had his own numerous duties. He advanced toward Brewster hesitantly, obviously acquainted with Brewster's order that none be allowed into the wing, and half-expecting Brewster to order him out.

Instead Brewster nodded pleasantly to him.

"Greetings, great Jev, son of—"

Brewster shook his head. "Never mind what I'm a son of," he said with a wry smile. "What's up?"

Akar looked uncomfortable. "Everything is in readiness."

"Fine," Brewster said. "I feel like a goddamned bride." His smile persisted. "Did you find my friends in time to get them here?"

Akar was silent a moment. "I bring poor tidings," he said.

Brewster said, "Look, just talk to me. Forget I'm a Jev. You used to be quite a talker. What are your poor tidings? Can't find 'em?"

"I have sent messengers everywhere, armed with the seal of the Ho-Ghan. There is no trace of them..." He hesitated.

"Go on—what else did you want to say?"

"I fear perhaps Jev Ahriman has taken them. He has not responded to the council or the Ho-Ghan and will not be present at the ascension ceremony."

Brewster said quietly, "I know it's not Ahriman. The question is whether you honestly think so or know better. If I find out that you consciously lied to me, I won't be easy with you. Remember that."

Akar inclined his head, saluted, and turned to leave. Brewster said, "One more thing," and stopped Akar. "This is something I meant to ask you before. You remember two days ago I showed you a batch of notes I'd gotten?" Akar nodded and Brewster said, "You asked me about the woman named Vrita mentioned in one of those notes. I know that you knew who she was. What I want to know now is—did you tell Thyle anything about it?"

"Yes."

"When?"

"A few hours after the meeting." Akar's face was stony. "First I checked on it. I discovered that she had executed every driver of the tyar that brought you to the lodge, and every servant or guard who knew."

Brewster looked puzzled. "How could you find that out?"

Akar's discomfort grew visibly. Finally he said, "I had a guard of my own to watch her." His coppery skin flushed.

Brewster made a low sound in his throat. He frowned and asked softly, "Then you, too?"

"It was before she met you. I knew I meant nothing to her."

"You didn't tell Thyle because you were jealous of me?"

"Thyle was my Jev. It was my duty to tell him."

Presently Brewster nodded. "I admire your loyalty," he said and nodded again, signifying Akar was free to go. When Akar left, Brewster went out on the balcony and stood beside Poro, watching the battalions of Argyres assembling below. A fever was running through the Inner City but Brewster was calm and thoughtful.

* * *

THE ceremony of the ascension had the extravagance and the almost intolerable slowness of a dream, and Brewster went through it like a dreamer. He scarcely saw the vast banks of people or heard their voices. There was color before his eyes and sound in his ears, and here and there would be a face he knew, a uniform he remembered, but nothing more. The sight of the Ho-Ghan, veiled as was his prerogative, hardly stirred him in his lethargy. He stood alone before the Ho-Ghan and the three Jevs and went through the ritual with the amber stone, his fingers aflame and the flames not burning the red robe he accepted from Jev Eblis, and he repeated the words he had learned by rote. When the parades had stopped and the music died away and the last ceremonial finished he went, flanked by great columns and warriors and Argyres, to the tower of the Jevs.

There he sat at the pentagonal table with Nastrond and Eblis and Azevedo and kept the word he had given to Lanae Iga at kotai. Seated and standing by the score all around the great table were the scientists of Jegga, waiting for Brewster to speak.

Then Brewster spoke, and began to explain the Earth science of making metal. His words fell in an awesome hush and he did not pause until he had spoken for more than two hours. Then the scientists and ministers spoke and he answered their questions, correcting diagrams, elaborating, explaining. The great Sinju screen that had been set up in the bowl traveled the length and breadth of Jegga, bringing the mines and smelters and roads of the vast system already built into close view, and here Brewster would comment, here suggest something.

It was as Joe Abbott had said—everything was ready. But now the hills and the Kardandan canals and the Pingui red mountains which Abbott had searched vainly with the Sinju, all these and more came into sharp, distinct focus.

It was dark when the council adjourned, and Brewster returned to the Krennian wing. He sank down to an exhausted slumber from which he kept awaking to stare bleakly at shadows. Late that night he began to wander through the quiet chambers, feeling the presence of guards everywhere though the chambers were empty. In the central chamber he found Poro sitting awake, and only then was he able to return to his uneasy bed and find sleep.

* * *

On the second day after he had become Jev, sixteen days after the coming of the Earthmen to Jegga, Brewster knew he was losing control of himself. It was a new sensation to him. He felt the remnants of his patience slipping away, and his newly found calmness with it. The cold fever that had run through him the night Thyle had died now returned and he could not fight it off. He was waiting for something, and when it did not come he knew he would have to go out and meet it, to force it to come.

What slight comfort he could gather from his mental state was the fact that he was still aware of what was happening to him. He could preserve his balance and hasten the end by losing himself in work, and there was work to be done.

So on this second day, he left Ho-Tonda for an extended tour of Jegga to supervise the beginning of operations in the great network of mines and hearths, which his knowledge had made it, possible to function. As a Jev he could not travel alone, but he excluded Vrita from his entourage at the price of a stubborn refusal. His action, and the actions that had preceded it at the ascension, was inexplicable, and he could not have afforded it had he not sensed the immediacy of the end. But it had been dangerous.

SHE had come to him in the Krennian quarter the night before. It was their first meeting in three days. She had looked at Brewster as he stood before her, troubled and faintly aloof, wearing the red robe as if he had been born to it, and she had spoken her mind.

"You have not seen me. You have not called me."

"It would have been violating the tradition. You are a widow."

"Was I not a widow three days ago?"

"I was not a Jev."

She had hesitated, then: "What of Ahriman and the Eye?"

"I am Thyle. It is enough for me now. I must not forget that I am a Krennian—it would mortify your people if I were to claim the seat of Ahriman."

"But what will you do with the Anzus eye?"

"Nothing, now. The decision can wait."

"The secret of Ahriman's death will not keep much longer."

"I know."

She had studied his inscrutable face and found nothing and then she had said, "You will not mortify those whom it is your privilege to mortify, yet you hurt me, who bestowed the privilege on you. What has changed between us? Do you love me no longer?"

He had taken her in his arms then, and kissed her. "Leave me now," he had said. "Don't come again until I send for you. I'm going away tomorrow. When I return there will be time to talk. But not now, not tonight. Try to understand."

When she had left, he wasn't sure whether he had acted wisely. There had been danger in both courses open to him. Four days before he would have chosen the other, but that night she had revived the memory of the words she had spoken to him, and fighting it he had taken the chance. It hardly mattered, he thought, that he had perhaps tipped the scales even further against himself. It was getting too late now to do much about it.

The next morning he had left for Pingui. From there he had gone to Kardandan, and then to the great blooming mills of Zorka, and then to the Totamangu mountains. There in the great open-hearth furnaces he had touched his amber stone and set the intelligence of Thyle's flame to its task. And seeing it do its work, he knew that he had given Jegga and this, its own fire, the spark that would spread to an industry greater by far than any on Earth. He had looked out upon the sea of faces of innumerable workmen drawn from the universe in all their variety, and it had been too great a thought for him to keep the end in mind.

So he traveled for five days, the center of great parties and feasts and celebrations, and surrounded as he was by his Lanae and ministers, and the numerous officials of every neighboring province and city, he knew a greater loneliness than ever before. And all this time he was waiting, knowing it would come...and yet beginning to wonder.

For in his mind he had built a structure of bits of information, of vague perceptions and ideas, and in more than one sense it might prove to be a house of cards. He was the same Sure Brewster, gambling for stakes beyond his comprehension, but forced to gamble now. He was waiting to draw his cards...

* * *

IT CAME in Ramusio on the fifth day, exactly three weeks after he had first landed in Jegga. He had almost been certain of it there, if anywhere, and he had given it every chance.

Ramusio was four thousand onum from Ho-Tonda. It ranked perhaps twentieth in size among the many cities of Jegga, but it was a sprawling giant of commerce. It was the hemispheric junction of four canals and its spaceport ranked with Kael, and through it flowed much of interplanetary culture. Yet it could be a wild and violent place. In its ancient streets the many-hued natives of the universe outnumbered those of Jegga, and its gay life was conducted in a hundred variant dialects of the Jeggian tongue. It suspended a large number of the planetary laws of Jegga and substituted its own, or sometimes none at all. From morning until night its skies were dotted with arriving craft, its canals clotted in perpetual traffic.

When Brewster first asked to go to Ramusio, Akar and his Lanae advised against it. Brewster listened and repeated his order and the matter was closed until they arrived in Ramusio. There Brewster decreed two holidays for the army of warriors that had accompanied him, and thus opened the door.

It was during the feast given in his honor by the Vice-Regio of the province that the staffs were rapped and a voice called:

"The *Fyavo* Abbott."

There, across the noisy, crowded hall, stood Joe Abbott. He was dressed in a blue civilian tunic, with nothing to distinguish him from an Estannar except the jagged emerald that hung from a cord around his neck. He gazed around the hall until his eyes lit on Brewster, then he smiled and came forward.

Akar had instantly gotten up beside Brewster and ordered one of the adjoining chairs vacated, but Brewster had risen a moment later and quietly ordered Akar to see that the feast continued until the time of his return. He met Abbott halfway across the hall and Abbott bowed and touched his hand to his forehead before he shook Brewster's proffered hand.

Abbott said, *"O brui ro, Jev Thyle,"* smiling faintly.

Brewster half-laughed. "Come outside," he said.

He led Abbott to a roof terrace and motioned to a Lanae to clear the place. Silently he took out a pack of cigarettes and saw the way Abbott regarded them and offered him one. He lit both cigarettes and watched Abbott inhale and exhale gratefully. The night air was still.

"You look as if you hadn't had one in a long while," Brewster said. "I'd have thought three cartons would last longer than a week." He grinned and added softly, "Unless you found six other guys who wanted a smoke pretty bad?" He tried to meet Abbott's eyes in the gloom.

Abbott looked at him and said, "You've done all right, Nick," in an emotionless voice. "I don't suppose you can go much higher, huh?"

Brewster glanced at him sharply and said, "Warn them off, Joe. It's no good here. This whole area is heavily guarded. Let me arrange it when there's a chance."

Slowly Abbott shook his head. "You're good, Nick, you're good. But this is different. Not even a smart cookie like you can break out of what's already been arranged." His face twisted into a hard smile. "But you knew we'd come for you, didn't you? You saw how things were beginning to shape up a little differently than—" He pushed Brewster's hands away angrily. "Not me," he said. "I'm not the boy. I couldn't hope to get through to you if I were armed. So I'm doing the next best thing—I'm the finger man, to make sure you're not confused with your adopted Jeggite brothers."

"You *fool*," Brewster snapped in exasperation. "You haven't a chance! I've been expecting something like this—"

HE broke off as Akar came hurrying out on the terrace, his face grim and purposeful. Two Lanae stood beside him and behind them were long columns of warriors who fanned out all along the terrace, at the ready. Others came up bearing a wandho screen.* Akar saluted.

"Your pardon, great Jev. Lanae Tuew declares the Fyavo Abbott to be carrying something with the substance of Estannar on it. Therefore, with your permission, the wandho is ready."

A slow baleful grin spread across Brewster's face. He turned to Abbott and said, "You see? Maybe you don't know what a wandho is?" He studied Abbott's tight lips and sighed. "I see you do, so you'd better hand over whatever it is."

"No," Abbott said. "Turn on your screen."

One of the Lanae barked an order, but Akar raised a hand and stopped the warriors who were adjusting the screen. A crafty look shone on Akar's intelligent face. He held a little green tube in his hand as he advanced to Abbott. "No," he said, "I will take it upon myself to search the Fyavo."

At that instant, as Abbott turned about and made a dash for the rail, Brewster quickly stepped forward and brought his fist down in a slashing blow on the back of Abbott's neck. Abbott went sprawling over and fell against the rail. Only two or three steps more and he would have hurled

---

* *Wandho* screen—a chemical detector used with high frequency light waves, capable of exploding hidden weapons, etc.-ED.

himself to the street hundreds of feet below. Brewster's hands were unsteady as he kneeled and searched the unresisting form. The blow he had given Abbott, because he had been prepared to give it, had knocked Abbott senseless. Now he stood up again, holding in his hand a small tube-like pink cylinder.

Akar accepted the cylinder and turned it over in his hands and nodded. "It is as we hardly dared hope. This is an Estannar signal flare. The wandho would have detonated it instantly—" he looked meaningfully at Brewster, "—and killed your friend the Fyavo."

"And the effect of a sharp fall?"

"The same. It has a delicate mechanism for so powerful a flare. I have seen these in raids on Boron." He paused. "There is but one answer—the Estannars are in position for an attack on your life."

Brewster nodded soberly. "You've been ready all this while?"

"At a moment's notice, mighty Jev. No onslaught, however desperate, could succeed against us, but now with the starting signal in our hands, my captains will look forward to another Charchan."*

Brewster looked down at the unconscious form at his feet with a look of contempt and pity. "Send him back to Ho-Tonda and keep him under guard in the Krennian quarter. See that no harm comes to him—I have my own plans for him."

"And you, mighty Jev? You must not—"

Brewster stopped him with a hard smile. "You would have the one you call mighty Jev run for safety, Akar? No. I am a great admirer of the Jeggian techniques. I will be with you."

*   *   *

NO OUTWARD sign of change was allowed. The feast continued and the wine flowed. Many of the Lanae remained and half the warrior guard, but Brewster and Akar left immediately in a tyar that landed on the terrace and took off again in the darkness. From the vice-Regio's palace they proceeded through guarded, nightbound skies to the military spaceport several onum from Ramusio. Here waiting launches shot them skyward to warships that lay at space-anchor high over the city, their sleek

---

* Charchan—the scene of a great massacre of Estannars who were caught with a huge fleet and no fuel for its ships after the Jeggians ambushed a convoy of fuellers. The one-sided battle of Charchan, and its effects on Estannar morale, ended one of the great modern rebellions. - ED.

bodies dark and their muttering rocket-tubes shielded.

Brewster recognized the warship in which he found himself as the one that Akar had previously commanded. Nothing in it had changed, and its new commander proudly led Akar and Brewster to the oval control room in the ship's bow.

The plans, as Akar had said, had already been prepared, but now every warship had time to build up its rocket-power before allowing its blasts to be seen. Since none of the military stations or lightships had reported more than isolated vessels anywhere within range of the signal flare, the Estannar plan was clear. They could not have hoped to storm the tower of the vice-Regio's palace with foot troops; thus it was a certainty that they had filled the dark skies over Ramusio with armed tyars, waiting to descend on the tower, overwhelm it, and flee before any power could be brought to bear against their scattering number. It was to be no more than a large raid, the only attack—as Akar explained with contempt—which the Estannars were capable of planning.

"Suppose it had been launched as planned?" Brewster asked. "How would you have met it, with only a few moments' notice?"

Akar smiled as his hands expertly played with the code keys on the control board. "A few moments' notice would have been more than we needed. You were in no ordinary tower, my lord. At the first sign of alarm the entire hall would have descended two hundred feet, and the tower itself filled with warriors. But now our warriors have been warned to keep out of the tower—we mean to sweep clean."

Akar spoke into the little phone beside him. Answers kept crackling back, and the control board danced with lights. Painstakingly, Akar repeated the changes in orders, apologizing to Brewster for speaking in Jeggian, though Brewster understood almost everything; the military language was a sort of simplified Jeggian, condensing even detailed and complex orders to a few words.

Half an hour after they had left the vice-Regio's palace, everything was ready. There was no tenseness visible on Akar's darkly smiling face as he began the action. He switched on the Sinju and under his nimble fingers the screen searched Ramusio for the palace, then held it. He pressed a button. Five seconds later a pale red streak shot into the black heavens from the tower. High above it the streak blossomed until the sky seemed to be overcast with a thin film of blood.

Suddenly the streets leading to the palace were cut across with hundreds of slender green beams. Other beams met them, falling back under the original onslaught. Then, just as the red glow in the sky came its brightest moment and began to die away, hundreds of tyars were revealed in its light, swooping down on the palace. For a moment Akar put on the speakers attached to the Sinju, and the whirring thunder of tyars and the shrieks of the city filled the control room. When Akar turned off the sound, he touched a glowing button at his fingertips and its light went out.

The warship quivered and came to life with a great roar. Suddenly the miniature city in the Sinju was flying off the edges of the darkly lit screen and the palace kept growing. Akar's hands rested on the control board gently, watching the Sinju intently. The attacking tyars had landed on the tower by the hundreds, and others buzzed in the air all around it like swarms of maddened gnats. But there seemed to be little fighting there, for hardly a streak of green was to be seen. And then several of the tyars began taking off.

"They've seen us coming," Akar said.

AT THAT moment three warships flashed across the screen and from their bows great forked tongues of blue-green lightning lashed out to hit the tower. Instants after they were gone, when the luminous afterlight of their bolts had died away, Brewster saw the enormous holes the bolts had punched into the tower. He caught but a glimpse of the tyars as they spilled into the streets, smashed to bits, and then three more ships and three more again dived in for the attack, and the rhythm of their attack made the Sinju, at so close a range, too brilliant to be of any more use.

But the Sinju flashed upward and great searchlights on the ground below probed white fingers to catch the remaining tyars as they scattered. Directly under the main deck of Akar's ship, Nastrond guns sent a shattering broadside into the air directly ahead. Looking up quickly through the glassite ports, Brewster saw the Sinju's scene come alive.

Akar's ship was in the fifth group of three, coming in last to crush whatever tyars had escaped. It swung through the sky, its arc caught in the lights below, and crippled, blazing tyars were swept off its sleek bow and sides as it knifed into the area around the palace and was gone, its wake a wide swath of destruction.

Now Brewster took the Sinju and manipulated it to hold the scene they had left behind. The upper tower was a ruin in which nothing stirred. Its crumbling upper walls were falling down into streets alive with flashing lights and red-orange pyres. The air over the entire area was empty, and only fiery particles discharged from the warships' rocket tubes were to be seen, drifting slowly down. Brewster sat gazing into the Sinju, lost in thought, hardly hearing Akar's voice.

"Action concluded, my lord. What are your orders?"

Brewster shook his head…

And so the thing for which Brewster had waited had come and gone and the opportunity with it. But it was not yet over, for the next day brought startling news.

CHAPTER TEN

ABBOTT had escaped! Brewster sat there and heard Akar speak, and he shook the weariness from his sleep-numbed brain. The blow crushed him.

"How did it happen?" he murmured. "Tell me everything."

"According to your directive, the Fyavo was sent last night to Ho-Tonda. He arrived there shortly before dawn and was confined to the Krennian wing under house arrest. Two hours ago the Argyre watch changed and it was discovered that the entire guard of picked warriors had been slain and the Fyavo gone."

Brewster swung his legs to the edge of the bed and reached for the robe he had hurriedly taken off when Akar knocked for admittance. He looked incredulous. "How was it done?"

"Three of the guards had been hurled over parapets and the other five strangled. The officers are at a loss to understand it, but they believe it was the work of a band of Konos searching for you under some previous, out-dated instruction."

"Konos," Brewster repeated thoughtfully. He got up and walked about the little room and noticed he had not wrinkled the bed sheets sufficiently, and he looked to see whether Akar too had noticed it, and to take his attention, he asked quickly, "But how could they get into the Inner City, let alone the palace?"

"For the past two days there have been mass attacks," Akar said grimly. "Last night, shortly before the attack here in Ramusio began, Konos descended on Ulatai and completely demolished the new forges. It was obviously an attempt to draw our forces to that area. It failed, if only because we knew they were already set to attack here, but the destruction at Ulatai was great."

Brewster was silent and thoughtful.

Akar said, "I bring you a message, therefore, from the council. It met this morning, and has decided, with your concurrence, to undertake drastic action. The Jev Eblis moves to arrest every Estannar in Greater Ho-Tonda."

Brewster cocked his brows. "Every Estannar? How many?"

"Perhaps seventy thousand."

Presently Brewster nodded. "Send my concurrence," he said, and as an afterthought, "Arrange everything for my departure to Ho-Tonda at once. Appoint Lanae Tuew to take charge in your absence."

"My absence, my lord?"

"Yes. You won't be going with us. I have a special errand for you— an errand I trust to no one else. Come back quickly."

When Akar went out Brewster hurriedly dressed, putting on the red robe he had worn for days. From under a cushion of a sofa he removed his holstered automatics and buckled them under his robe. Then, waiting for Akar, he began to pace the room.

In Ramusio, as everywhere else he had gone, he had chosen a tiny room in a military establishment as his own temporary quarters. His excuse had been unvoiced, but seemingly indicative of a fear of attack by Konos. But this would not have explained why he had slept sitting up in a chair or a sofa, starting at every sound though he was surrounded by a corps of warriors. Now, on the sixth day of a vigil that might have erupted into violence at any time, he was exhausted. Every nerve-end was raw, his cheeks sunken, his eyes haggard and red-rimmed. The Konos at Ulatai had unwittingly lengthened his life expectancy, but it could not go on. In Ho-Tonda the last links would be broken today. He had to act immediately, to hope—as he now saw there had been good reason to hope, that he was right. But most of all he had to act while he still retained some shred of sanity...

WHEN Akar returned, Brewster said, "Now you and I will go alone to the vice-Regio, where—" He shook his head, seemingly changing his mind. It had to be done carefully. "Take a tyar and come with me," he said. "I am sending you on a secret errand to Vrita."

Studying Akar's face he had seen nothing. They left the Argyre fort and took an armored tyar, which Akar drove. It started toward the sunlit spires of Ramusio, but halfway there Brewster seemed to come out of his reverie and told Akar to put the tyar down. They were then over an arid, deserted area between two canals, and when Akar confusedly asked Brewster whether he meant directly below. Brewster nodded. He had maintained his attitude of absent-minded musing.

Slowly the tyar settled to the ground, and as it touched, Brewster got out and was followed by Akar. Saying nothing, Brewster started walking toward the edge of the nearer canal. The morning had lost its early chill and the sun was emerging golden from its red mistiness. Here and there birds wheeled in a cloudless, white-blue sky that was otherwise empty. A warm breeze swept over the sandy lowlands, combing the vivid green weed-brush that lined the canal banks.

Here, on the edge of the canal, Brewster stood and looked down into the still waters, his reflection redder than the water and that of Akar beside him a black and clearly defined figure.

"It grows late, my lord," Akar said quietly.

Brewster nodded. "There is a saying among us on Earth," he said, "which is phrased: 'It's later than you think.' It is meant to reflect how time passes mortals more quickly than they know…" After a moment he went on. "It's very late now, Akar. This is my errand."

His hands fumbled at the jewel-encrusted oriflamme on his robe, and from the center jewel he took out an object that gleamed against the amber stone next to which it had lain. He held his hand to Akar and revealed the thin blue-black disc of the Anzus eye.

Akar's face grew tight and he looked at Brewster.

"Take this to Vrita," Brewster said. "Wait for—"

"But Vrita is in Ho-Tonda."

Brewster nodded and finished softly, "Wait for her," and he tipped his palm over so that the gleaming disc slipped from his hand and fell to the sandy earth between them.

Akar did not seem to have heard Brewster then. His eyes had focused on the disc and followed its fall. Now he kneeled to pick it up, and only then did he seem to understand what Brewster had said. Bent half over, his hand extended, he looked up to Brewster and the first dim flicker of alarm lit his eyes. His face was no more than three feet away from Brewster's, and for an infinite moment the two stared at each other and understood each other's thoughts.

And then as Akar started to draw away slowly, very slowly, as if what he saw had robbed him of the power to act, he tried to speak but no sound came from him. For as Akar had bent over, Brewster had reached under his robe and withdrawn one of his automatics. Its deadly snout was inches from Akar's temple. Now it moved down, and the hand that held it grew tight and the gun roared.

Akar fell as if he had been bludgeoned. Hunched over he took the blow and dropped on his side, then rolled over and lay on his side, his head near the water, his still moving legs higher up the bank. Blacker than his tunic, brighter than the jewels of his oriflamme, a wet stain spread quickly from the gaping hole in his belly. He was still alive, his eyes open and watching Brewster put the gun away.

Brewster stood over him. "Time ran out on you first," he said, his voice cold and sardonic.

HE touched a hand to the still open jewel on his chest and let a finger brush the amber stone within. A tiny flame, almost invisible in the bright sunlight, danced on his fingertip.

"I prefer my own toys," Brewster said, "but if you lend someone one of yours, he may find a use for it."

He leaned over a little and pointed his fiery finger to the deep wound. The breeze caught the flame and it leaped over the intervening space and settled in the bloody hollow, and there it found a new vigor and began to spread. Brewster took away the slender green tube fastened to a belt around Akar's middle and stood up.

For moments longer, almost until the consuming fire had reached his eyes, Akar kept staring at Brewster. There was no emotion in them but surprise.

When it was over, nothing remained and where his body had lain there were glazed, almost molten sand-grains and a tall figure's depressed outline...and the jewel of Akar's oriflamme. Brewster picked it up and opened it. Akar's jewel was smaller than the one Brewster wore but the amber stone within Akar's filled the jewel completely, and thus was actually larger than Brewster's.

Then he picked up the blue-black disc from where it had lain all this time. He turned it over in his hands a moment and then carelessly pitched it into the waters of the canal. The jewel he placed in a sewn pocket in his robe.

Without a backward glance he walked quickly back to the tyar.

THE journey from Ramusio to Ho-Tonda had taken six hours, and in that time, for the first time in days, he had slept with his clothes off. When Lanae Tuew, the dour-faced middle-aged Jeggite in command of the trans-Jegga tyar, came in to wake Brewster, Brewster's first request was whether Akar had reported via Borju.

He seemed faintly distressed when Tuew replied negatively, and searching Tuew's face he felt better. So far he was in the clear. He had wondered how far Akar had gone to protect his absence, and there had been uncomfortable moments when he had returned alone after purportedly having sent Akar on his mission. But no questions had risen and now he was playing to head them off.

"The air lanes around Ho-Tonda," Tuew informed him, "have been blocked by the military. Jev Azevedo sends his compliments and suggests a primary landing without the city."

"Of course," Brewster said. He washed and shaved while the vessel and its powerful escort landed at an Argyre field north of Ho-Tonda.

Disembarking, he was met by Iga, the council representative, and taken to the field house where the port officers were gathered around a Sinju, watching the operations Iga explained.

Jev Eblis had struck quickly. Armored tyars held control of the lower air and a fleet of warships cruised watchfully high above them. On the ground Argyres had combined with picked shock divisions of the three Jevs, in anticipation of a struggle which had not yet materialized. Indeed, the mass arrests were proceeding with singular lack of serious difficulty, and on the Sinju Brewster watched one small segment of the great undertaking.

A flying division had arrived to block off a freight canal. With the air lanes and roads closed, thousands had tried to escape along the canals. The sunlit red waters were clogged with vessels of every description, with rafts and even with swimmers. The troops hovered over the canal, stemming the horde. Again and again they would go in pursuit of someone who had broken through their cordon, diving down to within a few feet of the water to point out a swimmer to one of their patrol boats.

Two things Brewster noticed: that many of the fleeing people did not seem to be Estannars; and that no violence was being used. Wherever he saw them, the troops were merely herding people into the never-ending line of black tyar-vans along the canal. It was obvious that they were under orders to take live prisoners.

Presently Lanae Tuew came in and announced that an air lane had been cleared to the Inner City. When Brewster went out to the waiting tyar, it seemed to him that he could hear the massed voices of Ho-Tonda rising high in the air. But he could see little of what was going on below because his ship was surrounded by so heavy an escort. Landing to enter the Inner City, there was a new delay.

Few of the escorting vessels were allowed through. Enormous numbers of warriors swarmed the City's defenses, and unlike the handsome, decorative mounted warriors he had seen there so many times, these were hardened men, some grimy, with the smell of battle about them. Carefully they scrutinized each tyar though they held high officers. Brewster himself received a formal and impressive salute, both there and at the other walls, for the palace as well as the Inner City teemed with warriors, many of them in uniforms Brewster had never seen before.

Once at the palace, Brewster repaired to the Krennian wing, and there, surrounded by his staff officers he put through calls for Akar in Toctai and Kael and Cassia. Waiting for an answer he knew would never come, he paced the central chamber worriedly. The messengers returned to confess failure and at length, seemingly after an inner debate, Brewster called Lanae Catu, his chief of personal guard.

The concern on Brewster's face was far from sham now. He was about to test the first of his theories. Of all the ways it might possibly collapse, one of the most dangerous lay in too complete a success; if he was completely right, this first test was extremely perilous.

He said, "There was a Phyladian named Poro. This morning he was arrested. Bring him to me."

"I have heard of no such arrest, my lord."

"Then find someone who *has*," Brewster snapped.

CATU retreated and left, and Brewster went to the room he had occupied and replenished his supply of cigarettes. He had no hope of finding one of the ubiquitous notes and he found none, and he went out on the balcony of the central room where he stood and smoked. Inside, his officers, perhaps twenty of them, had ordered wine and were watching the Sinju's survey of the city with calm, deliberate comments, but Brewster could feel their eyes on him.

When Catu returned, bringing the Lanae and two captains of the palace guard, Brewster stepped in at the threshold of the balcony, and with the loudness of his voice kept the trio at a distance, stopping them in their tracks as they approached. Through his mind kept running the words he had spoken to the dying Akar—*"if you lend someone one of your toys, he may find a use for it"*—and he knew it was a time for boldness.

"I don't want to hear your excuses!" he called angrily. "Bring the prisoner Poro to me!"

There was an instant of silence, and in that instant the thoughts raced madly through his brain: what if they should answer that Poro was dead?...would Akar not have told him so?...but if Akar had arrested Poro he would not have had him killed...it all depended on whether Poro had been arrested...and logic inexorably said that he had...logic?...but it was no more than a house of cards... And so over and over he thought it through in that instant.

When the officers saluted and left without a word, he knew he had won the first round. The house of cards was still standing, but for how long?

He stood there waiting, watching the fleeting scenes on the Sinju across the room, while his ears were filled with the distant sounds of the beleaguered city. Presently the officers returned, and manacled to a heavy weight he carried was Poro, surrounded by Argyres. Brewster looked at the Phyladian's dull face and then walked to him.

He said to the Lanae of the guard, "What instructions did Lanae Akar send you this morning concerning treatment of this Phyladian?"

"This morning?" The Lanae was puzzled. "None, my lord."

"You are Lanae of the guard?"

"Yes, my lord."

"Then you *lie*," Brewster snapped. "Free the Phyladian."

"But he—"

"Silence," Brewster said curtly. "Free him."

The Lanae mumbled the order fearfully, and the guards assumed a new, tense watchfulness as the green-skinned, giant was unmannacled. Poro gently laid the heavy weight down and stood quietly.

"Order the guard changed and all who were in the palace on duty for the past night and day are to report to Lanae Tuew presently."

Again the Lanae gave the order, and the guard filed out.

Brewster said to Catu, who stood close by, "Summon a picked patrol of my best warriors. This Lanae and all his officers are to be put under arrest and—"

"My lord, it was not—"

He fell silent under the black fury of Brewster's eyes. "There will be time," Brewster said evenly, "to judge your guilt or innocence later." He turned back to Catu. "They are to be kept incommunicado," he said. "Keep them separate from each other, allow no talking among them and they are to see no one, nor to send or receive messages. This duty is entrusted only to men of my command."

Silently the Lanae and officers of the guard were led out. When Brewster looked around at his staff officers, he saw that none understood what they had witnessed—as he well knew by then, for understanding it they might have interfered. Now he addressed them.

"I see, my officers, that your thoughts are all with the events taking place in Ho-Tonda. The warriors of Thyle belong beside those of my brother Jevs. Therefore, it is my order that you, under the leadership of Tuew, present yourselves and your regiments to Jev Eblis for his disposal. This accomplished, Tuew will return here to await Akar and myself."

TUEW was confused. "And who will remain here?" he asked, looking at Poro distrustfully. "And what of your—"

Brewster said quietly, with finality, "Akar has arranged all." He nodded for them to go. "I am not one to fear a brute—" he grinned scornfully at Poro, "—I have bested with my own hands."

By the look that crossed the faces of Tuew and several others he knew they had heard of his fight with the Phyladian, and now understood that Poro was that Phyladian.

"Nevertheless I will post a special guard," Tuew said, and left at the head of the other staff officers. One by one they went out, some casting a last look back, others hurrying, until in a few moments they were all gone, and Brewster was left alone in the semi-darkness of the great chamber with Poro.

Brewster regarded the Phyladian, then said softly, "You speak my language of Kren?"

Poro nodded and put a finger to his lips. He moved with agility surprising for his bulk, walking swiftly to each of the four entrances to the central chamber and looking into the adjoining rooms. Then he returned and dialed the Sinju, and the screen swept across the city to a plaza surrounded by enormous buildings. One of these buildings was lost behind the streams of green fire that was being played on it from huge Nastrond guns. The Jeggites were attacking it in force.

Poro glanced at the scene and turned the Sinju off.

"They have found our Konos," he said in English, his deep voice hushed. "We must go to him before it is too late. Only he knows what is to be done now."

"But how can we go there?"

"You have done well thus far. Confuse your warriors further and order a patrol to take you there. You must continue to use your power while the Jevs are occupied." He started, listening to some sound he had heard, then said, "You have disposed of Akar for a time?"

"For a long time," Brewster said somberly.

"Good. Let us go then. And remember to answer no questions but show your might instead. To these people you are a Jev."

Brewster cursed bitterly and left with him.

* * *

THE military escort flew in a wedge, high over the embattled towers of Ho-Tonda, and in the protecting flank of their formation Brewster drove his own tyar. Beside him sat Poro. Brewster had carefully made sure every communicating instrument was functioning only one way—from the others to him—and then he spoke to Poro. He could hardly arrange his thoughts; a thousand questions clamored in his brain. Poro could not answer them all.

"I knew immediately it was you who freed Abbott," Brewster told him. "It was the only thing that made sense. I found that note telling me to go to the Imperial library and it couldn't have been there long or it would have been found—they searched my things regularly. The only one in the wing was you. You were practically telling me it was you but I couldn't take the chance, even after I found you watching me reading that book. Suppose you were a decoy?"

"But why should you have thought that?"

"I wasn't sure of anything anymore. Everyone was turning out to be someone else. The Jeggites had proven to be so fantastically clever that I just couldn't tell. I knew one mistake might be the end. Of all the planted coincidences I'd been maneuvered through, I had caught only one—the one with Vrita. Then I saw that your being in the palace, in the Krennian wing, wasn't the accident I'd thought it was. I remembered you had unobtrusively picked that fight we had—"

Poro smiled, and with his smile the dullness of his eyes lifted, as under a veil, and then he was again the stolid, stupid Phyladian. "It was a calculated affair," he amended. "I had been instructed better than to pick the fight. I was merely to offer the excuse, and I was assured you would seize it." He nodded reflectively. "From the very beginning he understood your nature and predicted many of your reactions."

"Thank God," Brewster said fervently. "He was playing against a gang who knew me pretty nearly as well as he did." His face was bleak and drawn.

Poro said, "So you reasoned that I had been sent to get to you?"

"Not all at once. You see, there was a hole in it. What if I hadn't caught on that my bodyguards meant to kill you? What if I hadn't cared if they did? For an emissary, your case had certain coincidences for it, but as many against it."

"You overlook one thing. Had you not seen that your guards were ready to kill me, or had you not cared, nothing more important than my death would have occurred. True, I would have failed as an emissary, but others in a variety of guises would have attempted to reach you. The very nature of your position was such that any attempt to draw you into contact would necessarily have to be the result of some coincidence."

Brewster nodded. "I saw that later, but this morning when Akar told me Abbott had escaped, my first idea was that Akar had killed him. When he told me the details, I understood it was true and that you must have been the one who engineered it. It was absurd to think of Konos, as Akar said, getting in here. Then who else could have killed and beaten a large guard? Only Poro, the quiet Phyladian, wandering unnoticed from room to room, had the freedom of action—only Poro was here—and he alone had the strength to overcome so many men quickly. And yet, even here I had doubts…I had them until the last moment, until you answered me…"

"You could not understand what nature of being I was?"

"Yes. Suba Marannes had told me of the Bheynor, the offspring of intermarriage between Estannars and those of other races, who look like Estannars and still retain the power to lie. But you did not look like an Estannar, and you acted with an intelligence that I knew was far from the Phyladians…"

A DEEP sigh escaped Poro. "I, and the beings like me, have been one of the Estannars most carefully guarded secrets until today. We too are the products of intermarriage, but we are Bheynor in reverse. We resemble those of the other races, but retain the intelligence of the Estannar. Our beings are called Temhor, which means, in the ancient language of Estannar—promise for the future. For more than a hundred years we Temhor have been bred scientifically, and in us the Estannars see the people of the future, the interbred racial being, combining the best features of all." He paused. "But you could not know this, naturally, and we understood the obstacle would be great."

"I had to gamble on some kind of explanation," Brewster said. "Everything else pointed to it. I kept saying to myself *'inexorable logic, inexorable logic'* when there was no logic to so much of what had happened. I had to take the chance even if I was wrong, because unless I was right about you, I would lose perhaps my last chance to contact the faction that held Abbott." He regarded Poro. "You explained it all to him?"

"As much as I had time. He left on foot, and the last I saw of him, he had gained the second wall. Certainly he would have gotten through to the others and warned them that you would come of your own will—but then the mass arrests started. I do not think he got past the cordons. They were already on guard early this morning."

"Then there's no hope for him?"

"Perhaps. He may have been arrested as an Estannar. The warrior patrols were ordered to kill none who did not fight. Only the Konos offer resistance. For the rest, it appears that the Jevs have found out about the many Temhor in the city."

"But how?"

"Panic, perhaps. You have seen the Sinju and you know what is going on. Did you not notice that many of those who sought to escape do not look like Estannars? Some doubtless are innocent Usaus, Anians, Ermosians—but many others are Temhor."

"But why do they run? They're giving themselves away—and if they're as intelligent as you..."

"They are not as fortunate as I, who was chosen to work with *him*. They know only that they have lost contact with each other. Our strength lay in our organization, and the arrival of great numbers of Konos broke that organization to bits, for the Konos have been killing recklessly for days, trying to get through to you. Accidentally they must have killed many members of our groups who were also trying to get you in contact, in case I should fall by the wayside. That was his precaution."

Brewster shook his head. "I still don't understand much of what you're saying. It can wait a little, but one thing does seem to be clear—that tremendous things have been in preparation here, and that suddenly everything has been let loose."

"Yes," Poro agreed, "the preparations have been ready here for a great many years, but much of what is happening now is not the result of those preparations—it is a series of desperate moves meant to head off your collaboration with the Jeggites, utilizing those preparations. It is as if one had stored munitions for a long planned battle and then had to blow everything up to hold the enemy back, because the enemy had struck first. The Estannars are wrecking the plans of many years just to gain a little time now."

"I see," Brewster said. A heavy, involuntary sigh escaped his tight-drawn lips. "What a tragic waste," he said quietly. "Here we were trying to get through to them and they destroyed every means we could have used. And now they're destroying the things we'll need later...if there is to be a later..."

Poro was pointing below. Their squadron of tyars had left the city and its environs not long before. Now they had approached the outlying state farms of the nearby Toctai province. Along an intersection of three roads below was the grouping of neat rectangles of white buildings that Brewster remembered. The escorting tyars ahead were already dropping.

"Now we will see him," Poro said. "He has expected much of this for many days. He has not lost heart. *He* will know what to do."

MANEUVERING the tyar into a long shallow glide, Brewster wondered. He had realized before that he had been no more than a tool in hands far more skillful than his own—or, in the imagery he had created, he was not the player of the cards but a card himself. A valuable one, to be sure, and perhaps the most valuable of all, if he could be played at the correct time. He was a loose Ace. He might be trumped out, or, if his own player called first, he might be made into the Ace of trump. But it was not in his hands now…

Suddenly his thoughts turned to a new channel, and Brewster saw that everything had inevitably led to it, to the question he now asked Poro: "But what if the contact with him has also been destroyed—" He broke off, seeing that Polo had been expecting the question.

"It is undoubtedly destroyed. To hope otherwise after these mass arrests would be foolish. Instead I have hoped that the Jeggites do not yet realize what has happened."

"The contact was through an Anzus?"

Poro looked at him and smiled briefly. "Yes," he said. "It was very intelligent of you to see that, I can understand now why *he* insisted that you had to be taken in as one of us."

One by one the tyars landed in a precise column along the apron of a field, nagged into position by Hruthians. The last time Brewster had been here, the field had been supervised by Argyres. Their conspicuous absence was mute testimony to the demands on military power that had been necessitated by the operations in Ho-Tonda. How much stranger, then, the fact that none of Thyle's army had been requested.

Getting out of the tyar, Brewster, accompanied by Poro, spoke a few words to his patrol captain, ordering a clearance from the field. The captain soon returned with word that it had been granted by the old warrior in command of the few Argyres within the central building. Then Brewster told the patrol to wait at the field for him, and went with Poro and one of the patrol warriors.

Entering the unguarded main square, Brewster kept thinking that Providence was still with him. The Jeggites evidently attached little importance to the area or to him. How simple, with a pliable communications system, it would have been to storm the place with suddenly gathered Konos. Yet here it was, open to attack, guarded by a handful of poorly armed Argyres. It was even possible that a simple bluff would do the trick, if it was necessary.

They were challenged only once, and after that the full guard assembly for formal salute. Accompanied to the medical staff chamber by the commanding officer, Brewster recognized the taciturn doctor he had met on his first visit. He spoke to the doctor for a few moments.

"How is he?" Brewster asked.

"No change, my lord."

"When did you last see him?"

"Yesterday. I'm due now. With your permission, my lord, I'll go with you."

"I prefer going alone. I'll send for you presently."

The doctor seemed glad to be relieved of what he obviously considered an onerous duty. He bowed and left. Brewster motioned to Poro, and together, led by a Hruthian orderly and his patrol warrior, they walked down the spotless green marble hall of the hospital. An oppressive silence lay over this building, as it layover the entire settlement. It seemed pitifully under-staffed. The rooms which Brewster glimpsed were all filled with patients, and now and then their murmurous complaining voices would drift into the corridors filled with male and female Hruthians, orderlies and nurses, but of the Jeggian doctors there were few to be seen. The hospital area here was equally distant from Ulatai and Ho-Tonda, and Brewster estimated that the first flood of casualties from both cities had been brought here. But where were the doctors? Had they been ordered to the combat zones? Then how great had the impending battle grown?

A FEW moments later the orderly stopped outside a door guarded by two Argyres. Brewster motioned his patrol warrior to wait outside and told Poro to enter with him. In every face Brewster had seen the wonder that followed his appearance with the silent Phyladian. Only his preeminent rank had forestalled the questioning that might otherwise have risen, and again, as it was to occur many times that day, Brewster remembered his words: *"...if you lend someone one of your toys, he may find a use for it..."* and a vast gratitude that Stevens too had banked on just that, filled his heart.

Brewster closed the door behind him and walked to the bed where Dr. John Stevens lay. He had not changed. The jaundiced, scarred face was expressionless, the gnarled hands trembling. The eyes that Brewster remembered as sightless yellow pools were closed now, and his deep, slow breathing was testimony that Stevens slept. But when he had quietly opened the door, Brewster had seen the old man close his eyes, and he conveyed the information to Poro with a shake of his head.

Poro nodded understandingly. He leaned over the bed and whispered, "It is I, Lau of the Anzus group. Brewster and I are here alone. If you hear me, open your—"

Before he had finished speaking, Stevens' eyes had opened. He did not move his head, however, and to meet his gaze Brewster leaned over beside Poro. He was shocked by the clarity; the fierce intelligence that lay in Stevens' eyes, and when, a moment later, Stevens began to speak in a well-controlled murmur that did not carry beyond the bed, a shudder ran through Brewster. It was like a voice from the grave. Prepared as he had been for something like this, the actuality of that soft, ghostly voice was almost too much.

"The Anzus is gone. Of my three doctors, two have been called and the last may go soon. You must hurry while there is still confusion enough to allow you freedom. Commandeer a warship and start for Usau. Allow as small an escort as possible. Do you understand?"

Brewster was not sure that he understood, but he said, "We can take you with us. It will not be difficult—"

"It has never been difficult. You must go alone, Nick. Do not try to save Abbott or the Marannes people. You must go quickly or it will be too late. Poro will explain everything." His eyes moved the least bit to focus on Poro. "I sent Kari to Ulatai yesterday. The work in Ho-Tonda is his doing, as are the warships off Usau. When you get through, tell Tartullian that Brewster may call the force wall off. He will understand. All my plans have been based on it, and the men lost in Ho-Tonda will aid its realization."

He closed his eyes. For all the clearness and control with which he had spoken, the few words had exhausted him. Brewster looked down at his quiet form and a dim realization of what Stevens was prepared to go through from now on came to him. Perhaps because he was still uncertain or perhaps because he knew it was not for him to question, Brewster knew also that he could do nothing with or for Stevens.

But Poro had been right, *he* had known what to do...

Silently Brewster and the Phyladian left the chamber. They returned to the field where their tyars waited, not a word exchanged between them there or in the tyar the way back. Poro had shaken his head, afraid that the communications system had been tampered with. And now, at the critical hour, it was imperative that no inkling of the mission Brewster would shortly undertake, should leak out...

Once back at the palace, however, and secluded in the privacy of the Krennian chambers, Brewster quickly pieced together the fragments that had invisibly bound Poro and Stevens and the others whom he had not known, and whom Stevens had mentioned.

"I haven't got it all yet," Brewster told Poro. "Let me talk it out as if I were thinking aloud and you'll help me."

PORO shook his head. "There is much you know that will be beyond me. Many of my actions have been based on instruction or faith, but in those matters concerning *him*, I can be of service." He stood before Brewster, waiting. "I must beg you to be quick."

"I've got a reason for stalling," Brewster said quietly. He lit a cigarette and drew the smoke into his lungs and watched the plume he blew out, frowning and meditative. Then he nodded and began to speak.

"Stevens knew what was happening to me and he built his plans on the expectation of my reactions. Now, from what he said, it appears that he could have been taken away from there by the Estannars, but chose to remain there as a voluntary prisoner?"

"Partly so. The Estannars could have taken him in the raid when they rescued the other three survivors of the first ship from Kren. But since he was already under the influence of their Anzus, the Estannars decided to leave him behind, hoping he would consent to act as their most necessary link between them and their agents in Jegga. And he did so consent."

"I see. I'll put it this way, there were Estannars in Jegga when the survivors of the first *Trailblazer* were brought here. These Estannar agents had an Anzus?" He paused.

"From time to time many Anzus have fallen into our hands, as have many of the weapons of the Jeggites. It was inevitable that such exchanges of trophies should occur between warrior nations. Just as the Jeggites captured many of our military secrets, so did we capture theirs. When it was known that the Jeggites had taken live Krennians, the Estannars knew that the Krennians had to be taken away before the secret of metal manufacture was forced from them.

"But the Estannars knew also that one day more Krennians would come to Boron and be captured by the Jeggites. They prepared against that day, and foreseeing the possibility of failure on Boron, they built a great underground organization here in Jegga. For the first time they used beings like me, the Temhor. We were taken from our secret lands in Estannar and sent in groups to establish ourselves in Jegga. We all had different assignments, and mine, fortunately, was to be a member of the Anzus group, among whom I was known as Lau.

"For, from the beginning, because Dr. Stevens was injured and was under the care of Jeggian surgeons, it was decided to try to establish him as the link. We set our Anzus within range. It was brought to the fields near the great hospital settlement, and its hypnotic power brought to bear on Dr. Stevens. He was still unconscious during those early days, and to the knowledge of the Jeggians, he scarcely improved. For we controlled his mind and his actions. Through our Anzus we were able to transmit our thoughts to him. What others of your people had learned from the most cruel experience, Dr. Stevens learned from us.

"It was not necessary to control his mind after those early days except to defend him against the Jeggians. We had kept his eyes clouded and his arms trembling, and though his mind was clear he looked still a dying, hopeless cripple. But to prove our side—for we had told him of the Jeggian plans to conquer Kren along with the rest of the universe in their hands—one day we released him from the influence of our Anzus. The improvement in his condition was immediately noticeable to his doctors, and that day he was subjected to a merciless grilling, until our Anzus rescued him. As it was, its influence returned none too soon, for the Jeggian doctors had sent for an Anzus of their own.

"It failed, because ours already occupied the field of his brain and he was saved. They kept him alive, hoping against hope. He was their only link with the secret of metal. In time, because the Estannars made no new move to get him, the Jeggians decided we too realized he was of no use to them, and were thus further convinced. But all this time he was in contact with us, directing us, counseling, keeping the contact alive among the various sections of our arriving Temhor and Bheynor and Konos. Why all this went on we did not know, save to realize that our leaders were planning an eventual blow here in Jegga itself. Our strength was growing steadily—"

BREWSTER interrupted. "I can see how you could keep in touch with him through the Anzus—at least I think I can—but I don't see how he got through to you. As far as I know, the Anzus works one way—from its controller to the controlled."

Poro smiled faintly. "He spoke to us. We had three Temhor doctors on the staff, two who appeared to be Darzizt and one Usau. In the course of their duties they occasionally visited him. Whatever we told Dr. Stevens through the Anzus, he could tell his three doctors and have it passed along by them to their own groups.

"I was of the Anzus group, and there were five of us. We lived on a great state farm near the hospital settlement. Three of us were, like me, Temhor-Phyladian, but as apparent Phyladians were highly desirable as farm laborers. We three kept the Anzus in our fields and transmitted to Dr. Stevens whatever orders were given to us. The orders came from the other two of our group; one, a Temhor-Anian, was the head of the farm; the other, a Bheynor, was his assistant. We never knew where they got their orders, but undoubtedly there were additional links all the way through to the leaders in Estannar.

"Thus, group on group communicated, and it all went through Dr. Stevens. But he was more than a central link. This I discovered when I was ordered to attempt getting into contact with you. Dr. Stevens had been sending you notes—"

"Then it was Stevens," Brewster said, startled. "It seemed to me that it had to be Stevens, but I heard an Estannar deny it..." He let his voice die away, seeing the answer. "But of course no Estannar would be allowed to know it," he said, as if explaining to himself. "That would be inviting disaster."

"More than that," Poro added, "the Estannars—all who came in contact with us—were purposely misinformed. Only we Bheynor and Temhor close to Dr. Stevens knew the truth. He wrote the notes and had them delivered. Before me there had been several Temhor-Hruthians in the palace who were links. The Argyres discovered them—without discovering the secret of the Temhor—and destroyed them. There were others too, scattered among shopkeepers, tyar-drivers—we even had a bearer to a Lanae in the army of Jev Nastrond. My task was to get into the palace in a capacity where I could deliver Dr. Stevens' notes, which were given to me by a gardener.

"But I knew all along that there was a division among us. Our communications had been broken all along the line. From the time you of the second Krennian ship arrived, the Jeggites killed thousands on the slightest suspicion. Shortly after I came to the palace I learned that both the Bheynor and the Temhor-Anian on our farm had been executed because they were known to be friendly with the Marannes family. It meant the end of our contact with leaders in Estannar until new ones could be established with us.

"But it did not affect Dr. Stevens' ability to send his own messages through his three Temhor doctors. The two Temhor-Phyladians on the farm remained unsuspected. Thus they were able to keep Dr. Stevens under the Anzus influence, releasing him for short periods sufficient to enable him to talk or write a note. Naturally, because the danger was now infinitely greater, these free periods became less and less, and the notes decreased in frequency—"

"Did you ever deliver any notes to Abbott?"

"Twice. Secretly, of course."

"You were able to read them, I gather?"

"Yes."

"Did you ever notice the difference in the way the notes were worded?"

"Naturally, but you must understand this by now?"

"You mean he was playing on my personality."

"YES," Poro nodded, "from the very beginning. The notes Dr. Stevens sent to Abbott were all factual. He merely told him to look in certain places, knowing that Abbott was already predisposed to accept the evidence. It was different with you..." Poro spoke gently, with no intimation of censure. "...You brought along different lines, and it was Dr. Stevens' opinion that you had to find out for yourself, no matter how long it took. Therefore the notes he sent you were meant only to pique you, to make you think a little, to wound, perhaps. He played on your personality, as you say, because he believed that you would find whatever evidence was needed once you decided to look for it..."

"And when I became the so-called Jev Thyle?"

Poro frowned. "It was a shock. You see, until then Dr. Stevens had held out hope. This new, incredible development appeared to have changed everything. He knew of the Konos who had been sent to kill you—the ones discovered in the Marannes quarter—and he had sent his own message through to the Estannar leaders that no such further attempts were to be made. Now he was puzzled. He sent one last note, which I put into your cigarettes when you returned to the palace as Jev Thyle.

"I saw you reading the note, and I saw you go to the Imperial library, and, if you recall, I watched you read that section in *Descoru es Jegga jon Jeg*. I reported this through to Dr. Stevens, and after that, no matter what you did, he was certain that it was meant eventually to hurt the Jeggites."

"Even when I gave the Jeggites the secret of making metal?"

Poro nodded. "We had a Temhor-Darzit among the scientists who later gave your report to one of Dr. Stevens' doctors. Dr. Stevens, too, knew the metal processes and he saw the errors you had committed. But all your errors were in the end processes, and this told him that you were playing to gain time—"

"I was trying to contact some element of the rebels. I was still afraid to try you, Poro, and I had guessed that Abbott's constant disappearances were linked with the rebels. I needed time until either Abbott showed up again or someone else contacted me."

"Ah yes," Poro said, "but since Dr. Stevens had no contact with them, they had no way of knowing that you had lied when you supposedly gave the secret away. They could only see the huge manufactories begin to function. To them you had been an outcast but now you were the lowest of all traitors. Thus, I was not surprised when Abbott was brought to the Krennian wing this morning under arrest as a conspirator in an attempt on your life. I killed his guards and freed him, and then I told him that you had read the *Descoru* and now understood everything. And it was his intention to bring this news to the Konos factions with whom he had been in contact. But I did not think that he had gotten through, and from Dr. Stevens' warning not to attempt to rescue him, evidently he was arrested."

"What about the other things he said?" Brewster asked. He had smoked three cigarettes, lighting them end to end. But a strange vigor ran through him, as at last he was beginning to understand so many of the things that had plagued him. "What was that about sending someone named Kari to Ulatai yesterday?"

"I perceived from that," Poro said thoughtfully, "that I had been in error on some of the things I told you previously. Kari was leader of a special band of Konos kept in Ho-Tonda for Dr. Stevens' use. They were a fairly large band, numbering several hundred at times. Because their only contact with the Estannar leaders was Dr. Stevens, they could not be used against you—thus special Konos had to be sent in. But last night Dr. Stevens sent Kari to destroy the forces at Ulatai. The Jeggites were already far advanced on some samples of the metal, and it was imperative to delay them, or they would discover that you had lied."

"Then it was an action calculated to give me time?"

"OBVIOUSLY. And now, from what Dr. Stevens said, it appears that the action in Ho-Tonda today was touched off by him. Kari and his Konos forced the Jeggites to a position where they could retain order only by some such gigantic upheaval as arresting all Estannars. Once this happened, evidently Dr. Stevens' orders and not panic, as I supposed, sent out Temhors fleeing with the Estannars. Thus new confusion is added and even innocent members of other races are joining the stampede to escape from Ho-Tonda. All this will keep the Jevs too occupied to know what you are doing and meanwhile you can make your—"

"But what of Stevens? He said the Anzus was gone, and two of his three doctors gone. Where does that leave him?"

"In a dangerous position, as he well knows. Something must have happened to the two Temhor-Phyladians who kept the Anzus, and Dr. Stevens is no longer under its influence. His doctors have doubtless been among those called to attend the wounded in the fighting in Ho-Tonda, for the Konos there would not submit without inflicting great damage. But while one of his doctors remains, Dr. Stevens is safe."

"And if he leaves?"

Poro shrugged. "They may see the change in Dr. Stevens or they may not. Perhaps he will pretend to sleep, as he did when he heard us come in. In any event, he has weighed the consequences and made his decision.

Evidently Kari was able to contact a group of Estannar warships off Usau. Your one hope is to get through to them, and to bring to Tartullian, a great Estannar leader, the message that may call the force wall into abeyance."

"As a Jev?"

Poro nodded and kept his expression unchanged.

Brewster looked at him and said, "You think I don't know?"

Poro said nothing. A look of keen interest came into his eyes.

"I've known all along." Brewster said. "It wasn't reading the *Descoru* that did it. If Stevens had thought merely reading that book would do it, he'd have gotten it to me earlier—or something like it—"

"But only as Jev could you have gotten into the library," Poro reminded him.

Brewster nodded. "All right, but reading those passages in the *Descoru* did no more than confirm what I already knew."

"But how could you know?"

Brewster countered, "How did I know Dr. Stevens was probably under the influence of an Anzus?" When no answer came from Poro, Brewster said, "Because I saw evidences of the division of command all through the actions of the rebels. One group tried to kill me—another sent me notes. If you were delivering the notes, as I finally concluded, then you also had the opportunity to kill me. Why didn't you kill me? Obviously because your faction didn't want you to.

"Again, there were things you don't know about. Akar told me that others of my men from the *Trailblazer* had gotten notes. He didn't know about Abbott or me, but he knew about them. Why? Because one faction used good methods and went undetected—that was your faction. But the other group, which I assume is headed by Harper, Crane and Burke—the survivors of the first *Trailblazer*—sent notes poorly and were found out. Which was clear evidence of a badly divided system.

"Everything kept pointing to Dr. Stevens. I had seen him and it seemed unbelievable. But two things convinced me. The lesser of the two was my own experience with an Anzus. I saw then that it might easily control one's every action, however involuntarily. Still, as I say, this was merely a confirming factor—something I deduced from the fact that major evidence pointed to it."

"And this major evidence?" Poro asked.

"The fact that I understood what lay behind my becoming Jev. I saw then, once I appeared to be a Jev, that the faction that sent me the notes still let me live...and I realized that whoever was behind it had banked on my realizing everything sooner or later. It was a tremendous gamble on my intelligence and there was no one—" he spoke somberly, "—not even Abbott, who would have done that except Dr. Stevens. He alone knew me well enough to hope—to know—I would see through it all."

PORO shook his head. He said quietly, "I see from your words that you have indeed realized the underlying farce, and though I see it and know Dr. Stevens' high estimate of you, it still seems incredible that you saw it by yourself…"

Brewster said grimly, his face suddenly flushed, "I'll go into the details some other time. I'm not proud of them. But you can have no doubt that I knew. Otherwise I would not have kept the amber stones and thrown away the Anzus eye." His smile was cold and empty. "I had a use for some of their toys, you see."

"And will have again before this day is through."

"Yes," Brewster agreed. "There's a lot to this being a Jev and I'm going to squeeze it dry." He paused meditatively. "But even though there are hundreds dying in Ho-Tonda," he said quietly, "this was probably the only way…"

"No," said Poro. "There were other ways, but after what has happened, this will be the shortest, if not the best, way. The great and learned Tartullian will show you. And now we must hurry, if you are to get through to him."

Brewster ran his hands down on his face. "I've been thinking," he said. "I've got one or two things I ought to do first." He looked at Poro. "They've got Abbott and the Marannes family. I'm going to get them out before I leave."

"You must not—"

"I don't care about the time. I know the Estannars captured the other six of the *Trailblazer* and they're safe—but just in case they aren't—and because Abbott and the Marannes family are blood on my hands, I'm going to wash clean."

"Think," said Poro. "It is not a question of time. You are to return here and still be the Jev Thyle. You must not burn bridges you will later need to cross. Everything must be left untouched, no matter what the risk, for in meddling with the Jevs you show them you know what they plan." He smiled regretfully. "Do you think they would want you to deny them the danger they all undertook…the danger in which you had to leave Dr. Stevens?"

Brewster said through tight lips, "You're right. But not all the way. We'll split that up…you'll go."

For an instant Poro looked at Brewster, then he nodded his head slowly. "You've gotten ahead of even Stevens, I see."

Brewster grinned momentarily. "Even Steven…that's good, Poro, if you knew it." He knit his brows reflectively. "Yes, I think I have. And I have my own ideas of what goes from here on. It's that divided plan again; I think it's still divided. If it wasn't, Stevens wouldn't risk everything he's planned on one cast of the dice. It's death for him, you know…"

PORO stood silently, his eyes fixed on Brewster with what was certainly nothing but wondering contemplation. It was helpless contemplation, too; as though he realized, just as Stevens had, that Brewster must follow his own line of reasoning. And it was apparent that suddenly a new line of reasoning had been reached, followed, and measured to a decision.

"What if Tartullian's plan doesn't correspond with yours?"

"You don't know my plan," said Brewster.

Poro shrugged. "You don't know Tartullian's—nor Stevens'."

"Stevens knows me," said Brewster calmly. "He knows me so well that there is but one line of reasoning he can follow. Only one way he can convince me that my place is here. Well, let's say I've skipped a step in his reasoning, and I'm convinced now? Then what?"

Poro looked at him. "You stay here."

"Exactly. But Tartullian can't know that. And he's got to know. So there's your answer. You go to Tartullian."

"How?"

"Just as Stevens directed. He must know why he planned it that way. I'll see that you go according to plan. A small ship—and a Jeggite warship convoy."

"That means a fight."

"Now you're catching on," said Brewster with a grin. "And if it means a fight, it must be because both Stevens and Tartullian want one— and if they want one, they must be ready for one. And if they're ready for one… Do you follow me?"

Poro's eyes gleamed. "The inner city."

"That's what Stevens and all Estannar have planned. Crack that, and you crack the whole set-up. What was it Stevens said: 'Tell Tartullian that Brewster may call the force wall off?' He meant *can* call it off, not *may.*"

There was blankness in Poro's face.

Brewster noted it, half-smiled. "You see, Poro, I do know an answer that you, anybody else, doesn't. Except perhaps two: Stevens, and…"

"Time is growing short," Poro took up after his deliberational pause as though despairing of understanding; even realizing here was a secret almost revealed, then held back. "What message do I give to Tartullian when I 'meet' him?"

"Tell him that Brewster has called the force wall down."

"Nothing else?"

"Nothing—except to hit hard and fast. And on time." Brewster looked reflective. "The time..." He launched into a series of verbal calculations, and except for a few interspersed corrections, Poro listened silently. When Brewster had finished, Poro's eyes were shining. The giant Phyladian strode to the window to stare toward the center of the city—toward the inner wall. His clenched fist rose, then fell with an unmistakable portent.

"Hard and fast!" he swore.

CHAPTER ELEVEN

FOR two days Brewster remained calmly in his quarters. Much of the time he spent sleeping; some of it in contemplation of the last remnants of the fighting in the outer streets, along the Kardandan canals. Most interesting was the Sinju. It showed him a scene of destruction at Ulatai. Kari and his Konos had done their work well. The blast furnaces lay in ruins, the mineshafts were blasted, and all work had ceased.

The battle had been a furious one, and sheer suicide on the part of Kari and his men. They had been slain to the last man, hunted down by detachments of enraged Jeggites. Jev Nastrond himself visited the scene, drove his armed forces to ruthless extermination of the Konos. Over the Sinju, Brewster watched his hawk face with interest.

Brewster called him on the Sinju the second day. But not before the news he had been awaiting came over the Tonju. The news was garbled, to be sure, and incomplete. Strict censorship had been clamped down, but enough had come through to give Brewster the news he wanted. There had been a battle in space between pirate Estannar ships, and the warships. There had been casualties. And nowhere any mention of the ship that carried Poro.

Brewster called the fleet commander. "I ordered a strong escort. You sent a weak one. My messenger has been kidnapped!"

"It was an unprecedently strong force, O Jev," protested the commander. "Already I have reported to the Regio. A powerful punitive expedition will be prepared..."

"See that it is," Brewster said coldly. "And report to me, not the Regio. Get that straight."

It was pure bluff, and Brewster knew it. But he smiled grimly. Today the thing would come to a head. Today would decide the real power of the Jevs—and the most powerful of the Jevs. He fingered the intelligent fire stone at his breast; thought of the anzus stone of Ahriman at the bottom of the canal where he had thrown it.

* * *

NASTROND'S lean face bore no friendliness on the Sinju. Brewster spoke first. "You're wrong," he said, anticipating his accusation. "Ulatai was not my doing. A bargain is a bargain." There was no apology in his voice, rather a scarcely hidden satisfaction that he meant Nastrond to discern.

Nastrond saw it. He scowled. "Still ambitious, O Jev?" he said. Perhaps your balance cannot match your stride."

Brewster remained impassive. "I make the threats," he said.

"That is presumption," said Nastrond. "You can make no threats."

Brewster frowned inwardly. There was a quiet definition in Nastrond's voice that spelled an uncomfortable certainty. Certainty about what? Swiftly Brewster knew that here was a man who knew something he did not. It wasn't good.

There was a queer tight sensation in Brewster's breast as he went on: "The mighty Jev Nastrond also presumes," he said softly. "He forgets the death of a man—a mighty man. He forgets, too, the existence of an imposter, and the reason for that masquerade. Perhaps it is because he remembers a law? A law that now operates on the side of his enemies; who wait to strike at his heart?"

Now at last the calmness of the Jev Nastrond was broken. His face became ugly, twisted. His eyes flamed with mixed emotions. But predominating finally; sweeping over Brewster like a wave, was hate; and murderous intention. "You ask for death!" he snarled.

"But you are not its minister," reminded Brewster. "You will be only a member of a council of four—no, of five. In the inner city. All of us know what we want. There is enough for all. Tonight, at the hour before midnight."

"You dare to bargain with me!" Nastrond was enraged. For an instant he seemed about to launch into a tirade, then suddenly craftiness crept into his eyes and his voice leveled out into a flatness that was so obviously sly that Brewster smiled. But there was no humor in his smile. Instead he looked squarely into Nastrond's eyes.

"Remember the law," he said. "It is written—*already* written—that one hour after midnight the truth will be made known, and a barrier removed. Removed for a year. If by any untoward chance, the Jev Thyle should not emerge from the conference of Jevs tonight, in time to erase what is written…" Brewster paused suggestively. "That is not bargaining," he finished softly. "A bargain is such that two or more concerned have a voice in the making of that bargain. You have no voice."

Nastrond's face was white now, but he calmed himself with what seemed an incredible ability; and slowly he smiled. "At the hour before midnight," he agreed. "A conference. Then we shall bargain."

The Sinju went blank as Nastrond broke the connection. Brewster frowned. Nastrond had smiled; an enemy who smiles is a dangerous enemy. But why? What was that disturbing thing that Nastrond knew that could make him smile in the position in which he now stood?

"Damn," said Brewster aloud, after he had turned off his own Sinju.

* * *

BREWSTER went to his room to sleep. But as he closed the door, he stopped and looked toward the couch with a flicker of annoyance crossing his face, to be erased as quickly as it had come. "Vrita," he said.

The dark girl's face grew tight. "You do not welcome my presence?"

Brewster advanced, stood beside the couch a moment looking down at her. She had apparently planned for the moment of his arrival very carefully. Even now, his mind surging with the plans of the coming hours, Brewster was forced to admit that she was disturbing. For a long moment he stared down, thinking. She saw his inner debate, but failed to recognize its nature.

"Why do you stand there? Am I not pleasing to you? Perhaps my hair is not well done…"

It might as well be now, Brewster thought. It was as good a time as any. He bent down, took her shoulders in both hands, lifted her face to his, and kissed her on the lips, forcefully, almost crushingly. Then he dropped her back, to lie gasping.

All at once hate flamed into her eyes. She leaped to her feet, screaming. She hurled herself upon him, fingers extended, clawing, scratching. Brewster grasped both wrists tightly, shook her savagely, and hurled her back on the couch.

"I know of the others," he said coldly. "Akar...Ahriman..."

For an instant startled hope flared into her eyes. "You're jealous..." she whispered.

Brewster laughed harshly. "Jealous of a harlot?"

She went icy now, and Brewster almost shuddered at what he saw in her eyes. For a moment he was puzzled. Here again was that uncomfortable feeling that another knew something he did not. All at once it was vastly disturbing. Real alarm flooded him.

She rose to her feet, crossed to the mirror and carefully rearranged her hair, straightened the flimsy transparency of her gown, and posed artfully. There seemed to be an unexplainable confidence in her; a sureness of her future course—a course with which she toyed before embarking upon it. "You know so little," she murmured. "It is a pity, for one so intelligent— and so ambitious. Ah, that ambition... If only it were founded on something substantial; on reality."

Brewster was silent. He knew that if he spoke, the secret she was implying would become a real secret by reason of his curiosity. Instead, he turned toward the door, walked deliberately toward it and threw it open. "I want to sleep," he said shortly.

"It was you who killed Akar," she said, still engaged before the mirror. There was no accusation, no emotion, in her voice. It was as though she had merely said, "It is warm today."

He snorted. "Melodrama doesn't become you, Vrita. Please go; before I throw you out."

It worked. Eyes flaming, Vrita turned to him, caution cast to the winds. "You are a fool, Krennian. Yes, I said Krennian; that's all you are. You think you are the Jev Thyle—do you believe that we are such fools? Do you think that we would bargain, when we can command?"

Brewster grinned at her tightly. "If you are babbling about Akar and his fuming stone, forget it," he advised caustically. "I took his stone away from him. He is no more Jev than your dead husband. Which is a point that nauseates me. A man is an idiot who sleeps among brambles whose scratch can become infected with filth—and thus be the death of him. No one knifes me in my sleep."

VRITA was obviously furious now. But once again the mysterious element of triumph superimposed her fury. It flooded over her now, sure and powerful. She laughed loudly at him.

"Husband!" she exclaimed. "What a dupe you are. I was no more the wife of the Jev Thyle than you are the Ho-Ghan! That was only a trick. A trick to give to you a Jev-ship that would keep you content. But it wasn't real any more than the Jev-ship that Akar thought was his. Yes, there have been many, Akar among them. It has pleased me to toy with them. Just as I have toyed with you." She laughed in his face and went on: "Jev? You think you are a Jev? Fool! There is no more Jev Thyle. Nastrond killed him, not I. True, it was my hand that held the gun, but it was Nastrond's plan. Then, when you forced your ridiculous bargain on the Jev's, he conceived the idea to bestow a worthless title and a minor flaming stone on you to keep you quiet."

"Rave on," said Brewster coldly. Inside him a real iciness was growing. Here, before his mind's eye, all his plans were crumbling. What he had written was now a worthless scrap of paper without the authority of a Jev to back it up. More than worthless because it was the statement of an enemy. In all the solar system, no enemy had more reason to be such than a man of Kren. No Jeggite would listen to his accusations— much less would the Regio himself.

She did go on, now, the dam of triumph releasing the floodwaters of enumeration. "Remember how you learned I was the wife of Thyle? Ah! Yes, you were duped. You gave the secret of making metal in return for a worthless title. Nastrond is the real Jev Thyle. You, who believed you held two Jev-ships, those of Thyle and of Ahriman, have only one, and a bit of the power of another—power that you cannot control. Remember? You know nothing of the flaming stone, except perhaps to start that which you cannot stop. And the Anzus eye... What about the method of using the Anzus? Even if you had any Anzus to use..."

"I haven't even got the Anzus," said Brewster calmly. "I destroyed it. I placed no trust in a gift of yours. You knew as well as I that it was the least useful of the five. *I* can overcome it—Even the Estannars use the Anzus. It was by no means foolproof."

Vrita lifted her eyebrows, then she laughed. "That leaves you with no power at all." She walked up to him, pressed her body tight against his, lifted her lips and kissed him warmly. Then she turned to the door. "Charity is good for the soul," she mocked. "Goodbye, *Fyavo.*"

"Just a minute," Brewster said. "I have a few things to say."

She stood with her back to the door, waiting. "Go ahead," she said with a careless toss of her head. "But make it brief. I have use for my time."

BREWSTER sat down on the couch, took a cigarette from his pack and lit it deliberately. Then he blew smoke in her direction and looked through it at her mildly curiosity-tinged features. "I just talked to Nastrond," he said casually. "Arranged a conference with him and the other Jevs and the Ho-Ghan for tonight. In fact, in a few hours, now. The proposed discussion might interest you, since you have a stake in Nastrond—the same stake, I presume, that you had in Akar, and Thyle, and myself." He paused, eyed her reaction to the insult.

She looked scornful. "You were not unwilling," she retorted.

"Back on my own world I eat ice cream," he said, "because it tastes good. You have a certain flavor, like fruit. The only trouble is that you are rotten to the core."

"Have your say," she snapped harshly. Her eyes glittered with hate now.

Brewster grinned at her. "All right. I'll make it brief. In plain words, I informed Nastrond that, as the Jev Thyle, I would call the force wall down tonight at one hour past midnight. I can do this, because I know something you obviously don't, that the Ho-Ghan is dead, murdered by the Jevs, and that the present Ho-Ghan is a fraud." He ignored her gasp of utter surprise and went on: "To insure my own safety, I arranged to have a message delivered to the Regio, ordering the force wall down if I do not emerge unharmed from the inner city."

Vrita looked at him a long moment as he stopped speaking. Then she spoke, the inferences that had followed one another in her mind emerging as words. "You *must* be a fool. You know, of course, that you will *not* leave the inner city, once you go into it. You know also that your message to the Regio will be worthless, once he knows you haven't the power to call the force wall down. And you know, too, that Nastrond knows you are not a Jev. Further, you know that I know."

Brewster carefully extinguished his cigarette by grinding it into the carpet beneath his foot. "Certainly, I know all that," he said calmly.

"Then why do you tell me of this ridiculous plan for a meeting, and of your foolish threats?"

"Don't you know?" Brewster lifted his head and stared straight into her black eyes.

"No. I don't."

He got to his feet, walked slowly toward her. "I intend to go through with the plan. In short, I intend to bluff it out."

"That's silly!" she exclaimed. "You are more of an idiot than I thought. You can't bluff anyone. Even I..."

Brewster said, "I've never killed a woman before."

Her face went ghastly white. For a startled instant her eyes met his, saw the truth in them. Then she whirled, tore at the door in an attempt to get it open and flee through it. But she was too late. He caught her shoulders, turned her around, and pinned her against the door. Her terror filled eyes glared into his, her lips writhed with a scream that would not come.

"This is war," he said. "War between my world and yours. And because my world doesn't know who's behind the eight ball, I've got to act in its name. And so, right here and now I declare war on Jegga. Unfortunately, I constitute the only Earthman on the fighting front. It's Earth or Jegga; and if you leave this room, it will be Jegga."

*   *   *

DARKNESS, and a semblance of order, the first in several days, lay over Greater Ho-Tonda like a soothing blanket. Nick Brewster piloted his own tyar low over the rooftops, heading toward the inner city and the gateway where admission was possible, operated from within. Here a gateway could be opened in the force wall, on signal.

It was still several miles to the inner city wall, just beyond which was the invisible and deadly force wall, with its constant circle of dead birds marking its boundary.

Below were the city streets, narrow and crooked here, and practically deserted except for patrols of Jeggite soldiers. Just ahead, marching rapidly down a narrow street, was a platoon of soldiers; and in their midst walked a captive. He was tall; looked like all Estannar. But suddenly Brewster dipped his tyar lower, eyes peering down intent on the captive's head. If that wasn't Joe Abbott's familiar shock of tousled hair...

Before Brewster could make certain, the soldiers halted beside a building, turned inward, vanished. Hurriedly Brewster brought his tyar down in the street, stepped out of it. He ran toward the building, which stood under the looming shadow of the great stone wall surrounding the inner city. There be stopped short, frowning. Facing him was a blank stone wall with no doorway visible anywhere in it.

He advanced, examined the wall closely, looking for cracks that might indicate a secret entrance. But there was none. Experimental pounding on the wall revealed no hollow sound. The walls were solid as Gibraltar, or very thick. Nothing here but gold stone. Brewster growled in annoyance, looked up and down the deeply shadowed narrow street.

It was quite possible that the party of guards and their prisoner could have made their way through these shadows and out of the street, while causing him to believe they had entered a doorway that it was obvious now did not exist. He shrugged and turned back to the tyar. That must have been what really happened. But had their prisoner been Abbott?

Again alert, Brewster scanned nearby streets without success. No marching soldiers were visible. More than half convinced he had been victimized by his own wishful thinking. Brewster resumed his way toward the entrance to the inner city. If there had been a prisoner, the chances were thousands to one he had been an Estannar. No prisoner as important as Joe Abbott would be dragged through the streets at night in such an unceremonious manner.

NEARING his destination now, Brewster's realization of the colossal bluff he was about to put up broke over him with growing conviction as to its million-to-one chance for failure. Jev Nastrond knew the secret. Nastrond had no reason to fear him, because he was not a Jev and in no position to carry out his threat to call the force wall down. And Nastrond would see to it that when his message reached the Regio, the truth about his status would also reach him. The least that could result would be an investigation, which would take fatal time. And time was the essence of victory for the Jeggites now.

Out in space the cat was out of the bag. The Jeggites knew now that they faced an enemy with ships—but they also knew that that enemy's hand had been forced, and that eventual victory was theirs. Only one thing could smash the Jeggite power, the smashing of the inner city, the death of the Jevs, the elimination of their amazing powers. And that would not happen unless the force wall went down before Tartullian arrived to attack.

Tonight. Just between midnight and the dawn, the attack would come. And Tartullian's fleet would come to its doom, unsuspecting, trusting in him, to lie in shattered wreckage at the foot of the force wall, just as unwary birds lay there, victims of the irresistible force that made the wall impregnable.

But if his bluff worked, the wall *would* go down. All he needed was access to the inner city, and then...

He would get in all right. Nastrond would see to that. And also, Nastrond would see that he didn't get out. But there was one factor that played in Brewster's hand—Nastrond, and the other Jevs still faced the danger that had forced them to secrecy regarding the Ho-Ghan up to now; the danger of the news leaking out, and the automatic lowering of the force wall by immutable and age-old law.

Brewster counted, too, on their doubt as to his real intentions. As yet, he was sure, they considered him no more than a rat seeking to gain what power he could by what treachery and double-dealing he could. They did not suspect the real depths of his intrigue—his alliance with Stevens; with the Estannars; with the rebel movements. Proof enough of that was Nastrond's acceptance of his denial that he had anything to do with the attack on Ulatai.

Brewster brought his tyar to earth before the entrance to the inner city and was immediately accosted by the guards. He found it unnecessary to say anything; he was instantly recognized and conducted forward. He was expected.

He was led through several doors, and finally stood in a great room, the opposite side of which was blank stone. Low in it he saw a small opening, large enough to walk through; and visible beyond was a lighted reception room. But between was a blank space. That blank space, Brewster knew, marked the force wall, extending on down into the ground.

A bell rang once and the captain of the guard motioned Brewster forward. Brewster looked at him, then shrugged and walked boldly toward the opening. He didn't hesitate as he strode into the lethal area, through it, and into the lighted room beyond. Here several more guards stood, eyeing him speculatively. Inwardly, Brewster shuddered with relief, a nervous reaction that was purely involuntary. Walking through that opening was like walking under a bucket of paint, only on a vastly more potential basis for disaster.

He was led now into the inner city, where he saw ahead of him the fantastically imposing palace of the Ho-Ghan. He made his way down the open street, which was brilliantly lit from concealed light sources. At length he reached the palace and walked up its broad marble steps.

Here a page met him, conducted him deferentially into a small, but luxuriously furnished room.

IMMEDIATELY the page had left the room, Brewster followed, peered down the corridor outside. When he was certain it was deserted for the moment, he ran cat-like toward a door on the opposite side. He opened it, stepped in, found himself in another anteroom. He left the door ajar, sat down casually in an easy chair, took his heavy pistol out of his belt and laid it across his knees. Then he waited.

In a moment the sound of footsteps came; and two guards took up their station outside the door across the hallway. Then other footsteps came—these softer as though the owner was clad in sandals. Brewster, sitting in the shadows of his own room, caught just a glimpse of the man as he passed. It was Jev Nastrond. Brewster grinned.

A few seconds of silence followed, then an angry question in Nastrond's voice. There was a flurry of excitement; running footsteps faded toward the entrance of the building. Brewster sat stiff, waiting.

The sound of the sandaled feet came again, returning, and as the owner came abreast of the doorway, Brewster called out in low tones. "Here I am, Jev Nastrond. Please come in, and don't make any fuss; I've got you covered with a primitive, but effective, weapon."

Nastrond stopped, his face flushing an angry red. But he came into the room without hesitation.

"Close the door behind you," directed Brewster. "We'll have a private conference before we proceed to our scheduled business—which I observe you had no intentions of carrying out."

Nastrond closed the door and stood eyeing Brewster warily. "You have a flair for intrigue and drama," he observed coldly. "Also a rather erratic imagination. What is all this child's play?"

"You mean switching reception rooms?" Brewster grinned mirthlessly. "I didn't like the upholstery in that other place. Besides, I don't want to talk in any antechamber. Our business is around the council table—with *everybody* present."

"Exactly," snapped Nastrond. "And now, if you don't mind, we'll proceed to the conference as was intended."

"But not under armed escort," corrected Brewster. "Remember, I hold all the aces. If I don't come out of here unharmed, the force wall will go down for a year. I can imagine you have an idea of what will happen once that news gets out. From nameless sources, I've learned that you have reason to fear certain elements which could conceivably get past even the Jeggite war fleet."

Nastrond laughed nastily. "Yes," and he repeated Brewster's words, "you hold all the aces. And we fully expect you to play them."

Brewster waved his pistol; Nastrond led the way from the room and down the corridor. After a seemingly endless passage through a complex maze of rooms, they entered a large one, vastly more splendid than all the rest. Incredibly beautiful paintings hung on the walls, the most magnificent Brewster had ever seen. Marble mosaics made up the floor and walls, an intricate design so painstakingly laid that it must have taken years to complete. The design was such that it automatically led the eye to an ornately carved door, which seemed to be cut from a single opaque, cloudy blue crystal. Brewster's eyes fastened on it momentarily, then he shifted his gaze to the three men who now stood facing him silently, waiting for him to speak.

"No deal, gentlemen," he said easily.

The Jev, Azevedro, spoke. "No deal? What do you mean?"

"Just that there's one missing," said Brewster. "This is between us all. We'll begin when the party's full up."

"Don't be a fool," said Jev Eblis. "You know as well as any that Ahriman has been missing for many days. No one knows where he is."

"No one?" Brewster's glance fell only casually on Nastrond, then swept on to Azevedro, and back to Eblis. The glance had been enough. Jev Nastrond did know of the death of Ahriman. And he also knew who had killed him. There was a sardonic gleam in his eye that he was at no pains to conceal. But could it be true the other two *didn't* know? Brewster would have sworn it was so. Brewster went on. "Let's skip that. I am not referring to Ahriman. He is unimportant. I am referring to the Ho-Ghan. Where is he?"

OUTWARDLY Brewster was calm, but inwardly he was seething with tension. Who was the new Ho-Ghan? That was the question that he had been unable to answer through all of his deductions. And somehow, he sensed that in the answer to that question lay a great deal of significance. Certainly the Ho-Ghan was no puppet. He was a person high in Jeggite circles. And here, now he was gambling much on the mysterious Ho-Ghan's identity. Would his bluff work? Would the Ho-Ghan come forward? Brewster counted on the cupidity of his enemies; and on their curiosity. Certainly these Jevs were not so foolish as to underestimate an enemy—or even a rival, if they supposed him as such—to the extent of being so careless as to pass up learning his plan, no matter what they planned to do about him afterward.

These Jevs were one with the new Ho-Ghan, that he knew. There could be no duplicity nor secrecy between them. Such an empire as the Jegga Empire could not have been built on constant treachery and double-dealing. And because of that Brewster felt sure that a simple demand would bring forth the one person in all this set-up he wanted to see. The one person he *had* to see!

Because of what lay back in his apartment, they could not know that he knew what they thought he didn't—that his power was nil. All the cards, apparently, were stacked in their favor. They could not suspect his real reason for demanding that the Ho-Ghan be present—that he had any reason other than simply a desire to arrogantly put on the screws just as a matter of throwing his weight around…

Azevedro spoke up angrily. "Keep your place, Jev Thyle. You have come here to dicker. Such trivial matters need be brought to the attention of the Ho-Chan only when…"

"Wait," Nastrond's sharp voice cut into the sentence like a knife. "All right, Brewster. If you would see the Ho-Ghan, then *look*."

Swiftly, as Brewster stood with a frown of incomprehension that gradually blackened into anger, Nastrond strode to a cabinet, drew forth a long robe, a mask with a peaked top, and threw it over himself. Then he turned to face Brewster. "Behold the Ho-Ghan!" he cried.

Brewster laughed in his face. "You fool your companions more than you do me," he said. "That's a gag that won't go, Nastrond, I know better than that. And so do your two companions. Just look at the jealousy in Azevedro's eyes. And the surprise in Eblis'. First, Nastrond, you aren't tall enough. Remember, I saw the new Ho-Ghan at the reception; and remember, too, that you stood at my side at the time. The man who sat in the throne was no stooge—you wouldn't risk that. He's a man as important in all this as you! Come on, Nastrond, cut out the kidding."

The three Jevs stood stock-still. Then Nastrond spoke. "You are right, Brewster. We'll make a deal with you. What do you want?" As he spoke he moved back a few paces. Brewster leaped instantly toward the crystal door, stood with his back against it. His pistol appeared in his hand, covering the three in the room.

"I want to see the Ho-Ghan," he said. "Right now. Open the door, Nastrond, or I'll kill you all where you stand and blast it in myself!"

Azevedro's face flamed, and he reached for his belt, at the same time stepping forward.

"Stop," barked Nastrond. "Let him go, Azevedro. Let him go in." He crossed to a wall, pressed a hidden lever. Behind Brewster there was the sigh of air, and he sensed that the door was ajar. He turned toward it. But as he did so, Nastrond's hand streaked for his belt beneath his borrowed Ho-Ghan robe. Then, before Brewster could whip his gun up, a flash of flame came from Jev Elbis, and Nastrond toppled to the floor with a ghastly scream of agony.

Moving swiftly, even in his astonishment, Brewster sent a slug crashing into the brain of the forward-plunging Azevedro. He cast one startled glance at Jev Eblis, who was smiling oddly, then the outer door crashed in and Brewster leaped through the crystal door as a swarm of guards entered. He slammed the door shut behind him. Oddly they did not follow.

BREWSTER had no time to debate on the inexplicable action of Jev Eblis. For standing before him was a tall figure clad in a snow-white robe, his face covered by the tall peaked headgear that Brewster had seen in the reception hall on the only other occasion he had viewed the false Ho-Ghan.

"We meet at last," said Brewster, still holding his gun level, its barrel trained directly on the tall figure. "I've been wondering for a long time about you."

The Ho-Ghan remained silent, standing motionless, apparently unperturbed by Brewster's advent. The only sign of emotion might have been the rapid rising and falling of his breast as he breathed.

Now that he confronted the false Ho-Ghan, Brewster was not anxious to strip his mask from his face; rather he stood with eyes intent, roving his gaze up and down the Ho-Ghan's tall, almost slim figure. Tall as himself was this imposter, and with an erect, unfaltering carriage. Brewster's deductions strove to pierce the mask, to guess the man's identity. He failed. And still the man remained silent. Brewster could sense his dark eyes, behind the mask, returning his scrutiny.

"Somehow," Brewster said, "I've got a lot of respect for you. And just on a guess, something just happened behind this door—maybe you heard the commotion out there just before—that makes your part in this just a little deeper than I figured. It's too bad it has to end."

Still no answer from the hooded figure. Brewster smiled grimly. All right, it suited him. There'd be some real drama in this unmasking. "Where's your Sinju?" he asked. "We're going to do a little calling."

The tall figure turned slightly, indicating the instrument at one side of the room. Brewster nodded and strode over to it. He laid a hand on the control switch, then paused to face the Ho-Ghan.

"Before we begin, I might as well tell you what this is all about. In brief, your game is up. And Jegga's game is up. With the help of a man named Stevens, perhaps the greatest hero the Earth has ever known, the age-old dream of Jev is going to be shattered. Earth, or Kren, will never become the slave of Jegga; and further, Estannar and Boron and all the other worlds will be free. No longer will Jegga rule. Here, tonight, in the inner city, the power of Jegga will be smashed. And do you know what will smash it?" Brewster paused suggestively, smiled grimly, toyed with the gun in his hand. "One little bullet," he said softly. "One little piece of lead from this primitive weapon of mine. A weapon that pales to insignificance besides your own, but curiously, wrought of the one thing that has kept the dream of Jev from becoming a reality ever since that dead day when he killed himself in insane frustration on the surface of Boron, the world he longed to conquer plainly visible, but ever unattainable, just above him. It's ironic, isn't it, oh Ho-Ghan?"

There was a long moment of silence while the two looked at each other. Then Brewster went on. "One little bullet; and with your death, in plain view of the Regio, the force wall comes down. The only thing he doesn't know is that when it does come down, a man named Tartullian will lead an Estannar fleet to attack and destroy the inner city, and with it the defenses of the outer city. Jegga will fall, and the slave worlds will be free."

Brewster's fingers tightened on the Sinju switch and he leveled the gun. Then he stood there frozen, the blood draining from his face in sudden shock. For the Ho-Ghan had thrown off his mask with one motion and stood revealed before him. And a soft, musical voice came to his stunned ears: "Would you kill me, Nick Brewster?"

"*Suba*," Brewster's voice came hoarsely from his lips. "*Suba Marannes...* Oh, my God..."

CHAPTER TWELVE

THE girl's face was pale. "At last you are on our side, Nick Brewster," she said. "But what is this about Tartullian?"

Brewster returned his gun slowly to his belt, advanced toward her, still dazed by the unexpected shock of the revelation. "I can't believe it," he whispered. "How can it be possible? You, an Estannar, the false Ho-Ghan! It's *impossible!*"

"Impossible? For a *bheynor?*" she asked.

"You? A *bheynor?*"

She nodded. "Yes. And my grandfather too. What about him; what happened out there?" She indicated the door.

Brewster looked bewildered. "I don't get you. Your grandfather? There are no Estannars out there."

"The Jev Eblis," she said impatiently. "Is he all right?"

Brewster looked at her silently for a second, then he nodded his head. "I begin to see, slightly," he said. "Yes, Eblis is all right. In fact, he killed Nastrond, and I took care of Azevedro. Eblis didn't follow me, and I gather he had something to do with the guards not following. In fact, it seems to me he led them off somewhere else."

"*The plan*," she breathed. "He's gone to put it into execution. The Konos in the city—and the Estannars. The prisons will be opened. There will be battle in the streets. The rocket of Eblis has become a weapon."

"Wait a minute," Brewster halted her. "Let's sit down and get this clear in my mind. What's going on? How did you get here? How did you get to be the Ho-Ghan? Were you the Ho-Ghan that night at the reception? How did your grandfather get to be the Jev Eblis? And a million other things…"

Suba smiled, but there was anxiety in her smile. "Yes, of course, but quickly. There are things you must tell me, too. There is much work for us to do… The story is long, so I will give you only the high points. It began long ago. You realize now that I am happy. That I've been working for the Estannar cause for years.

"Our methods had to be complicated, by necessity, and although I could lie, being a *bheynor,* many others of our agents could not. So they could know only their particular phase of all plots, so that their capture would not give away the ramifications of the plan, nor endanger their companions. Still, messengers had to be gotten through. I was the means of that."

"How?" Brewster was puzzled.

"Very simple. Every time a messenger came, I married him. Then, when it was time to go back, I divorced him. You see, as an Estannar, he could never have gotten by the Jeggites. By marrying me, whose reputation as that sort of a woman had been carefully built up, the Jeggites never suspected the truth—nor could they refuse entry to the city of my husband. My grandfather was twice decorated by the Regio for distinguished service to Jegga. He was a trusted man."

Brewster was smiling. "That's wonderful!" he said. For an instant Suba looked at him, then she went on hurriedly. He interrupted her. "About you're not really being married, I mean," he persisted. Their eyes met, then she went on without further interruption, but he continued to smile.

"TWO of the Jevs were killed, and my grandfather took the place of one of them. That was how it came about that I became the Ho-Ghan. Remember that night in the palace, when the Ho-Ghan was killed? Remember how, later, I left you before we entered the ballroom. It was then that I took my place as the new Ho-Ghan, without even the knowledge of the other Jevs. Actually, another false Ho-Ghan was placed there by the Jevs, but he lived no more than a few minutes after he donned the robe. His body was yet burning as I sat on the throne.

"I have been here ever since. Except for the time you saw me at the burning of the Marannes section of the Estannar quarter. Many wondered, then, where my grandfather was. None could have suspected he was acting as the double of the Jev whose place he had taken. No one would have suspected he could accomplish this feat, because no one knew he was a *bheynor*. Now he has gone to release the Estannars and arm them, together with the remaining Konos with new weapons he devised from the Eblis rocket. They are powerful weapons, easily comparable to the green ray of Nastrond. With them we stand a chance in the outer city."

Brewster sat calmly for a moment. "But not much of a chance," he said. "Perhaps a momentary victory, then disaster when the Jeggite fleet attacks in force. Only by capturing the inner city could they hope to win."

"That is impossible," said Suba. "The Regio's troops guard the entrance, and besides, the entrance will become one with the whole force wall at the least sign of trouble—and none but the Jev's and the Regio could open it again. My grandfather, unfortunately, does not know that secret. And once he leaves the city, his masquerade will be over, and he cannot return."

Brewster's face was pale now. "You mean we can't get out of here?"

She shook her head. "Not while the force wall is up. And now there will be no chance to get it down."

"And Tartullian's fleet will be utterly destroyed by the force wall when he attacks," groaned Brewster.

"Come," said Suba. "Let's go up onto the roof gardens. Perhaps we can signal them from there."

Brewster followed her, his heart lead in his breast. He knew that it was hopeless. Tartullian's fleet would come in like lightning, staking all in one smash. His complete success depended on his speed and power. Once he gained the inner city, and the outer city with its defense ray, he could fight off the Jeggite fleet, and be master of the situation. But he would be coming in expecting the force wall to be down. And before he knew that it was not down, his fleet would be dying in crushed wreckage at the walls foot, just as those dead birds lay there, victims of a force they could not see or understand.

There was one answer. His hand went to his breast...

ONCE on the roof, they could see far over the city, and now, as they watched, they could see that fighting was beginning. Tiny figures were running through the streets, attacking the giant ray stations, and one by one they became the center of flashing maelstroms of green rays and red flames.

Suba looked for a while, then buried her head in her hands. "All for nothing," she moaned bitterly.

Brewster took her by the shoulders and lifted her up. "Suba, darling," he whispered. "I had hoped there would be something else for us. But this is something that is beyond even my imagination. Before I say another word, I want to tell you that I love you. And before we proceed to make an emotional mess of it, I want to tell you what I'm going to do." He turned and stared down at the turmoil in the outer city. He waved a hand outward. "Just how much does that mean to you?"

"Everything," she said tragically.

"Even your life?"

Slowly her eyes turned until they stared into his. "What do you mean?"

"Are you willing to die so that all that will not be for nothing?"

"Need I answer?" she asked.

For an instant he considered her tear-streaked face, then he shook his head. "No, I don't. Then, here's the answer..." He fumbled at his breast and in an instant the flaming jewel of Thyle lay cupped in his palm. He added another, smaller jewel from its pouch in his tunic, then stood there, gazing down at the beautiful flame of them. "I know how to start their action, but not how to stop it," he said reflectively.

For a long time there was silence on the balcony of the roof garden, then Suba Marannes spoke. "Start it," she said simply.

He looked out over the city. "The force wall will stop it. Nothing can pass through that, not even the intelligent fire. But everything inside will be utterly destroyed. When Tartullian arrives, he will find this inner city and all its weapons and the city's defenses a mass of flame. It is the only way to stop him from attacking it and destroying himself."

HE HELD the shimmering stone in his palm, his fingers caught the flame, coaxed it forth. Then, with a quick motion, he tossed it over the rail, to fall in a shower of coruscating sparks to the courtyard below. The other stone he carried to the opposite side of the roof and hurled it into the darkness as he had the first. Down below, now, with incredible swiftness the flame grew, hissing with a loudness that rapidly assumed terrifying proportions.

"Death by the fire of the living stone is so clean," whispered Suba, staring down at the holocaust that was growing instant by instant. Already a smaller building collapsed in a rush of brilliant sparkling fire. Suba turned to Brewster and looked up into his face. Then she leaned forward and kissed him long and tenderly on the lips. Just once. He returned the kiss, and they stood looking at each other silently. "No dramatic emotions," she said.

He nodded. "Somehow they seem a sign of weakness."

"And weakness isn't in your makeup, is it?" Suba said. It wasn't really a question; more an admission of a fact.

But Brewster wasn't paying any attention to her now. His gaze was fixed on the courtyard below, where the small building had collapsed. Down there a man's figure was running, toward the outer wall.

"Abbott!" bellowed Brewster in an amazed shout. *"Joe Abbott!"* Even above the hiss of the flames his voice carried like that of ancient Stentor. Abbott heard it, stopped in his tracks and stared around bewilderedly. Brewster yelled again. This time Abbott looked up. The shock and surprise in his stance was patently evident. He looked up, then looked around at the flames again, constantly growing in violence, but without any smoke or fumes.

He waved an arm desperately at Brewster. It was obvious what he wanted.

"He wants us to come down," said Suba.

"It looks as though he knows something we don't," agreed Brewster. "He was running for some place. And not long ago I saw him do a vanishing stunt very similar to what he'd have to do now, judging from the blank wall he was heading for."

Without another word Suba led the way down from the roof garden. In a few moments they were running down the street toward the waiting Joe Abbott, who was critically gauging the advancing wall of flames. Behind them, a portion of the palace crumbled. Toward the opposite end of the inner city, where the exit through the force wall lay, many Jeggites were running. Some of them were too late, and they could be seen trapped behind a wall of flames that advanced rapidly, cutting off their escape.

"Hurry!" yelled Abbott. "This way. I know a way out!"

Brewster and Suba reached him, and Brewster clutched Abbott's hand warmly for an instant before they all ran in the direction Abbott had originally been heading. As they ran, Abbott panted out: "How'd you get here, Nick? And what's Suba doing in that get-up?"

Brewster grinned. "Believe it or not, my boy, *she's* the Ho-Ghan."

Abbott gaped, faltered in his stride, then went on, gasping.

"It was as big a shock to me when I found it out," said Brewster. "But what's important now is that we get out of here. I'll tell you the rest later."

"How in hell did this fire get started?" asked Abbott, looking back with apprehension at the wall of flames roaring down on them. "Man, this will burn the whole inner city out like tissue paper."

"I started it," Brewster said. "It was the only way to save the day for the Estannar fleet under Tartullian..."

"YOU know about that?" exclaimed Abbott. And almost in the same breath: *"You* started *this?"*

"Don't get confused," said Brewster. "I'm on the right side. Always have been. But I had to know first what the big plan was. Stevens had one, and the Estannars had one, and they weren't getting together any too well. I had plans to call the force wall down, but that got knocked into a cocked hat. There was only one thing to do, burn the city out..."

"And yourselves along with it," interrupted Abbott. They had reached the wall now, and Abbott's fingers roved over it, found a rocky protuberance, and pressed it. A section of the wall sank back. They went inside.

"Yes. Because in less than an hour, maybe minutes, Tartullian's fleet will attack with all it's got—straight for the inner city, thinking the force wall is down..."

"No!" exclaimed Abbott. "For God's sake, no!"

"The fire'll stop him, if he doesn't get here too soon. If the whole inner city is a mass of flames, he'll have sense enough not to waste time on it. He'll proceed to section two of his plan, and go after the outer city defenses."

"They'll be tough to crack."

"They're already being cracked," said Brewster. "We saw it from the roof. The Estannars have been released and armed. Don't ask me how—that's a long story, and I don't understand all the angles myself, yet. But Suba, here, can explain it all. It's her grandfather, more recently the Jev Eblis."

Behind them a roar of flame cut off his voice for an instant, and Abbott shouted, "I don't know how to cut off that stone door. I have to leave it open. But further on we pass through the force wall and I can close that. This is a secret entrance Nastrond knew about. I don't think even the Ho-Ghan knew it existed. He had me brought in for some reason not more than an hour or so ago."

"I saw you," said Brewster. "And I can give the reason. But I got to the outer wall and you'd vanished as though the earth had swallowed you up."

The noise was terrific now; and the tunnel through which they were passing amplified it. After a hundred more yards, in which the heat grew more terrific by the second, Brewster began gasping. Ahead of him Suba faltered, would have fallen. He caught her.

"The oxygen…" he panted. "It's going fast—being sucked out by that damned flame. How much farther, Joe…?"

"Here," came Abbott's voice, almost as though he were answering, although Brewster realized he hadn't heard a word Brewster had said. Even Abbott's triumphant yell had came to him only as a whisper.

Abbott pushed Brewster ahead, then followed. A few yards farther, and as though it had been cut off with a knife, the roar of flames ceased. They were in total darkness.

"I never want to run a gauntlet like that again!" Abbott's voice came fervently, sounding startlingly loud in the silence. He lowered his tone a bit when next he spoke. "We're okay now, Nick. It's a few hundred feet to the other stone door. Then we'll be in the street."

"Let's go," said Brewster. "I've a hunch we're going to be needed out there. There's fighting to do."

"That's for me!" exclaimed Abbott. "I've been itching to get my hands on some Jeggite throats for ages now."

BREWSTER put Suba on her feet. "You're going to stay right in here," he said. "Nothing can happen to you behind these walls. And right now, I don't want anything to happen to you. We've got important matters to discuss after this is over…"

"Nothing doing…about staying in here, I mean," she said. "I'm the next in line in command among the Ho-Tonda Estannars, and if anything should happen to Grandfather, I'll have to take over. I'm going out there with you both."

"You'll have to let her come," said Abbott. "She'll only follow. I know these Estannar women, believe me."

Brewster grinned. "I didn't expect her to stay," he said. "It was just my way of saying I think a lot of her. But come on, let's get going. If my ears don't play me false, there's hell beginning to pop out there!"

*   *   *

HELL had begun to pop. There was no doubt of it when they stepped into the street. High in the heavens over Ho-Tonda a vast fleet of warships wheeled and rushed in battle. And everywhere ships were falling; both Estannars and Jeggite. But as they watched, it was evident that the proportion was three to one on the red side of the Jeggite ledger.

On a rooftop nearby a group of Jeggites were preparing to put a green flame cannon into operation. Even as they watched, its first bolt shot skyward and an Estannar ship fluttered like a broken leaf; came down out of control.

Brewster took his pistol from his belt and with six deliberately spaced shots, picked off the entire crew. The sound of his shots was lost in the roar of battle, and the absence of any flame streak gave the gunners no clue as to what was striking them down.

Abbott whooped with joy. "Got another of those cannons?"

Brewster grinned, pulled out the other one and thrust it in Abbott's fist. He also whipped a belt of cartridges from beneath his robe and Abbott strapped it on. Then Abbott plunged down the street in search of something to shoot at.

* * *

THE next few hours were a maelstrom of action that culminated finally in the exhausting of Brewster's ammunition. They found themselves in a large square, not far from the former Estannar quarter, which was still blacked with fire. Other sections of the city were aflame now, and the sounds of battle were diminishing. A large Estannar ship landed in the square, and troops poured out, took up stations all around. Two figures emerged from the ship.

"Rogofsky!" yelled Brewster.

"Tartullian!" exclaimed Suba Marannes.

The little spaceman rushed forward, clasped Brewster's hand and pumped it up and down. "You old son-of-a-gun," he babbled. "You pulled the trick after all, didn't you? Even better, you beat us to the punch and burned that inner city joint out! We Earthmen did all the invasion navigating..."

Brewster grinned. "Wrong, Rogofsky. The force wall's still up. I couldn't call it down. You see I'm not a Jev at all..."

But Rogofsky's face had gone sickly pale. "You mean...Lord! The only reason we didn't dive in was the fire. No use attacking something that's already burned out. Thanks, Brewster! You never did a better job of playing with matches."

Tartullian advanced and shook Brewster's hand. He was an old man with white hair, but his face was young. And now it was wreathed with triumph and the realization of a lifetime dream. "We've won, *Fyavo*," he said. "Ho-Tonda is ours, and most of the battle fleet of Jegga is smashed. The master world is no longer master."

Brewster grinned. "I wonder how I'm going to tell them how lucky they are back in Brooklyn. Nobody'll believe me." He turned to Suba. "One more thing, Suba. Take me to the nearest telescope."

"Telescope?" she was mystified. "What do you want with a telescope?"

"I just want to show you something." Brewster turned to Tartullian. "How about a company of men to guard us, while we go?"

The question in Suba Maranne's face never left it, but she led the way through the city to a building whose top was the familiar dome of an observatory. They entered and when they reached the telescope, they found an old man sitting calmly studying a book of star maps.

"We want to take a look at Kren," said Brewster. "I'll show you where when you've got it in the screen."

The old astronomer got to his feet, and in a few moments the familiar globe of Earth lay glowingly green on the screen. It grew rapidly larger, until finally only the North American continent was visible. Once more Brewster saw that peculiar shifting phenomenon that brought patches of the surface into startling magnification. He took over the instrument himself, and the scene on the screen moved until the eastern seaboard of the United States came into view. Then, more delicately, he maneuvered until the scene on the screen showed a broad river, and across it a giant bridge. Brooklyn bridge.

"There," said Brewster, taking Suba by the arm. "That's where we're going. Just as soon as we can get the metal works at Ulatai back into operation. That's Brooklyn, your new home." He looked at her. "Okay?"

She looked at the screen, then turned to smile at him. "Okay," she said.

THE END

NOTES ON
The Introduction to the Civilization of the Empire of Jegga

By Raymond A. Palmer

The Introduction to the Civilization of the Empire of Jegga was as complete a compendium as any of the Earthmen could have wished. It not only gave illuminating accounts of the history of Jegga, but of its customs and language, and of the interplanetary system as well. It seemed to answer everything; even the dead birds that Brewster had seen within the wall of the inner city were explained, and the explanation turned out to be simple indeed. The inner city had been built to protect the life of the Ho-Ghan, and just as there were walls and warriors to defend it on land, there were walls of *force*, invisible and unexplained, that kept the skies above the inner city inviolate. Anything that came in contact with these walls, either from above or below, was killed by the force, though the wall could not be penetrated. These same force walls were in effect on the ground, sheltering the inner city, but the walls of masonry and the warriors who guarded them were added for purposes connected with tradition and grandeur.

The force walls were the invention of the Lyrio dynasty, and to it the dynasty owed its existence. It was a secret passed on from generation to generation, though occasionally, when a Ho-Ghan was banished and his rule taken away, and a new member of the Lyric dynasty elevated to Ho-Ghan, the force-walls were discontinued for a year, to demonstrate that the Ho-Ghan ruled by agreement of the Jevs, as well as his own power. The person of the Ho-Ghan was sacred and inviolate. He might be banished but never killed, never, in fact, touched.

As the Ho-Ghan was inviolate, so too were the Jevs. The title Jev itself came from the name of the greatest Jeggite warrior in history, the one who had commanded the armies that first conquered the universe. And as the dynasty of Ho-Ghans owed their eminence to their force walls, so too did each of the five Jevs owe their position to some invention of an ancestor, and the title and its secret was handed down through the years. To these inventions and secrets the Empire itself owed its security and existence, which accounted for the Imperial hexagon. The force walls were deemed the greatest because they alone provided the impregnable defense. Without it, no weapon, no knowledge, could continue to dominate.

The five Jevs were of equal rank. The Jev Azevedo was known by his symbol of star-fields, for the first Azevedo was the one who had devised the secret of celestial navigation, who had constructed the great navigating boards that were still in use. Their construction was secret, and kept by the Azevedo family. No navigation board could be opened without wrecking it. No navigation was possible without it, unless for short distances—but the Empire was vast.

The Jev Eblis was known by his symbol of the fiery rocket. The original Eblis had lived thousands of years before, preceding even Azevedo, and he had invented the rocket ship, and its means of propulsion, so powerful that interplanetary commerce became possible.

The Jev Nastrond was known by his symbol of green bolts. His was the weapon that had made conquest possible. Since the first Nastrond, his descendants had perfected other weapons, all based on the same principle, the heat ray. It was used in small weapons and large, as automatic rayguard and many other ways. Every derivative of the Nastrond Ray was made by the Jev Nastrond and his family.

Supporting the Nastrond Ray was the Jev Thyle's Flaming Stone. It was as strange and inexplicable a phenomenon as the Jev Ahriman's Anzus, for it was more than a weapon; it was a natural force. The Flaming Stone was the symbol for the Jev's control of *intelligent fire*. Against this fire only the force walls were impregnable. The fire could devour anything, organic and inorganic, for it was a living thing in its own right and needed no fuel for its existence. Or so it was believed, for the Jev Thyle had said so and there were none to dispute him. The fire could be directed and controlled perfectly. It could, for instance, eat in a straight line, or to a predetermined point, and nothing could put it out except a secret knowledge, which only controlled it. But it was used also as a guard. For example, on Boron, the Earth's Moon, it served as illumination for landing fields, but also because its strange light could illuminate Borons without illuminating anything else. In the years following the conquest, when the Estannars began using Borons as their warriors, in the years when all the system waited for the first Earthmen to come, the fire became incalculably valuable. It was universally symbolized as a flaming stone, demonstrating its power, and was kept in jewels and stone bowls. The original flame was believed to be still in the possession of the Jev Thyle.

The Jev Ahriman's Anzus was a formless animal. It had at least a hundred eyes, usually more, and these eyes, properly controlled, had hypnotic power. The range of this power depended on the size of the animal and the focus of its eyes. An Anzus with two hundred eyes could hold more than a thousand men, dictating their thoughts and actions, directing their will. But the Anzus could be cut up so small that it was only the size of an eye. The eyes could hold men as far as a bright beam of light of 1000 *dures* (or some 5000 candlepower) could be seen, but if it could be seen, seeing it was not dependent on volition, for it could travel, unlike light, through closed eyes. In effect, it was a transmitter of the thoughts of those who controlled it. There were believed to be countless thousands of them in the possession of the Jev Ahriman, and it was probably the most secret. But it had its limitations. In space its eyes could be seen, or felt, for fabulous distances, but the ships of the Jev Nastrond were known to be impervious to it, and it was believed he had used the Nastrond Ray in some new way to overcome it. Moreover, for some reason it would not live long away from Jegga, though it had first come from Phylades. It was, when large enough, very cumbersome and difficult to move, with no method of locomotion except by means of pseudopods, and if it had to move it often rolled over its own eyes, blinding itself. It had a distinctive characteristic odor, moreover, which was not pleasant, and which sometimes could be smelled, if several were together, farther than its effects could be felt.

These were the Jevs. There had been others, but their titles were lost in antiquity, or their secrets had been fathomed and their right to the title of Jev stolen and made common property. For the Jevs owed their positions to their might to their lack of continued defense against each and their consequent interdependence. Each had his army, his warships, his domain, but since their power to govern was superseded by the Regios, the boundaries of these domains were fairly tenuous.

The Regios governed by virtue of a decree from the Ho-Ghan. They were supreme in their regios, or domains. They were appointed for life, and their office could not be inherited, though frequently the Ho-Ghan would appoint a descendant of a previous Regio. The Regios had their own armies, known as the *Regiis,* or, in Ho-Tonda, as the Argyres, and the name Argyre spread until all the armies of the Regios were known by it. Of all the armies of the Empire, only the Argyres possessed all the weapons of the Jevs—but none of their secrets. The weapons were only lent to them to enforce civil law, and as tokens of the Jev's loyalty to the Ho-Ghan and their subservience to the Regios.

Of the extent of the Empire itself, and of its nature, much was said. The most recent census had counted more than two thousand heavenly bodies in the Empire. Though most of these had been uninhabited during the centuries of conquest, they were later settled by various peoples of the System. There were several chapters outlining the hardships of life on some of these bodies, and the amazing nature of compensations that the Jeggite scientists had developed to make life on these bodies possible. They had, for instance, had to irrigate, to produce oxygen, to prevent the continued splitting of some planetoids, to duplicate comfortable gravity levels, equalize air pressure, and so on. Here too was to be found a survey of the nature of interplanetary commerce, listing some five or six thousand different articles of manufacture, chemicals, vegetation, and other things.

Included also were several essays of a philosophical nature, examining the phenomenon of life in the universe. Life had been found on all of the other eight planets of the universe, Earth alone excepted from the Empire. Not only was this Life more or less intelligent, but, within certain limitations, it was similar, at least in its dominant form. For while there was a bewildering variety of interplanetary life, with creatures of every size, shape and description, the ascendant form was more or less alike. The colors of their skins might be different, or the ears pointed or longer, or the chests larger, but basically they were alike. And this, said scientists, showed that Nature repeated a pattern, and this pattern had everywhere proved superior to the other patterns of Life. Some went further, to the history of the Sun and the planets, but their arguments were theoretical. The essential sameness of dominant Life throughout the System was demonstrated by the fact that inter-marriage and inter-breeding was possible among all of them, and, in fact, there were countless numbers of variously interbred peoples along with the pure types.

The Regios governed as follows: One Regio for *Jegga,* or Mars; one Regio for *Estannar,* or Venus; one Regio for *Usau,* or Mercury, and *Hruthes,* or Uranus; one Regio for *Ermos,* or Saturn, and *Darziz,* or Pluto; one Regio for *Ania,* or Neptune, and *Phylades,* or Jupiter. In addition, *Boron,* the Moon of *Kren,* or Earth, was governed by the Regio of Estannar. The rest of the Empire was colonial, split among the Regios, and administered by a great many vice-regios and minor officials.

There followed several chapters describing the physical and intellectual characteristics of the various races. Aside from such frank statements as those which referred to the brute strength of the Phyladians, or the stupidity of the Hruthians (though they were docile and good natured) and the ugliness of the Ermosians (which caused them to be barred from most public places), there were accounts of the virtues and vices of the Jeggites and Estannars. Both were admittedly the most intelligent, but the Estannars were said to be without true inventiveness, without organizational ability, undisciplined, stubborn, and worst of all, effete.   But, withal, they were often charming, witty, talented, and frequently rose above their inherent weaknesses.   The Jeggites were strong, inventive, highly disciplined, natural leaders and governors, imaginative, and with little patience for weakness or inefficiency or stupidity.

The end of the volume concerned itself with history and law. Curiously, there were several essays that claimed the Chinese people of the Earth had originally come from the Earth's Moon. Actually, they were Jeggites who had, countless centuries before, gone to the Moon on their way to the Earth. All their attempts failed, and through the years a quarrel among them developed which split them into factions. These factions then attempted, individually, to reach the Earth. Finally one such faction did break through, landing in Asia, as Earthmen called it. But the entire faction went together and none ever returned, and the secret was gone with them. In time these people populated parts of Asia, and thousands of years later they produced the geniuses of the Jenghiz Khan, who was followed in six generations by the great Kubla Khan. The evidences of the same racial inheritance showed, however, in the similarity of many of their names and cities, and, in fact, the palace of Kubla Khan was a smaller replica of the palace of the Jeggite Ho-Ghans. And the symbol of modern China was still the Moon.

Going back further than that were accounts of early life on Jegga, how it had overcome its aridity with the genius of its canal builders, how the canals had influenced its early civilization. At first they had traveled along these waterways, developing vessels of great speed, which were still used in modern times.   So too, the great cities of Jegga were still on the waterways, and though they no longer served their original purpose, they reminded Jeggites that these canals, with their red water, had been the arteries and life-blood of early Jegga. For this reason, the color of the Emperor was red.

Last was a catalogue of law—the laws of the colonies, of the various planets, of the Regios, of military law, and of the Ho-Ghan. Here were the laws of superiority and inferiority, worked out like tables of equality, so that, for instance, the same act performed by a Hruthian and a Darzizt was, on the one hand, a crime, while for the other it was a legal act. These laws filled fifty pages of fine print and concerned everything from property to ethics.

There was also an appendix that listed many common phrases in Jeggian and their translation, and a great map of Jegga. *—Raymond A. Palmer*

If you've enjoyed this book, you will not want to miss these terrific titles...

ARMCHAIR SCI-FI, FANTASY, & HORROR DOUBLE NOVELS, $12.95 each

D-1   **THE GALAXY RAIDERS** by William P. McGivern
             SPACE STATION #1 by Frank Belknap Long

D-2   **THE PROGRAMMED PEOPLE** by Jack Sharkey
             SLAVES OF THE CRYSTAL BRAIN by William Carter Sawtelle

D-3   **YOU'RE ALL ALONE** by Fritz Leiber
             THE LIQUID MAN by Bernard C. Gilford

D-4   **CITADEL OF THE STAR LORDS** by Edmond Hamilton
             VOYAGE TO ETERNITY by Milton Lesser

D-5   **IRON MEN OF VENUS** by Don Wilcox
             THE MAN WITH ABSOLUTE MOTION by Noel Loomis

D-6   **WHO SOWS THE WIND...** by Rog Phillips
             THE PUZZLE PLANET by Robert A. W. Lowndes

D-7   **PLANET OF DREAD** by Murray Leinster
             TWICE UPON A TIME by Charles L. Fontenay

D-8   **THE TERROR OUT OF SPACE** by Dwight V. Swain
             QUEST OF THE GOLDEN APE by Ivar Jorgensen and Adam Chase

D-9   **SECRET OF MARRACOTT DEEP** by Henry Slesar
             PAWN OF THE BLACK FLEET by Mark Clifton.

D-10   **BEYOND THE RINGS OF SATURN** by Robert Moore Williams
             A MAN OBSESSED by Alan E. Nourse

ARMCHAIR SCIENCE FICTION CLASSICS, $12.95 each

C-1   **THE GREEN MAN**
             by Harold M. Sherman

C-2   **A TRACE OF MEMORY**
             By Keith Laumer

C-3   **INTO PLUTONIAN DEPTHS**
             by Stanton A. Coblentz

ARMCHAIR MASTERS OF SCIENCE FICTION SERIES, $16.95 each

M-1   **MASTERS OF SCIENCE FICTION, Vol. One**
             Bryce Walton—"Dark of the Moon" and other tales

M-2   **MASTERS OF SCIENCE FICTION, Vol. Two**
             Jerome Bixby: "One Way Street" and other tales

If you've enjoyed this book, you will not want to miss these terrific titles...

ARMCHAIR SCI-FI & HORROR DOUBLE NOVELS, $12.95 each

D-11   **PERIL OF THE STARMEN** by Kris Neville
THE STRANGE INVASION by Murray Leinster

D-12   **THE STAR LORD** by Boyd Ellanby
CAPTIVES OF THE FLAME by Samuel R. Delaney

D-13   **MEN OF THE MORNING STAR** by Edmond Hamilton
PLANET FOR PLUNDER by Hal Clement and Sam Merwin, Jr.

D-14   **ICE CITY OF THE GORGON** by Chester S. Geier and Richard Shaver
WHEN THE WORLD TOTTERED by Lester Del Rey

D-15   **WORLDS WITHOUT END** by Clifford D. Simak
THE LAVENDER VINE OF DEATH by Don Wilcox

D-16   **SHADOW ON THE MOON** by Joe Gibson
ARMAGEDDON EARTH by Geoff St. Reynard

D-17   **THE GIRL WHO LOVED DEATH** by Paul W. Fairman
SLAVE PLANET by Laurence M. Janifer

D-18   **SECOND CHANCE** by J. F. Bone
MISSION TO A DISTANT STAR by Frank Belknap Long

D-19   **THE SYNDIC** by C. M. Kornbluth
FLIGHT TO FOREVER by Poul Anderson

D-20   **SOMEWHERE I'LL FIND YOU** by Milton Lesser
THE TIME ARMADA by Fox B. Holden

ARMCHAIR SCIENCE FICTION CLASSICS, $12.95 each

C-4   **CORPUS EARTHLING**
by Louis Charbonneau

C-5   **THE TIME DISSOLVER**
by Jerry Sohl

C-6   **WEST OF THE SUN**
by Edgar Pangborn

ARMCHAIR SCIENCE FICTION & HORROR GEMS SERIES, $12.95 each

G-1   **SCIENCE FICTION GEMS, Vol. One**
Isaac Asimov and others

G-2   **HORROR GEMS, Vol. One**
Carl Jacobi and others

If you've enjoyed this book, you will not want to miss these terrific titles...

ARMCHAIR SCI-FI, FANTASY, & HORROR DOUBLE NOVELS, $12.95 each

D-21   **EMPIRE OF EVIL** by Robert Arnette
THE SIGN OF THE TIGER by Alan E. Nourse & J. A. Meyer

D-22   **OPERATION SQUARE PEG** by Frank Belknap Long
ENCHANTRESS OF VENUS by Leigh Brackett

D-23   **THE LIFE WATCH** by Lester del Rey
CREATURES OF THE ABYSS by Murray Leinster

D-24   **LEGION OF LAZARUS** by Edmond Hamilton
STAR HUNTER by Andre Norton

D-25   **EMPIRE OF WOMEN** by John Fletcher
ONE OF OUR CITIES IS MISSING by Irving Cox

D-26   **THE WRONG SIDE OF PARADISE** by Raymond F. Jones
THE INVOLUNTARY IMMORTALS by Rog Phillips

D-27   **EARTH QUARTER** by Damon Knight
ENVOY TO NEW WORLDS by Keith Laumer

D-28   **SLAVES TO THE METAL HORDE** by Milton Lesser
HUNTERS OUT OF TIME by Joseph E. Kelleam

D-29   **RX JUPITER SAVE US** by Ward Moore
BEWARE THE USURPERS by Geoff St. Reynard

D-30   **SECRET OF THE SERPENT** by Don Wilcox
CRUSADE ACROSS THE VOID by Dwight V. Swain

ARMCHAIR SCIENCE FICTION CLASSICS, $12.95 each

C-7   **THE SHAVER MYSTERY, Book One**
by Richard S. Shaver

C-8   **THE SHAVER MYSTERY, Book Two**
by Richard S. Shaver

C-9   **MURDER IN SPACE** by David V. Reed
by David V. Reed

ARMCHAIR MASTERS OF SCIENCE FICTION SERIES, $16.95 each

M-3   **MASTERS OF SCIENCE FICTION, Vol. Three**
Robert Sheckley, "The Perfect Woman" and other tales

M-4   **MASTERS OF SCIENCE FICTION, Vol. Four**
Mack Reynolds, "Stowaway" and other tales

If you've enjoyed this book, you will not want to miss these terrific titles...

ARMCHAIR SCI-FI & HORROR DOUBLE NOVELS, $12.95 each

D-51   **A GOD NAMED SMITH** by Henry Slesar
WORLDS OF THE IMPERIUM by Keith Laumer

D-52   **CRAIG'S BOOK** by Don Wilcox
EDGE OF THE KNIFE by H. Beam Piper

D-53   **THE SHINING CITY** by Rena M. Vale
THE RED PLANET by Russ Winterbotham

D-54   **THE MAN WHO LIVED TWICE** by Rog Phillips
VALLEY OF THE CROEN by Lee Tarbell

D-55   **OPERATION DISASTER** by Milton Lesser
LAND OF THE DAMNED by Berkeley Livingston

D-56   **CAPTIVE OF THE CENTAURIANESS** by Poul Anderson
A PRINCESS OF MARS by Edgar Rice Burroughs

D-57   **THE NON-STATISTICAL MAN** by Raymond F. Jones
MISSION FROM MARS by Rick Conroy

D-58   **INTRUDERS FROM THE STARS** by Ross Rocklynne
FLIGHT OF THE STARLING by Chester S. Geier

D-59   **COSMIC SABOTEUR** by Frank M. Robinson
LOOK TO THE STARS by Willard Hawkins

D-60   **THE MOON IS HELL!** by John W. Campbell, Jr.
THE GREEN WORLD by Hal Clement

ARMCHAIR SCIENCE FICTION CLASSICS, $12.95 each

C-16   **THE SHAVER MYSTERY, Book Three**
by Richard S. Shaver

C-17   **THE PLANET STRAPPERS**
by Raymond Z. Gallun

C-18   **THE FOURTH "R"**
by George O. Smith

ARMCHAIR SCIENCE FICTION & HORROR GEMS SERIES, $12.95 each

G-5   **SCIENCE FICTION GEMS, Vol. Three**
C. M. Kornbluth and others

G-6   **HORROR GEMS, Vol. Three**
August Derleth and others

If you've enjoyed this book, you will not want to miss these terrific titles…

ARMCHAIR SCI-FI & HORROR DOUBLE NOVELS, $12.95 each

D-61   **THE MAN WHO STOPPED AT NOTHING** by Paul W. Fairman
TEN FROM INFINITY by Ivar Jorgensen

D-62   **WORLDS WITHIN** by Rog Phillips
THE SLAVE by C.M. Kornbluth

D-63   **SECRET OF THE BLACK PLANET** by Milton Lesser
THE OUTCASTS OF SOLAR III by Emmett McDowell

D-64   **WEB OF THE WORLDS** by Harry Harrison and Katherine MacLean
RULE GOLDEN by Damon Knight

D-65   **TEN TO THE STARS** by Raymond Z. Gallun
THE CONQUERORS by David H. Keller, M. D.

D-66   **THE HORDE FROM INFINITY** by Dwight V. Swain
THE DAY THE EARTH FROZE by Gerald Hatch

D-67   **THE WAR OF THE WORLDS** by H. G. Wells
THE TIME MACHINE by H. G. Wells

D-68   **STARCOMBERS** by Edmond Hamilton
THE YEAR WHEN STARDUST FELL by Raymond F. Jones

D-69   **HOCUS-POCUS UNIVERSE** by Jack Williamson
QUEEN OF THE PANTHER WORLD by Berkeley Livingston

D-70   **BATTERING RAMS OF SPACE** by Don Wilcox
DOOMSDAY WING by George H. Smith

ARMCHAIR SCIENCE FICTION & FANTASY CLASSICS, $12.95 each

C-19   **EMPIRE OF JEGGA**
by David V. Reed

C-20   **THE TOMORROW PEOPLE**
by Judith Merril

C-21   **THE MAN FROM YESTERDAY**
by Howard Browne as by Lee Francis

C-22   **THE TIME TRADERS**
by Andre Norton

C-23   **ISLANDS OF SPACE**
by John W. Campbell

C-24   **THE GALAXY PRIMES**
by E. E. "Doc" Smith